# TRANSFORMATION!

## Ogre's Assistant

## Book Three

DJ Martin

*To everyone whose patience is better than mine: thanks for waiting on this one.*

# PROLOGUE

"You're getting better at this," Gregory said as he placed his marble directly opposite mine. We were playing Chinese checkers and drinking wine at his house on a Saturday night. Gregory wasn't only my boss' driver, he was also my magical teacher. The marbles we used weren't the standard glass ones you usually see; they were stones. We'd started playing it when I was learning about the different kinds of crystals and gemstones used in magic and discovered we enjoyed simply playing the game. It became our relaxation after my weekly lesson with him.

I took a sip of wine as I contemplated my next move. Gregory had almost two hundred years' experience on me, not only with magic, but also using strategy and tactics. I had yet to beat him but each week I lost by fewer marbles. Once I'd decided what to move where, it was a simple matter to enclose the stone with my will and *think* it to the selected indentation on the board. No touching required.

As Gregory started to peruse the board in search of his next move, my cell phone rang. I sighed. It had to be something to do with work. The boss was out of town so the office phone had been forwarded to mine instead of his. We frowned at each other as I answered, "This is Amy."

"Amy, it's John. I can't find Ev and he's not answering his phone. I think he may have gotten himself into some trouble."

"Hang on, John. I'm with Gregory and I'm going to put you on speakerphone." I hit the button and put my phone in the center of the playing board. "How do you know Ev is in trouble?"

"You know Ev and his fondness for women."

Gregory coughed. "Now what?"

"Well, one of the actor's assistants is a rather handsome woman and Ev started making eyes at her at a party the other night. And before you ask, yes, she's single and unattached as far as I know. Anyways, Mark, the actor, didn't like Ev paying attention to her and said so. Ev asked if she was Mark's lady and when the answer was negative, essentially told him to take a hike.

"Mark then talked to his assistant who, apparently, didn't mind the attention. He left the party in a huff but on set the next day, things sort of escalated. I'm assuming Mark is a wizard because lights started flickering on and off during a heated argument. The director told Mark to take a break and cool off while Ev started talking to the assistant again. He left a short time after concluding their conversation.

"That was two days ago. We were supposed to have a meeting with the financial people yesterday but Ev never showed. I called his cell but there was no answer. Then I went over to his hotel and the staff said his bed hadn't been slept in the night before."

I interrupted his story. "Has the assistant been around?"

"Yes. She went to dinner with him the night of the argument on set. According to her, he was a perfect gentleman and dropped her off at her door afterward. She says she hasn't seen him since."

I looked at Gregory whose face had gone blank. I knew by now that he was checking on the beacon spell he'd put into the ink on Ev's one and only tattoo. It had come in handy more than once when the boss disappeared without telling either of us where he was going.

"He's alive and still in your part of the country," Gregory told the agitated guy on the other end of the phone. "However, if you're worried, that's saying something. I will catch the first flight out in the morning and track him. Will you sleep tomorrow, or may I call you when I find something?"

(John was an *old* vampire who rarely slept. He just made sure he was out of sunlight during the day.)

"I will undoubtedly be awake so yes, do please call." John hung up.

Gregory and I looked at each other once more.

I let out a sigh. "Here we go again!"

# Chapter One

**Four months earlier**

It had been about a year since my magical powers had manifested, my boss found out, fired me simply because I was a witch, then finally rehired me. The first few months after I was rehired had some amusing moments. He harbored a fear of witches for some reason he wouldn't divulge and each time he pissed me off, was afraid I'd turn him into a frog or something. That spell was beyond my fledgling abilities, but I wasn't about to tell him that. It was fun to see him think better of what he was about to do in an effort to avoid incurring my wrath.

Ev, despite being an odiferous, irascible ogre, excelled in the people-end of his private security business. He'd hired (and rehired) me to handle the paperwork and money. Most of the time I let him spend his money as he saw fit. It was, after all, *his* company and I was just his employee. One particular day, though, I wished I could manage that frog spell.

I was reconciling the monthly brokerage statements and a transaction stood out as if someone had run a highlighter pen over it: a wire transfer of two hundred fifty thousand dollars out of his personal account to "In The Limelight Partners, LLP." A quarter-million and the investment manager hadn't alerted me? Something was fishy. I hit the intercom button on my phone.

"Ev, would you care to explain that two hundred fifty thousand wire last month?"

A cough then a clearing of throat preceded, "An investment. I'm promised a hefty return in just two years."

"And?" I prompted. There was more to it, I knew.

"It's a movie one of John's clients is starring in. I've read the script and since I'd pay good money to see it, I figure others will, too. It could even be a blockbuster in which case, I'll more than double my investment."

I was going to kill first John and then Martin. The former was a long-time friend of Ev's, a vampire who was agent to several high-profile actors. Our firm provided security to some of his clients. The latter was our investment manager. He usually called me when Ev wanted to do something stupid with his money and gave me an opportunity to avert disaster.

"I assume you told Martin not to tell me," I growled. Unfortunately, my voice was too high to produce a proper, deep-throated growl but it was usually enough to make Ev pause.

"Yes, I did. I get tired of you telling me what I should be doing with my money. I wanted to prove I could make good investment decisions on my own. It's a done deal, Amy. You'll see I'm right in less than two years. Now, was that all? I have phone calls to make."

There was a downside to using the intercom on speaker. You couldn't slam the receiver. So I punched the button as hard as I could.

I heard *"Control yourself"* clearly and loudly in my mind. My familiar, a cat named Fudge, unfortunately had unrestricted access to my brain. Distance didn't seem to matter, either. He was back at my apartment, three blocks away.

But he was right. Bad things could happen if I lost my temper. At the least, I could kill any electronic device within six feet or so. At the worst, I could cause an earthquake. Both had happened before and I didn't want a repeat. I especially didn't need the Witches' Council punishing me, which they would if I didn't keep a lid on my anger.

I closed my eyes and took deep breaths until my heart rate returned to normal and I heard *"Better."* Fudge's presence withdrew from my mind. Unfortunately, Ev was right both in the fact that it was his money and that it was a done deal. I just looked forward to gloating somewhere down the road when he not only didn't realize a profit but probably saw part of the principal disappear.

I could take part of my anger out on someone, though. I picked up the phone and called Martin, the investment manager.

I wasted no time when he answered. "Since when do you adhere to Ev's wishes and not call me when he wants to throw away money?"

"Sorry, Amy. I probably should have but he gave me the same-day wire instructions the day before the full moon. I was more than a little distracted and forgot. He also told me not to tell you, so there's that."

Martin was a were – the same as my now-deceased boyfriend – so I understood about being distracted once a month. Yes, they only involuntarily transformed on one day but they all had to ensure they were out of range of people or locked away, so in reality, it took more than just twelve hours out of their lives.

"If it's any consolation, his principal is protected by collateral. Yes, I know if things go belly-up there will be legal fees, but at least it's something."

I snorted. "Based on the little I know about Hollywood, Ev is a minority investor. If it comes to that, he'll probably see pennies on the dollar because the big hitters will take most of the collateral."

"You're probably right. I'll offer my apologies once again but all I can do is hope the market will make up for any losses there."

I accepted his apology, graciously I hoped, and hung up. No use crying over spilt milk and all that, eh? With another sigh, I entered that investment into the computer and continued on with my work.

The next afternoon I was in Gregory's cottage for my weekly magic lesson. Gregory had taken over as teacher from my best friend – he had more time to do so. At first, I had read books and been drilled every day, topped off with a practical lesson (I thought of them as Labs) every Saturday. Six months in, however, Gregory had decided just a once-a-week practical would suffice.

We also moved the classroom from my apartment to his cottage behind Ev's house. Like Cassandra, he had a garden which enabled me to work with plants. Also like my best friend, he had a workroom, but his put hers to shame. At over two hundred years old, he'd had time to collect all sorts of interesting things from the four corners of the world. Where Cassandra just had jars of dried herbs, piles of stones, and bottles of oil, in Gregory's workroom, reindeer antlers gathered in Lapland vied for space with jars of herbs, bottles of oil, and jars of poisonous bugs like bullet ants from South America. (Those were dead. Thank goodness.) It definitely broadened my studies!

While I was learning to draw the essence from one of those dead bugs for a potion, I related my frustrations of the prior day.

"He's such an idiot!" I exclaimed. "Yeah, okay, he's got some play money but to invest it in something as risky as a movie? Why won't he learn he doesn't have much common sense?"

"No, you're going about it wrong. Feel for just the poison and draw that energy, not the spent life force." Gregory's voice was quiet but held a note of admonishment. "As I've reminded you before, Ev is still just a child in many ways. I know that's a lot of money but he has the lifespan to make it up if need be. Maybe losing that amount will be what he needs to learn that particular lesson."

"What are we using bug poison for anyways?" I asked. "Did someone hire you to throw a curse?"

A soft laugh then, "No. It's for a protection spell. My client lives in a not-so-nice area and is having difficulty with break-ins. We will use the poison's essence as a deterrent. Now, once you've got hold of that energy, direct it into this bottle. I will do the rest."

Fudge, who always accompanied me to my lessons, padded over to the workbench and put his paw on my arm. I felt his familiar presence as a slight pressure at the back of my brain. With his help, I was able to separate out the poison energy still in the bug's dead body, pull that out and push it into the glass bottle in Gregory's hands. Once I'd accomplished that, Fudge promptly ate the carcass.

"Eeew, gross!" I cried.

*"What? With the poison gone, it is healthy protein. You should try it. Bugs are crunchy and tasty."*

Nonetheless, I was glad it had been a while since I'd eaten. To distract myself I turned to watch Gregory finish the potion.

There had already been a watery liquid with floating pieces of herbs in the bottle. Adding the poison energy turned the liquid from almost clear to brownish. As I watched, Gregory enveloped the bottle with his carmine-red personal energy and while muttering something under his breath, that energy became a tornado that dipped itself into the bottle and stirred the ingredients even further. The tornado disappeared and as the watery whirlpool calmed, the liquid became clear once again. Gregory put a cork in the bottle, scribbled something on an adhesive label and after slapping that on the bottle, declared it good.

I grabbed the bottle and read, "One teaspoonful sprinkled every five feet around perimeter. Apply one dab with cotton swab on each windowsill. *Not for internal use. Avoid skin contact.*"

I set the bottle back down. "I have two questions."

"You always have at least one," Gregory smiled. "Ask."

"Why do witches and wizards always mutter? Can't you speak spells out loud? How am I supposed to learn spells if I can't hear the words?"

I felt a metaphysical slap from Fudge as Gregory let out a guffaw. "And here I thought I'd been teaching you about how energy manipulation equals intent. I was apparently mistaken. Okay, I will give it another try.

"Magical people use their intent to manipulate energy, right? Like when you want to move something, you just will it to do so. Do you talk to whatever it is you're moving? No."

*"Pay close attention. I believe he is losing patience with you."* Even though Fudge was talking in my head, I waved him off with my hand then had to apologize so Gregory wouldn't think I was blowing him off. He nodded. He was used to Fudge's interjections even though he couldn't hear them.

"I'd guess some folks *do* say something out loud and others may only think things but for most of us, muttering is just a way to focus our intent. There is no set wording for any spell. I won't tell you the client's name but I was just muttering 'Protect the client's hearth and home' as I infused the potion with my intent. Now does it make sense?"

"Yes, I guess so," I said as I mused on how to phrase the second question.

"And your second question?"

"If our intent and energy is all it takes, why the extra stuff? I mean, take this potion for example. It's got oil, herbs and bug poison in addition to your energy. Couldn't you just go over there and wrap her house in a protection spell?"

Gregory blew out a breath. "When you first learned to shield, before your powers manifested, did the shield stay put without you thinking about it?"

"No," I shook my head. "I had to concentrate on it every morning and whenever I needed it to be stronger, like before one of Ev's parties."

"And now that your powers have manifested?"

"It's there all the time but if I need to tighten it, I still have to think about it."

"So, if I were to go wrap the client's house in a protection spell, would it continually maintain itself or would I have to refresh it occasionally?"

"I get where you're going with this but can't you sort of make it self-feeding, like drawing energy from the ground around the house?"

That elicited a frown and given that Gregory was the smiling type, I knew I'd said something wrong.

"You learned early on about drawing energy from the ground and affecting plants and trees growing around the area. How do you think the area lawn and trees would fare?"

He had me there. My first practical lesson with Earth energy was learning to draw it so it didn't affect the growing things. In some places, that was difficult to do because of intertwining roots. I felt like an idiot.

"So, you know the spell can't be truly self-sustaining, you know I don't have time to go refresh every long-term spell I cast, and I know you've learned a little about plants and other things having their own inherent magical capabilities. What conclusion do you draw?"

Although a good teacher, Gregory could be a little stern at times, which I didn't like. On the other hand, he made me think, which was a good thing. So, I thought. Like the proverbial light bulb going off over my head, I finally understood where Gregory had been leading me.

"The extra stuff keeps the spell going without your presence. You use things with magical signatures appropriate to the situation and let *them* do the heavy lifting, as it were. You just get the spell started."

"Bingo. In this case, the two herbs I used have protective properties. The bug poison essence is in case someone ignores the 'stay away' admonishment of the herbs. It won't be fatal but whoever breaches the ward will end up in hospital with some odd symptoms, making them easier for the authorities to find."

"But isn't your client a witch? Can't she do this stuff on her own?"

"She lives in an apartment, just as you do. Do you have a large, varied stock of herbs, oils, and other supplies right at your fingertips? Also, her element is Water. She doesn't relate as well to earth-based plants. She does a bang-up job with ponds and such in landscaping, though."

That made sense. The more I learned about magic, the more I saw why people turned to a witch or wizard of a different elemental affinity for some things. That said, I *still* didn't see where using magic could really benefit me, except for being able to open and then slam shut a wooden door without touching the knob. I found that particular ability a good outlet for my red-headed temper.

"I think it's time you concocted a potion of your own," Gregory said. "You've been studying for a year and apart from practical lessons, I haven't heard a thing about you using magic. I want to see how you'd go about something."

"But I don't have a need for any of this," I whined. "Except for Ev's temper tantrums and stupid money management skills, my life is just fine. What do I need a potion for?"

"*Practice, if nothing else.*"

I glared at my cat. As a familiar, he was here to help with my magic. Since I didn't do much of anything with it, I guessed he was more bored than most mundane cats appear to be.

*"Yes, I am bored. However, as I have stated before, you have a long life ahead of you. Some day you may want to put a potion together. Would it not be better to do it in the presence of someone with experience rather than botch something when you really needed it?"*

I hated school and since Fudge seemed to be immune to my whining, I turned my glare on Gregory.

"You need to get a feel for putting ingredients together, if nothing else." My teacher echoed my cat. Damn. They were ganging up on me.

"So what should I make?"

"I have another client who needs a protection spell. Her daughter is being unnecessarily teased in school. We need to put together a perfume that will not only smell nice but deter the offenders. It's an easy potion but I want to see what you come up with."

Chapter Two

I never took chemistry in school and now was thrust into an experiment. Where were my goggles and rubber gloves? I grabbed my reference binder and flipped back to the section on herbs and their properties. I needed something for protection, something that would make the creeps' energies bounce back on them, and something that smelled nice to boot. On a teenager. Who probably didn't even wear perfume and dressed in all black complete with combat boots. Joy.

"What's the kid like? I mean, is she a girly-girl, a nerd, a goth, a cheerleader? Wait, probably not that last. Cheerleaders don't get teased; they do the teasing. But how am I supposed to make it smell?"

Gregory smiled. Finally. "You are on the right track. She is what you would call a geek, I think. Spends a lot of time on computers; has even designed a couple of applications for mobiles."

"Apps," I automatically corrected.

"Yes, as you say, apps. She does not wear makeup and dresses mostly in denims and T-shirts. From what I'm told, she is quiet."

"Okay, then something subtle and not very flowery." I started perusing my list of herbs with protective properties. Then I got to thinking about her. I got teased in school but except for being suspended for throwing a punch when a flouncy bitch wouldn't get out of my way in the hall, I mostly just shrugged it off. Depending on what the teasing really amounted to, she needed to let it roll off her back or stand up to her aggressor. Maybe a little of both. That should probably be incorporated in there somewhere, too.

"*You cannot change a personality.*"

"I know. But you can help someone to realize they're just as good as anyone else, can't you?"

"*I do not understand human feelings of inadequacy, so I do not know how you expect to change her emotions with magic.*"

Fudge may be old and have witnessed a lot in his time, but he still didn't get humans or their society very well. I wasn't about to try to explain it – again – to a cat with a superiority complex. I sighed and turned my attention back to the ingredient choices. She needed a spine-straightening nudge, in my humble opinion.

Gregory came out of the kitchen where, if my nose didn't deceive me, he'd been brewing a pot of coffee. We were both addicted to the stuff and I loved visiting him and his special-roast beans. "What have you come up with?" he asked, handing me a steaming mug.

"Something to form a shield, something to give her a straighter spine, and something to make the shield rubbery so any negative energy will bounce back at the sender," I told him after a sip and a moan. His coffee was – almost – as good as sex.

"Sounds reasonable. What ingredients?"

"Since it's something she's going to apply like perfume, mostly essential oils in a grapeseed oil base. But, I need something rubbery. I don't suppose you have a rubber plant growing anywhere, do you?"

"No, but I see where you're going. I have a SuperBall or two in the odds and ends drawer. I'll dig one out while you mix up the rest."

While Gregory rummaged in one of the drawers, I pulled out an empty bottle and filled it partway with grapeseed oil. Then, a couple of drops of cedar oil, a drop of frankincense oil, and a few drops of borage oil. When Gregory plopped a small, iridescent ball into the bottle, I pulled a little energy from the air around me and aimed that along with my intent – that she be protected, learn to stand up to aggressors, and any negative energy should bounce back on the person sending it – into the mixture. I saw sparkling green energy pour itself into the bottle from my hand. (Horrors. I caught myself muttering.) Just as the last green sparkle floated into the bottle, the ball shot out and hit me squarely between the eyes, ricocheting from me to the table, ceiling, floor…and I lost track of it. Fudge didn't, though. True to his current form as a cat, he found it under a side table and batted it around the floor for a minute or two.

I dropped the bottle with the shock, sending oil and glass flying everywhere. "Ow. What the hell?" I cried as my eyes started watering from the pain.

Gregory just chuckled. With a sweep of his hand, the oil and broken glass found its way into the trash can. There were times I wish I had his Air affinity. I'm a klutz and always breaking something. Another wave of his hand over my forehead had the pain subsiding to a dull throb.

"Subtlety isn't one of your strong suits, is it?" he asked.

"Not usually, no," I replied, still rubbing the spot where the ball had hit. "I prefer to face things head-on. Why?"

"Your intention provoked a physical response rather than an emotional one. If you'd been a little gentler in what you were trying to accomplish, the ball would have just bobbed in the liquid. Translating that to our problem, the client would have used physical force in her attempts to protect herself *or* the aggressor would have been thrown back, thinking he or she had been attacked. Either way, it's not the response we want."

*"Persuasion rather than force."*

"Yeah? And where were you when I was doing all this? I didn't feel you like I normally do. I thought you were supposed to help." I thought back.

*"Sometimes experience is indeed the best teacher."*

I grunted. Some experiences I could do without. Getting smacked by a hard rubber ball was one of them.

"So, oh wise master and unhelpful familiar, how do I change what I did so I get the proper outcome?"

"Don't use your own personal anger in the spell," Gregory said.

"I thought Fudge was supposed to suppress that stuff when I was working." I glared at my cat.

Gregory fixed Fudge with a stare. "He is. I have a suspicion your familiar is in teaching mode. Or, he's just being a typical cat not concerned with anything but themselves. I understand they do that sometimes."

Fudge licked a paw. *"I was teaching. If it had been very important, I would have aided you."*

"With or without Fudge's help, you need to re-do your potion," Gregory said as he retrieved the ball from where Fudge had abandoned it on the other side of the room. "Start over."

Once again I mixed up the oils, plopped the ball into the bottle and infused it with my intent. This time I tried to keep it low key but given how much I hated bullies of any kind, it wasn't easy. Once again, I felt no evidence of Fudge putting a damper on my feelings. It was all up to me. As the last of my green energy sparkles disappeared into the liquid, I held my breath. The ball only looked like a fishing float, quietly bobbing on top. I'd done it!

"Very good, Amy," Gregory congratulated me as I put the cap on the bottle. Once again, he wrote instructions on a label and after sticking the label on the bottle, placed it next to the other bottle awaiting delivery.

I left Gregory's shortly thereafter, having the taxi drop me at Cassandra's deli, downstairs from my office. First, I wanted another cup of coffee. Unlike the year before, this March was still cold and snowy – and I don't do cold and snowy. A hot beverage was in order and her elixir was better than mine. Second, their first wedding anniversary had been a couple of days earlier and I wanted the lowdown on what they'd done. Oh, not *that*. Get your mind out of the gutter. But she said Tommy had a surprise for her and they hadn't been at work on Friday, leaving Charlie to run things on his own.

I got my coffee but not any information. Charlie was still flying solo, telling me my best friend and her husband were still away. I'd have to wait until Tuesday for my gossip session. (The deli was closed on Sunday and Monday.) While I was happy that she'd found Mr. Right, I still missed our almost-daily girl chats. I felt a little bereft as Fudge and I walked the rest of the way home.

Sunday saw me back at my laptop, finishing up the last of my contracted novels. Oh, you didn't know? I write paranormal romance under a pseudonym, basing a lot of my characters on people I'd met working for Ev. (It was a *huge* pool of quirky players.) When the first book had been accepted by a publisher, they asked for a total of ten. At that time, I didn't have much of a life outside work, figured I was good for it, so signed on. I hadn't anticipated turning into a witch who needed to study so I was frantic at times, trying to work, study, *and* write to fulfill my contractual obligation.

Late in the afternoon, I typed *The End* and heaved a sigh of relief. Oh, I wasn't done by a long shot – this was just the first draft. But I could see the light at the end of the tunnel – in three months or so when the editing was finished, I'd have more down time. I dreamed of taking a vacation somewhere warm and sunny, sipping fruity cocktails garnished with umbrellas served poolside by handsome cabana boys, and maybe even whittling away at my reading pile.

*"If you go somewhere like that, be sure to find a pet-friendly hotel."*

"I thought you liked staying at home. Elinda and Marge always do a good job of taking care of you when I go out of town," I replied in my mind. It had taken me a while to get the hang of thinking to Fudge when we talked instead of out loud like a normal conversation.

*"You are still a fledgling witch who may need my assistance. Although I am with you wherever you go, contact is easiest and stronger when we are near each other. I would feel remiss in my duties if you needed me and distance diminished our bond."*

"Although I'd love to leave this sloppy, wintery weather, it's not going to happen anytime soon. I still have too many things going on to take a vacation. I'd say I'll let you know but because you always know what I'm thinking, I won't have to. But I promise to find someplace I can take you to. Deal?"

Fudge didn't reply, just hopped from his supervisory spot on my desk over to the sofa where, after a couple of kneads and turns, he settled down for another nap. I followed…Sunday afternoons were made for napping.

Chapter Three

Mid-morning the following Tuesday, I heard the outer office door open. Ev never arrived at work before eleven and my assistant, Sally, didn't come in until one, so I poked my head out of my office to see who'd arrived.

"Hi, how may I hel…" I didn't get the whole sentence out of my mouth before I lost concentration. Standing before me was the most gorgeous man I'd ever seen. Around six feet tall, and I could tell there were six-pack abs and bulging biceps under his exquisitely tailored suit; sharply chiseled features complimented blue-green eyes, reminiscent of the sea; and Spock-type ears peeked out from between strands of thick, straight, glossy black hair long enough to kiss his waist.

An elf? Ev had told me they didn't have much to do with other races. What was he doing here?

*"Pull yourself together."*

"Yeah, no shit. But thanks." Fudge's presence in my mind snapped me out of my undying admiration. I cleared my throat.

"…help you? Sorry, had a catch in my throat."

A delicious baritone voice intoned, "My name is Perchaladon. I have an appointment with Evander Angelich for ten in the morning. I am somewhat early."

"Not a problem. He should be here shortly. May I offer you coffee or another beverage while you wait?" I moved toward our kitchen in anticipation.

"If your coffee is organic, I would be pleased to sample it without adulteration. If not, I am content without."

Thanks to Gregory (and his Italian friend), our coffee *was* organic. So, I poured him a cup of coffee, assuming "without adulteration" meant black, and wishing I'd brought my own to refill. He was still standing just inside the door when I returned to the reception area, which earned him a bump in the rear end as Ev barged into the office.

"What the…oh, sorry. I assume you're Perchaladon. Come on into my office." Ev started to roar but his voice immediately modulated when he saw who he'd hit with the door. I handed the coffee to the elf, who glided behind Ev – with a slight crinkle of his nose. I'd heard elves had a keen sense of smell and I could imagine his olfactory receptors being more than a little irritated by Ev's odor, despite the scented candles burning everywhere *but* Ev's office.

"What did you want to talk to me about?" I heard Ev say as he slammed his office door behind them. Their voices muted to the point I couldn't hear any more without putting my ear right up to the door, so I went back to my own work.

An hour later, I heard Ev say, "Thanks for coming. I'll read everything over and be in touch." A low murmur was followed by the sound of the outer door closing softly.

Then his usual roar, "Amy, my office!" It was right around eleven and Ev was ready to pay attention to work. I brought my coffee and notes, sat in my usual seat and got right to business.

"What did an elf want to see you about?"

"An investment. Sounds good but I'll not answer him for a day or so. Don't want him to think I'm too eager. What'cha got for me?"

Oh, god. Another investment. "Why would an elf come to you about an investment? You told me they usually stick to their own kind."

"We met at Club Tread last night and hit it off. He told me he had an idea for a new company, so I asked him to come here this morning to talk about it."

An elf at Club Tread. Although that was a favored watering hole of most non-human species, I'd never heard of an elf going there. This sounded fishy. "May I read the prospectus?" I asked.

"Sure, here." He tossed a tome across his desk. It had to be more than five hundred pages and weighed a ton. I'll admit, my curiosity was piqued. Most prospectuses were fifty pages or less – it didn't take a novel to present a business idea with as much financial projection as possible without any kind of track record. Without looking at it, I tucked it under my notepad while filling Ev in on what had happened overnight and that morning, what I'd done and what he needed to do.

When I got back to my desk, although I had other things to do, I glanced at the book and figured out why it was so thick. It wasn't written on a computer – rather than the standard Times New Roman font, calligraphy graced every page. I'd heard elves didn't like technology. I guess this just proved it.

Before getting back to the important stuff, I placed a call to Gregory.

"Hey," I said when he answered. "Ev's looking at another investment but this time it's through an elf. What's up with that?"

I could hear the frown in his voice. "Going outside their race isn't unheard of, it's just rare. What's his name? I don't know many, but I can try asking around to see if anyone knows why he approached Ev. Do you know what it entails?"

"No, but I got the prospectus to read. I may have Martin take a look at it, too. His name is Perchaladon. It just feels fishy, you know?"

"It may be legit but there's no harm in getting Martin's opinion, too. I will let you know what I find." Gregory hung up.

As always, Cassandra brought my lunch at noon. At least this part of our routine hadn't changed. She got a quick break from the counter and I got a yummy meal without having to leave my desk.

"Did I see an *elf* go up the stairs a bit ago?"

"Yep. Gorgeous, isn't he?"

"I only got a glance as he went by our door, but it was show-stopping. I can't imagine how you managed to say a word without drooling."

I paused in the slurping of my soup. "Fudge helped. He's good at slapping me into coherence. And before you ask, it was about some investment or another. I haven't had time to look any further into it."

"An *elf? Investment?* I thought they didn't do business outside their race."

"That's what I thought, too, but apparently it does happen on occasion. Or so Gregory says."

"He'd know, wouldn't he? I gotta go. See you when you drop your dishes later."

Not soon enough, it was quitting time. Because I started work really early (brought on by Fudge's inability to keep from climbing and shredding bedroom-darkening drapes), I got off work early, too. I hauled the prospectus home with me, determined to find out what Ev thought would be a good use of his money – *this* time.

After my nap and shared dinner with Fudge, I curled up on the sofa but instead of recreational or magic-type reading, I dug into the opus.

Three hours later, I determined that Martin needed to read this as well. I'm fairly good with numbers but I wanted someone else to tell Ev he was off his rocker if he thought this was a good investment.

Essentially, it was an idea to determine what in non-human species' DNA gave them the longer lifespan, then, after perfecting whatever formula, sell that to humans. Their "market research" said the vast majority of humans were jealous and would pay just about anything to live longer.

As a former human (I came into my magical powers relatively late in life), I knew there were some people who craved immortality, but I certainly wasn't one of them. Before learning I'd live two or three (or more) hundred years longer than the normal life expectancy of about eighty, I was perfectly content to live a comfortable life, grow old (hopefully with a special someone), and die. I doubted the veracity of their research. But Ev wouldn't believe me.

The next day, after looking at the calendar to determine it was only a quarter-moon, I arranged to meet Martin for a drink after work to give him the prospectus. Over a glass of my favorite merlot, I gave him a synopsis.

"Not another one," he sighed.

"Another?"

"These schemes surface every fifty years or so. Do you think this is the first time someone has wanted to delve into our DNA to find out the whys and wherefores of our existence? They have. From what I've read, every scientist who's tried can find anomalies between the rest of us and humans, but no one's had an 'aha' moment."

I thought. "But they've made such strides in identifying all sorts of markers. Perhaps this guy has the right scientist on board."

"I'll read it, do some research and let you – and Ev – know. But I'm doubtful there's anything new under that particular sun. In the meantime, keep Ev's checkbook close to you and I'll try to delay anything else."

The following afternoon I heard Sally exclaim, "Oh, my" after the outer door had opened. Curious, I got up from my desk to investigate and found Perchaladon standing at her desk in all his elfin glory.

Swallowing hard to stop myself from slavering, I asked what I could help him with. Sally sat at her desk slack-jawed.

"I would like to see Evander if he's available. Time is of the essence."

"I'm sorry but he hasn't yet returned from a lunch meeting. Is there a message for him?"

I heard Sally audibly gulp as she tried to get control of herself. If I hadn't had the same experience, I may have been taken somewhat aback. Sally looks like a chic Valkyrie and generally has the cool to match.

"I'm sorry but this is a private matter. May I wait?"

I wanted to tell him that Ev and I had very few secrets but not only wasn't it my place to do so, it wouldn't have been entirely truthful. Ev kept as much as possible from me. Even stuff I really should know.

"Of course. Please have a seat. Sally, I know Perchaladon likes our coffee and you know I'll always drink some. Perhaps you'd make a fresh pot?"

That should give her enough time to come to terms with an example of manly perfection sitting in her office. As the elf sat, I went back into my office and tried to go back to my work. Unsuccessfully. I assumed he was here to badger Ev about giving him money and I hadn't yet heard back from either Martin or Gregory. I started fidgeting in my seat, wondering how I'd get Ev to say, "not yet" or preferably, "no".

"Who *is* that?" Sally whispered as she refilled my cup for me.

"He can probably hear you with those ears," I whispered back. "Later."

Shortly, the outer door banged open and Ev's odor announced his return from lunch. "What are you doing here?" I heard.

The dulcet baritone replied, "I was in the area and thought to see if you'd come to a decision regarding the investment in my company."

"I'm sorry but I've been terribly busy. I'm still reading your proposal and speaking with my advisors. I said I'd let you know and I will."

"I understand but please do not take long. The subscriptions are going quickly." I heard the door close once again.

"You told a bald-faced lie," I said from my office. "You haven't read the prospectus because you gave it to me."

Ev peeked around the door. "Yes, and I'm waiting for you to tell me what you think. It sounds wonderful, doesn't it?"

"Actually no, it doesn't. I'm not an expert but I don't believe it would be successful for one minute. Martin has it now. He's better with that sort of stuff than I am. He said he'd call you once he'd read it and had a chance to look a little further."

Ev sighed. "You both are going to tell me no, aren't you?"

"In all likelihood, you're right. We will. But wait for Martin's call. And Gregory's. He's looking into Perchaladon's background, if there's anything to find."

Ev shrugged his shoulders, left, and Sally replaced him in my office door. "An elf going outside their race for an investment? That's weird. But oh god, what a specimen!"

"Yeah to both. I take it you've never seen an elf before, either."

"No. In a way, I wish I hadn't. I think Jack is handsome, but he can't hold a candle to that guy. It'll take a while to get that image out of my brain."

I laughed. "Jack is more than a pretty face or you wouldn't have married him. Looks aren't everything."

"No, but they certainly don't hurt!" she shot over her shoulder as she headed back to her desk.

That night I put all thoughts of elves and investments aside. I had a lesson with Gregory the next day and hadn't done a lick of my assigned reading. We were still working with liquid stuff and I opened *The Big Book of Potions and Philtres*, copyright 1856, to the section on philtres.

"Philtre, originally a word used to describe a love potion (from the Greek *philein*, to love), now means any drink imbued with magic, generally herbs brewed in hot water." My eyes started glazing. I was going to spend the night reading about *tea*.

*"Tea is a kind of plant. Continue reading."*

I could never slack off. Not with a damned cat supervising, listening to everything I thought. It wasn't fair. I read, jotting salient bits of information in my big notebook.

Chapter Four


Saturday saw me once again at Gregory's, this time making all sorts of *tea* for health, attitude, and love issues. As with everything else, I had to learn how to brew what herbs for which issues and to inject appropriate energy into each one. I snorted when we got to the love philtres.

"You have the right attitude." Gregory told me. "Although most people say 'love', they really mean 'lust'. You can't make someone go against their own nature but if there's even a hint of interest in the other party, you can amp it up. It generally doesn't last long-term, though."

"Why would you want to use magic to influence someone's love life?" I mused.

"Believe it or not, love is the second-most requested spell from most humans. I believe it was Gilbert who said, 'Love makes the world go 'round.' People want that, you know?"

I snorted again. "If, for some stupid reason, someone came to me for a love spell, I'd just laugh them off. Since long-term spells have to be maintained somehow, that sounds like a lot of work to hold interest."

"It is. And if the maintenance is slackened, the affected party will come to their senses quickly. It can make for some ugly scenes. But it's still something you need to know."

"Okay, I know it. Can we move onto something else?"

*"As the wizard said, philtres or charms can enhance a feeling that is already there. I have seen them work. It may someday suit your purpose to have someone highly interested in you for a while. Do not discount short term effects."*

Someday. Someday. Everyone kept telling me I might need to know all this stuff for someday. But grousing wouldn't get me anywhere, so I sucked it up and went back to my Labs.

Mid-afternoon, I was in the middle of putting together what would become an herb-infused wine for someone's tension headaches when Gregory stopped in the middle of a sentence and listened.

"The morning weather person was mistaken about timing. The storm front is arriving more quickly than anticipated," he told me. "We will have to either leave now to get you home safely or you will be stuck here tonight and possibly tomorrow."

The prediction was for the blizzard to arrive during the early evening, so I thought I'd be safe in coming to Gregory's for my weekly lesson. His Air ability just told me that assumption was in error.

"Will you be able to make it back from my place okay if you take me home?" I asked.

"It will be tricky."

"Then if it's okay with you, we'll stay here. I'd hate for you to get stuck in a whiteout."

"Thank you. In that case, please continue with your infusion. That's the last we have to do today and then I think it's time for a game of Chinese checkers." Gregory grinned. I still hadn't beaten him in that game and I knew he loved winning.

*"If you would let me suggest moves, you could easily beat him at that game."*

"I want to learn strategy on my own, thank you very much. I get better each week, don't I?"

Fudge didn't reply but curled up in a chair by the fireplace. I think he was a little peeved that I wouldn't let him play.

True to Gregory's prediction, the wind starting howling and snow started swirling within the hour. He paused in moving a stone from one indentation on the board to another to listen again. Without making his move, he stood.

"Bundle up. I need to capture some of this snow," Gregory said as he handed me my coat.

"Huh?"

"If I'm not mistaken, this is going to be thundersnow. The energy in the melted snow will be excellent to use in preparations to rile someone up. So, I need to put out collection vessels and you're going to help."

I bundled myself in my coat, swaddled my head and neck with my scarf and pulled on my gloves. Gregory did the same and handed me two small cast-iron pots.

"These should be heavy enough to stay put. While I place a couple farther away, I want you to put yours on the west side of the garage, ensuring they don't actually touch the garage wall."

Why you'd want to get someone mad was beyond me, but I duly leaned into the wind, made my way to the garage and put the two pots down a few inches from the wall. As small as I am, I nearly flew back to the cottage with the wind at my back. Gregory grabbed me before I could slam into the still-closed door.

"Excellent. Thundersnow is rare so this will be some potent water," he said as we unbundled. Even just a few minutes into the storm, enough snow had collected on our clothing that it dripped a bit as we hung everything up.

We returned to our game but before Gregory could make the move he'd interrupted, his phone rang. He listened for a moment after answering then grimaced as he said, "Are you crazy?"

A clap of thunder punctuated his statement.

"Ev, I know the Hummer will go in heavy snowfall. It doesn't help me see in whiteout conditions. Look out your damned window. Can you see the cottage? No? I didn't think so. You will just have to entertain yourself tonight."

Another boom sounded as Gregory hit the off button on his phone. Based on the expression on his face, I wasn't sure if the rumbling was him or the natural storm. "That boy will be the literal death of me, yet. He wanted to go clubbing in this weather!"

Somehow that didn't surprise me. Ev was notorious for making impromptu bad decisions. It took all his friends and acquaintances to save him from himself at times. I was laughing as I gestured at the board, indicating Gregory should make his move.

One advantage to staying over is I didn't have to come up with anything for dinner that night. Gregory, in addition to being a fantastic coffee barista, was a better chef than I. He thawed some fish and grilled it in the fireplace, cooking enough not only for us but Fudge, as well. For that, he got quite a bit of affection from the cat.

The sky's rumbling finally quit but the howling of the wind didn't. The power went out and there was another pause in our game while we went around the room, lighting candles. A few minutes later, there was a thumping at the door. Gregory opened it just a crack to prevent the snow from swirling into the house.

"Power's out and I'm bored. What are you guys doing?" Ev asked as he pushed his way in past Gregory, the wind blowing snow in with him. Fudge lifted his head, sniffed the air and retreated from my lap to a far corner of the house.

"Well, come in, then," Gregory said as he picked Ev's coat off the floor where the ogre had dropped it and hung it on the rack with the others.

"Hi, Amy. Hope you don't mind me barging in on your love fest."

I made a face. "Love fest? With someone two hundred years older than I? Honestly, Ev. I swear you have a one-track mind. We were playing a board game."

Ev grinned. "Oh, I know there's nothing between you two. I just like to get your goat. What game? Can I join in?"

"We were playing Chinese checkers, Ev. Amy, reset the board for three players. Since it appears we're going to have a party, what does everyone want to drink?" Gregory moved toward the kitchen.

Surprisingly, Ev not only knew how to play the game, he wasn't bad at it. Board games, much less something involving, you know, *thinking*, weren't something I'd have associated with Ev but then again, he also knew which utensil to use at the table. Wonders never ceased.

There *was* a slightly uncomfortable moment at the beginning of our first game. I was so accustomed to moving the stones with my mind when playing with Gregory that I forgot how Ev felt about witches. When I made my first move, Ev choked on the swig of beer he'd just taken.

Gregory slapped his back and then punched him on the shoulder. "Get over it, man. You should know by now she's not going to turn you into a toad, although at times I wouldn't blame her."

Ev coughed some more then cleared his throat. "Sorry. Habit, I guess. I'll try harder not to let it bother me."

I punched him on the other shoulder. "Good. Because there's not a damned thing I can do about it. Your move."

A few hours and a couple of glasses of wine later, I was trying to hide the fact that I was yawning. Ev may be able to stay up until all hours of the night and Gregory with him but due to my getting to work at such an early hour, I had no choice but to be a morning person. I felt like a real night owl if I made it to midnight.

"Sorry," I said through another yawn. "I'm not used to staying up very late."

"My fault," Ev replied. "I'll go home after this game, okay?"

I almost fell off my chair. Ev was being *nice*. To the final game, I nodded. Both men had won one game each and this would be the rubber. I stifled another yawn and tried to concentrate so I wouldn't lose by too many stones.

Thirty minutes later, Gregory had won (by just two stones) and Ev was pulling on his coat.

"That was fun," he said. "We should do this more often. Good night you two, and thanks." He let himself out, the snow blowing past him into the room before he could get the door shut. Or actually, slammed shut. Ev didn't know how to be quiet.

"I'm shocked," I said as I helped Gregory clean up our mess. "Ev was not only sociable, he didn't even mention business."

"As I've said before, he's really not a bad guy. We've done this in the past when the power went out, so I'm used to seeing this side of him," Gregory told me.

"I have a question."

"And I'm not teaching? Okay, what do you want to know?" Gregory had a quizzical look on his face.

"I just sat next to Ev for about four hours and didn't want to vomit from his body odor once. What did you do?"

A chuckle escaped him. "It's another advantage to being aligned with Air. If you noticed, I ensured Ev was sitting between me and the fireplace. I just created a small air current that blew away from me. It took his aroma up the chimney. Because of where you were sitting, you got the benefit, too."

"You need to teach me that. It would help so much in the office."

He made a face. "As an Earth affinity, I'm not sure you could do it. It's a rather gentle touch so he doesn't feel like a fan is blowing on him. It won't work in the office, anyways; the same way it won't work in the car with the windows rolled up. You need a direct conduit outside, like the chimney. If you can convince Ev to open the office windows all the time, you could try it."

I knew that wasn't going to happen. Ev disdained fresh air and if the heat wasn't on, the air conditioning was. I sighed. It was a thought, just not a good one.

A small argument ensued. Gregory wanted me to take his bed and I insisted on the couch. I fit easily on his two-seater where he'd either slop over the ends or wake up unable to walk from being in a cramped position. I, naturally, won and he finally handed me a pillow and a lovely, handmade down-filled quilt. When I commented on the workmanship, he told me it was one of the few things he had left from his *mother*. Way more than two hundred years old and it was still completely intact! I only nodded – if I'd said anything, it would have been sappy (oh, the loving care) and would probably have embarrassed him.

As Fudge and I snuggled under the quilt, I stared into the banked fire and listened to the sounds of pages turning in the other room. Gregory was obviously reading by candlelight. His mother, apparently, had never told him reading in low light was bad for your eyes. I snickered to myself, closed my eyes and fell asleep.

Only to be awakened a few minutes later by a paw batting my face.

"*Sorry, but you need to wake up,*" Fudge sounded apologetic.

"What? Is something wrong?"

"*I need to relieve myself but there is no litter box here. I cannot wait until we get home, whenever that may be.*"

"It's snowing and freezing outside. Are you sure?"

"*I do not have a choice, do I? Please open the door for me.*"

I climbed out from the warmth of the quilt, pulled my pants, shoes and coat on and walked outside with Fudge right on my heels. The snow was already deeper than Fudge was tall, and he plowed his way through it toward the back of the cottage. The door opened and Gregory poked his head out.

"Is something wrong?" Gregory's voice sounded concerned.

"Fudge had to pee."

"Bollocks. My apologies. Call him back. I will get his things from your house."

I'd totally forgotten that as an Air-affinity, Gregory can transport things through the ether. I called to Fudge in my mind, telling him that Gregory was getting his litter box from our place and he didn't have to freeze his balls off any longer.

*"Now he remembers. I am nearly through and will join you shortly. But thank him. I do not wish to repeat this experience anytime soon."*

"Why didn't you remind me sooner?" I asked as I attempted to dry Fudge off with a towel Gregory had thoughtfully provided.

*"I did not think of it. On the days you study, I am used to waiting until we get home to do my business. It was only when the urgency struck that I remembered."*

"His litter box is in the bathtub," Gregory called from the kitchen. "I also took the opportunity to get his food in case you can't go home tomorrow. I'm putting that down next to the bowl of water in here."

*"Enough with the towel,"* Fudge told me as he batted my hands away. *"Please convey my thanks to the wizard."*

Fudge hopped back on the couch and started to finish drying himself. I thought that would take longer than the towel, but he *was* a cat, after all. I gave Gregory both our thanks and heard him head back into his bedroom as I crawled back under the quilt, wrapping myself tightly to dispel the chill from standing outside. It took a bit, but I finally got warm again and drifted back off to sleep.

It was still snowing and blowing the next morning, although it wasn't quite whiteout conditions – I could just barely make out the garage and main house, when I hadn't been able to see them at all the previous afternoon.

"Unless it blows through by mid-afternoon, I would prefer you stayed here another night," Gregory told me as he refilled my coffee. "The Hummer may go where other vehicles will not, but it would still be tricky driving until we got to the main roads."

I heaved a sigh. I may fit on the couch, but it wasn't as comfortable as my own bed. Not to mention just being *home*. "I understand. Since I don't have any of my stuff here to work on, what can we do today?"

"Read? I have no more client work and can't think of anything I need done for you to practice on. Or you could lose some more games of checkers." The corners of his mouth turned up.

"I think I'm checkered out," I grinned back. "I'll just peruse your library for something to read. You undoubtedly have one or two I haven't seen."

At over two hundred years old and an avid reader (once he'd learned how), Gregory had filled an entire wall of the cottage with floor-to-ceiling shelves of books. Most of them were history or science but he had a lot of mythology, too. Current fiction? Not so much.

So, as Gregory hauled in several armloads of wood for the fireplace, I curled up in a chair next to the window and started re-reading *The Complete Fairy Tales of Hans Christian Andersen*. At least I thought I was re-reading them. I must have gotten through them at least once as a child, right? But I discovered I either hadn't, or my memory had totally failed because there were many that seemed brand-new to me.

As I read, I was aware of the almost complete silence. No refrigerator humming, no thrumming of the furnace, just the crackle and pop coming from the fireplace and the quiet sounds of Gregory puttering. I looked up to see what he was doing, and my jaw almost hit the floor. He was dusting! A man, actually doing housework!

I cleared my throat. "This is an unusual sight."

He paused, the feather duster poised above a book shelf. "What?"

"You're cleaning. I mean, with a duster. Why don't you just blow the dust away with your magic?"

He chuckled as he put the duster down. "Where would I blow it to? I could certainly gather it all up and dump it in your lap, if that would make you happy."

"But…"

"I've charmed the duster so it catches it all instead of just moving it around. Besides, I like the physical act. It's satisfying to see the fruits of my labor. I like a clean house."

Well, that certainly wasn't the reason he was single. Any woman would kill to have a man who liked housework enough to do it himself. I smiled and went back to reading.

*The Elf of the Rose* brought to mind Ev and the "investment."

"Did you ever find anything about that elf?" I asked.

"No, but it's not surprising. They don't usually have much to do with anyone outside their race and those that do, don't speak of their own kind. At least not the few that I know. Why?"

"Just wondering. I'm sure that Martin is going to tell Ev not to have anything to do with it and I thought if you'd turned up anything shady about the guy that it would help the cause. You know, the more ammunition we have…"

He took a sip from his ever-present cup of coffee and went back to dusting. "I know but you and Martin will just have to argue with logic."

I snorted. Ev and logic were mutually exclusive. But I'd already said my piece, so it would be up to Martin. If Ev was adamant, there was nothing we could do about it – it was his money, after all.

My phone rang, shattering the peaceful, electricity-free world.

"Hiya," Cassandra's voice came through. "You staying warm?"

"We're at Gregory's. I take it the power went out over that way, too?"

"Yep. News sites are saying it's out in various sections of the city and because of the snow and wind, it'll be a day or so before they get it all back. Did you stay overnight?"

I filled Cassandra in on the weekend thus far, including playing a board game with Ev. At that last, she choked on whatever beverage she was drinking.

"He's good at something that requires *strategy*? That means *thinking*."

I laughed back. "Believe it or not, yes. He even won a game off Gregory." As my BFF, she naturally knew of my miserable failures at Chinese checkers when going up against the wizard. As the landlord for our office, she also knew Ev quite well.

"Okay, I'm picking my jaw off the floor now. I also gotta go. Don't want to use too much battery or I'll have to go out and start the car to charge my phone. Tommy's already had to do it once."

We hung up and I went back to reading as Gregory continued cleaning. I couldn't help but sneak a peek every now and then. It was just *weird* to see a man enjoy doing housework!

Chapter Five

The wind quit blowing, the snow quit falling, and the power finally came back on sometime in the middle of the night. Monday morning dawned bright, the sun glaring off the snow. Gregory managed to maneuver the Hummer through unplowed streets and around stranded cars, dropping us off at my doorstep about the time I'd normally be leaving for the office.

Someone had obviously already been at work because the sidewalk in front of my building and the stairs down to my apartment had already been shoveled. For this I was glad. That stairwell collected snow like a vacuum and in storms like the one we'd had, the pile was high enough to make traversing the stairs treacherous.

An hour later, I made it to the office – after I'd luxuriated in my own shower for far too long. The city had plowed the main drag and most of the building owners had shoveled their portions of the sidewalk so the walk wasn't too bad. I still had to peel off the wet pants and boots I'd worn. I'd put on the heels I'd carried when Ev made it to the office. When no one else was there, my shoes sat under my desk and I walked around in bare feet. I hate shoes.

Although the sidewalk in front of the deli was clear, there was no sign of Cassandra. Even though it was closed on Mondays, she was usually in the back, catching up on paperwork. This day, though, the door was locked, even to me (it was spelled to allow certain people through when she was closed) so I had to make do with my coffee instead of a latte from her. Not my favorite way to start my least-favorite day.

I had just finished reading the weekend's reports and emails, compiling a list of things to talk to Ev about, when he stomped in the door.

"I need to move back to LA," he growled. "I'm sick of snow and cold."

"What's your beef?" I called from my office as I gathered my notes in preparation for our morning meeting. "You don't have to drive in it, don't have to shovel it, and are only out in the weather from door to car to door."

"I hate cold. When it snows hard, Gregory won't drive me anywhere. And I'm tired of looking at nothing but white out the windows," he groused some more. "My phone didn't ring at all, so I assume there were no emergencies. What happened over the weekend?"

"Nothing much," I said from the kitchen, where I was topping off my coffee. As I walked toward his office, I continued, "Myron knows his contract is up in a month and wants a raise; John called about providing a guard for a possible new client he's speaking with…"

I sat in my usual chair, continuing down my list of notes. Ev listened, making an occasional comment and notes of his own. I finished and handed him a list of calls to return. I'd just risen to go back to my own office when the phone rang. Reaching over Ev's desk, I answered it from his extension, listened for a moment and handed the receiver to him.

"It's Martin. He's finished that tome of a business proposal from the elf and wants to talk with you about it."

"Oh, good. That was on my list of things to do today."

I headed back to my office with *my* list of things to do longer by half since talking with Ev. Thankfully, Sally would be in shortly and I could hand off some of it to her. I tackled the phone calls first.

Less than an hour later, I was working on a contract for a new hire when the outer door opened. Knowing Sally wasn't yet in, I slipped my shoes back on and headed out to the reception area.

"Good morning, Miss McCollum," that heavenly voice greeted me. My eyes were treated, too, as Perchaladon took off his outer coat, revealing another exquisitely tailored suit showing off his …um…assets. "Is Evander in? I'd like to speak with him."

I really hated when people didn't make appointments. "He is," I replied, only drooling a little bit. It really was difficult to look at him and stay focused on work. "I'll ask if he has time to see you." I didn't want to offer coffee or anything, just in case Ev had other ideas.

I poked my head in his office. "Perchaladon is here and would like to see you. I wasn't aware you'd made an appointment with him."

"I didn't but it's okay," he said. "Show him in."

I walked back out to the reception area. "Ev can see you. May I offer you a beverage?"

"No, thank you. I am fine for now. And I know the way to his office." I stayed where I was and watched him walk down the hall to Ev's office, sighing when he closed the door behind him. I shook my head clear of un-work-like thoughts and went back to my desk.

Not too much later, I heard the door open and Perchaladon say, "I am disappointed in your decision. It is one I believe you will come to regret." I watched as he strode past my door and heard the outer door close.

Ev and his aroma drifted into my office. That reminded me: I needed to order more scented candles. I made a note. "You should be proud of me, Amy."

I looked up from my work. "You said no?"

"I did. Martin told me the history of these sorts of companies and how much money he was sure had been lost over the years. After that, I decided not to invest. See? I can say no!"

"It's about time you listened to one of us," I told him. "While I have you, what do you want to do about the workers' comp insurance? The premium is going up by a third this year."

"Don't we have an agent for that stuff? See if he can find something else." Ev left and I heard his office door close once again. The light for one of the phone lines blinked on. I added a note to call said agent to my list. An administrative assistant's work was never done.

***

And life went on. The snow melted and spring finally arrived. It felt like I'd only blinked and the heat of summer was upon us. My Saturday sessions with Gregory moved from his workroom out to his garden. Although Cassandra's garden was larger and lusher (she was, after all, an Earth witch), Gregory's was nothing to sneeze at. While I helped him weed, we discussed the properties of all the herbs and vegetables he grew.

"Your book contains correspondence lists but if you get to know the plant, you may find a different use for it," he intoned. Gregory didn't drone like the college marketing professor who'd nearly put me to sleep but he was definitely in teaching mode. "Therefore, you need to really *listen* as you're weeding a bed. You never know what you might hear."

I sighed as I pulled another piece of grass out of the bed of catnip. "I know. Cassandra said the same thing. I do get some flashes but so far, nothing that's not on any of the lists."

"You just don't spend enough time with the plants. Once a week definitely isn't going to build up any relationships."

"*I have a* wonderful *relationship with catnip. It smells so good!*"

I laughed. There was a reason Fudge was still inside the cottage while we were out in the garden. Gregory didn't trust him around the herbs. After Fudge's reaction to a valerian plant in Cassandra's greenhouse, I understood why. He and Merlin, her cat and familiar, had tried to dig it up to get at the roots.

My life wasn't all work, though (and I considered my lessons with Gregory work). I'd finished my final manuscript and fired it off to the editor in May and made her suggested revisions in June. Ev was on the party circuit, which always was at its height in the summer when people could gather on patios and lawns instead of cramming themselves into living rooms. That meant he wasn't in the office as much. I spent a lot of my free time biking around the lakes, enjoying the exercise – and the people-watching.

As Cassandra and I sat on the deck of an ice cream parlor with a couple of other girlfriends, admiring the tight behinds of the male rollerbladers who skated on the path mere feet from our perch, I mused aloud that maybe now I was done with my writing contract, I had time for a love life again.

"You *have* been a hermit lately," Louise quipped. "Every time I've suggested a girls' night out in the last several months, you've been too busy. It's time you were in circulation again!"

"Oh, I know," I sighed. "I really have been. Between regular work, studying this magic stuff, and finishing with my writing, I haven't had a lot of time. But now one of those things has dropped off my list so I can at least *think* about getting involved again."

"I wish I could do magic," Elsa moaned. "You three are so lucky."

"It depends," Cassandra replied. "Sure, we can do things you can't but on the other hand, we have twice the homework as teenagers, or sometimes as adults, like Amy's finding out. I hated all the studying I had to do between regular school and Mom's assignments."

"Yeah, but it's still cool," Louise grinned. "I love being able to warm a snifter of brandy from across the room if I'm interested in the guy holding it!" Louise was a rare Fire witch and had the temperament to match. "But back to your love life, Amy. I hear that new country bar out at the mall has lots of cute guys and mostly our age!"

I grimaced. Country music wasn't my thing. "I hate cowboy boots," I ventured a lame excuse.

"You don't have to wear them, just snare a guy who does!" I should introduce Louise to Ev. Their minds ran along the same track. Ev had started trying to fix me up with a multitude of guys within a month of Tony's untimely death. I kept telling him I wasn't ready. Ev's taste in men and mine didn't exactly match up and given that I knew most of the men he mentioned, I could have come up with even more excuses if that one didn't fly.

"Oh, come on," Elsa added. "One night out watching guys in tight jeans and fancy boots won't kill you. It's Saturday. We can go tonight. At least three of us could." She eyed Cassandra.

"It'll have to be just the three of you," Cassandra rejoined. "Tommy and I have dinner plans with his dad and some other people tonight. And since I left the deli early today, it wouldn't be fair to skip tonight, too, leaving Tommy with *all* the work." She looked at her watch. "As a matter of fact, I need to run. It's a dressy dinner and I have to get ready."

"Okay, then, the three of us?" Louise fixed a stare on me. "We'll pick you up at seven."

I sighed. "Okay, fine. I'll go. But no promises."

"None asked for. It'll be good just to see you out and about."
We parted company, Cassandra and I taking the city streets
eastward while Louise and Elsa headed south on the path around
Lake Bde Maka Ska. They lived together in an apartment right on
the western shore of the lake.

I left Cassandra at her driveway and continued home, hauling
my bike down the stairs, through my apartment and into the boiler
room across the hall. While I could have locked it on the bike rack
at the corner, I wanted to see it again. Although where I lived was
fairly safe, one didn't leave belongings outside unattended for very
long in any neighborhood, not just mine.

I had about three hours to get ready to go out. Apart from
the occasional party Ev had thrown where my attendance was
mandatory, I hadn't been out in quite a while. I may not really
enjoy country music, but I couldn't argue with the blue-jeans-
atmosphere of that type of bar. It made the choice of outfit so
much easier!

Promptly at seven, a car honked outside. I shoved cell phone,
identification, money and credit card in my pocket, grabbed my
keys, blew a kiss goodbye to Fudge and headed out. Once I'd
thought about it some, I was actually excited to be going out
partying, regardless of the venue. It *had* been a long time!

Elsa was driving. She made the perfect designated driver.
Even a sip of alcohol and she got violently ill. Didn't matter what
sort, either; beer, wine, and hard liquor all made her sick. But she
had enough "fun" genes to make up for it. We chatted about what
we might see that night during the ride over.

"Saturday is usually couples' night," I moaned. "We picked
the wrong night to go out."

"Not necessarily," Louise retorted. "This is supposed to be a
singles' bar. There may be some couples, sure, but I bet not as
many at the beginning as at the end of the night!" We all snickered.
The majority of the DJs around town always used the phrase

"hotel-motel time" when it was closing time. It was truer than not in many places.

# CHAPTER SIX

"Twenty dollars?" I squeaked. "That's an awful lot to pay just to get in the door!"

"It's obvious you haven't been out in a while," Elsa said. "That's pretty much the going rate. Besides, you can afford it."

It wasn't the money that concerned me. It was the principle of the thing. Cork didn't charge a damned thing to walk into his place and I had a lot of fun at his pub.

"Hey, we're in time," Louise grabbed my arm and pulled. "There's still an open table right by the dance floor. C'mon, let's grab it!"

Elsa grabbed my other hand and we followed in Louise's wake, threading our way through what was promising to be a wall-to-wall crowd. We plopped in the chairs a split second before two couples, who'd obviously also seen the empty table, were able to make it that far.

"That was close!" Louise laughed. "I didn't want to stand all night. Now, who've we got so far?" She craned her neck to check out the room. Subtlety was not one of Louise's attributes. Elsa and I did the same, but I like to think I was a little more circumspect in my perusal. I didn't see anyone who caught my fancy, but the night was yet young.

A couple of hours and a couple of drinks later, the evening was in full swing. The band was playing at full volume and the dance floor was crowded. Louise and Elsa danced with several different men while I kept the table occupied so it wouldn't get taken. That's not to say I hadn't been asked. I just hadn't been asked by anyone I cared to dance with.

The band was playing a song I'd never heard (not that I kept up with country music, you understand) when I felt a hand on my shoulder and a sweet baritone voice shout in my ear, "May I have this dance?"

I turned to see that gorgeous hunk of elf, Perchaladon, leaning down. Immediately, alarms sounded in my head. Not that there weren't some paranormals in the crowd – there were – but he was the only elf. What was he doing here? I smelled a rat. But there was only one way to find out what he had on his mind.

"Of course," I replied with a faked smile. He took my hand as I rose and, guiding me onto the floor, disregarded the current fad and led me into a foxtrot. I silently thanked my mother for her ballroom dance lessons and followed easily.

"What's an elf doing in a mostly-human country bar?" I shouted up to him. "I thought your race didn't mix with others?"

Thanks to my high heels, he didn't have to bend down too far to answer me. "Unlike many of my own, I prefer to mix with all types of people. I find them interesting. You, for example. What's such a lovely witch doing working for that overly-aromatic ogre?"

Uh-oh. He knew I was a witch. How did he know? I was certain I'd left my "I'm a witch" placard at home. He must have seen the confusion in my eyes. Or maybe smelled it. Or something. I wasn't certain what capabilities elves had.

"Every paranormal being has a different aura than humans. I can see those auras, as can every other elf. Yours has magic in it."

Ooookkaayy. They can see auras. So, no hiding what I was from elves. Got it.

"To answer your question," I hollered. He winced.

"You do not have to shout. I have the ability to filter out the music and hear what you say clearly when we are this close."

Better hearing than I'd imagined. Filed away for future reference.

"Sorry," I said in a normal tone of voice. "To answer your question, it's a job. And a good paying one, at that. Why?"

"I was just wondering. Evander does not seem like a very intelligent being. You do. The two normally do not work well together."

I smiled. "He doesn't have skills in some areas, that's true. But he's very good at what he does and so am I. We make a good team." What was this guy after?

"So, it was you who told him not to invest in my company."

"Not entirely, although I didn't think it an appropriate investment for him. His financial advisor put the nail in your coffin."

A frown marred that handsome face. "And who is his investment advisor?"

"I'm sorry," I frowned back. "Not that it's a big secret, but Evander's affairs are his own. It's not my place to tell you. Perhaps you should ask him."

The guy might be handsome *and* a good dancer, but this was getting creepier by the minute. People chose not to invest in companies, startup or not, all the time. Why was he so bothered? I was getting uncomfortable with the whole thing. Thankfully, the song ended, and I was escorted back to the table where Elsa and Louise were sitting with their eyes and mouths wide open.

"Thank you for the dance, Miss McCollum," Perchaladon bowed. "Perhaps we will do it again sometime."

As soon as he'd walked away, I heard, "Who was *that*?" and "How'd you snare a handsome elf when I got a pimply-faced human?" from Elsa and Louise, respectively.

"He tried to get Ev to invest in a company. Ev said no and he just showed up here. Apparently wanting more details than Ev gave him and thinking I'd pony up. I'm glad the song ended. So, how was the human?" I tried to change the subject.

"He stepped on my toes more than once. I thought elves stayed within their own race."

I was supposed to be out partying, not thinking about work, and was saved by a not-pimply-faced man asking me to dance. I escaped the inquisition – for now.

By eleven, I was yawning. It really was irritating, not being able to stay up late. Louise and Elsa were still enjoying the night, dancing nearly every song with a different guy. I didn't want to spoil their fun, so I hollered that I was going to take a taxi home and they should stay. They both nodded and waved as I left the table and made my way out to one of the numerous taxi stands around the mall.

As I was walking along the sidewalk, a limo cruised up and the rear window rolled down.

"May I offer you transportation?" Perchaladon said from the back seat. I'd thought he'd left the bar two hours earlier. This was getting creepy.

"No, thank you." I tried to be polite. "I prefer to take a taxi rather than get into a car with a relative stranger."

"I can assure you, Miss McCollum, that my kind does not take advantage of a woman when she does not wish it. I am simply offering to share my vehicle with you."

Yeah, right. He obviously wasn't like the rest of "his kind." Therefore, untrustworthy. I said nothing, turned my head away and continued walking. His limo trailed me. I wasn't sure how elves reacted to magic, but I knew for a fact that the car's engine wouldn't work if, *somehow*, all the dirt in the street made its way into the tailpipe, clogging it.

I was just about to gather all the dirt I could find and magically shove it up the tailpipe when a second limo came screaming around the corner, cut Perchaladon's limo off and screeched to a halt at the curb, nearly causing the first to rear-end it.

The front window rolled down and I saw Gregory leaning over from the driver's seat. "Get in. Ev's in hospital."

"What?" I yelled as I climbed into the front seat. "What happened?"

I'd barely had time to close the door before Gregory pulled away from the curb and quickly maneuvered his way out of the parking lot.

"He got into a fight with another ogre at Club Tread. Although weapons aren't supposed to be allowed, the other guy had a knife and before I could react, he managed to stab Ev in the side, puncturing a lung. It's not life-threatening but he said he wanted you there when he got out of surgery."

I clicked my seatbelt and relaxed a little. "How did the knife get past security? And I assume it was over a woman?"

"Of course. But Ev was in the right this time. He was behaving himself. For a change. As to the knife, the head of security is still looking into that. I know Charles. Heads will roll."

Now that I knew what was happening, I could completely relax. Although Ev usually didn't get so hurt he needed surgery, this wasn't his first scrape over a female and probably wouldn't be the last. One question begged.

"How did you find me?"

"Your mobile. Sorry, Amy, but I've had you on my locator application since last year. I wanted every opportunity to keep you safe from anything that went down with Ev."

In case you didn't know, one of Ev's girlfriends went crazy about a year earlier. She wasn't the first and probably wouldn't be the last, but that time I got caught up in her madness. She had the weird idea she could take Ev's company, so she kidnapped him. When I wouldn't let her do anything, she and her minions kidnapped me and because Fudge was with me at the time, he got taken, too. It was thanks to his abilities that it only took the authorities a day or so to find us.

"Why didn't you just call?"

"I tried. You didn't answer."

I pulled my phone out of my back pocket and looked. I indeed had a missed call, which was weird. I should have felt it vibrate but I obviously didn't. I ought to have been angry that Gregory had activated the locator function on my phone without asking but instead, I wasn't bothered by it. I trusted Gregory with my life. Literally.

Thanks to light traffic at that hour, we pulled into the parking lot of St. Aloysius Hospital in about half the time it would have taken on a week day. Given that it was a Saturday night and the police were out in force to catch drunk drivers, I had a sneaking suspicion Gregory had cloaked us so he could grossly exceed the speed limit.

St. Aloysius is the only hospital in the Twin Cities that caters to non-humans. Most paranormals don't get human illnesses but they do require stitching up, poison treatment, and other medical services. Human doctors don't know a lot about paranormal physiology, hence the specialty hospital. Because ogres and trolls are frequent patients, nearly everything is oversized to accommodate them. I felt rather tiny, walking through the huge doors.

We were ushered to the waiting room just outside surgery. St. Aloysius may be an atypical hospital, but their coffee was no better than that found at ones for humans. Gregory and I both grimaced as we sucked down enough caffeine to keep us going for a few hours.

An hour or so after our arrival, a man dressed in scrubs came into the room. We were the only ones there, so it wasn't difficult for him to figure out who to address. "I assume you are here for Mr. Angelich?"

Gregory nodded. "Yes. I am his driver and official next of kin. How's he doing?"

The doctor raised an eyebrow at the "next of kin," then chuckled. "Starting to wake up from anesthesia, madder than a hornet, and asking to see you both. Surgery-wise, he'll be fine. Uncomfortable for a few months but he will heal. Come on. I'll take you through to recovery."

The man turned on his heels, presumably expecting us to follow. Which we did.

This wasn't the first time I'd seen Ev in the hospital and probably wouldn't be the last but to see him in a hospital bed, hooked up to all sorts of machines with tubes and wires running all over the place was still a shock. He opened his eyes as we walked in the room.

"Did you get that sonofabitch?" he slurred his words.

"Yes, Ev, Charles has him and will deal with it," Gregory soothed. "You should concentrate on getting well now."

Ev groaned. "I know I'll heal. I just can't believe they let a knife into the club. Or that I got stabbed with it over a woman."

My thought was that it probably wasn't the first time that had happened, but I kept it to myself.

"Amy," he turned to me.

"Ev," I tried to sound upbeat, "Whatever it is can wait. You need to recover from this."

"No, it can't wait," he mumbled. "Perchaladon…" He fell back asleep.

"He's going to be out of it for at least twenty-four hours," the doctor said. "We've got him on some pretty hefty painkillers. I suggest you go home and get some sleep. We'll call you immediately if there are any complications, but I don't expect any."

I grabbed Gregory's arm and headed toward the car. It was now after two o'clock in the morning and even with the coffee, I was almost dead on my feet. With a promise to keep me informed, Gregory dropped me at my apartment and sped off.

*"You need to sleep but first you need to feed me."* I knew Fudge knew what had happened by virtue of his always being inside my head but a little sympathy for the situation would have been nice. I told him so.

*"Your ogre is always getting into trouble. You should be accustomed to it by now. My food?"*

I duly put a scoop of food in his dish, ensured his water was topped off and dragged myself into the bedroom. I didn't even bother to put my clothes in the hamper, just stripped where I stood and fell into bed.

Once again, I cursed my cat for shredding my drapes. The sun woke me just four hours later. Between that and Ev's last "Perchaladon," I couldn't go back to sleep. At least it was Sunday and I could nap in the afternoon.

While inhaling my coffee, I mused on what could have bothered Ev so much about the elf. I didn't think Perchaladon was stalking *him.* Then the more I thought about the previous evening, the more pissed I got. I assumed he'd tracked me down just to ask me those questions, but how? And why?

*"Elves are not the nice creatures in your fairy tale books."*

"I know that," I shot back. "I'm just trying to figure out his angle. If he wanted Ev to invest in his company, it should be Ev he's stalking, not me. So, why me?"

Fudge yawned and started a bath. *"You are not unattractive for a human. Perhaps he is pursuing you romantically. Or not. Time will tell."*

Such a helpful familiar! Not. I knew in my gut it had something to do with business, not romance. I didn't have enough information to go on, though. Just then, my phone rang. It was Gregory.

"What happened last night before the fight?" I asked after we'd exchanged greetings.

"That's why I was calling. Perchaladon was at Club Tread last night, harassing Ev about his investment opportunity. Once again, Ev blew him off but it has me concerned. I wanted to know if Ev said anything to you that he didn't say to me."

"I don't think so. You should know, however, that it was Perchaladon's limo you cut off at the mall last night. And he was in the nightclub I was in."

"WHAT? Why didn't you tell me this?"

"Um. Other things on my mind until now. Like Ev?"

I could hear the deep sigh. "Sorry. I haven't had enough sleep and am on edge. So, tell me now."

I related the dance, the question game, and then the issue with the limo.

"Why accost you? Ev made the decision not to invest," Gregory mused.

"I've been asking myself the same question. Do elves go bonkers just like humans…or vampires?"

(A crazy vampire had once fixated on me. It wasn't fun.)

"I honestly don't know," was the reply. "Because they tend to keep to themselves, we don't know a lot about their race. But I rather doubt it. Otherwise, there would be stories and I don't know any. I'll ask my contacts. In the meantime, he can't hurt you as a vampire might so if he comes around again, treat him like you would anyone else of that caliber. I'm going to the hospital to check on Ev. Want to come?"

"Thanks but no. He's just going to want to discuss business and I don't think that's good for him at this point. I'll just keep the home fires burning until he's able to come back. They *can* keep him in the hospital even if he wants to leave, right?"

A chuckle and then, "Yes. Well, sort of. They will just keep pumping drugs into him so he sleeps rather than move and possibly tear his stitches. He won't feel like much for about a week, anyways. Even with his healing abilities, he's going to be mighty sore. And the doctors can't do anything magical for him to speed up the process. You're safe for a bit. I'll let you know how he's doing."

Gregory ended the conversation and my phone immediately rang again. It was Louise.

"Hey, just checking to make sure you're in one piece today. And what about that mouth-watering hunk of elf?"

I related what had happened after I'd left them.

"Sorry about your boss but knowing ogres, it doesn't surprise me. And sorry Mr. Handsome is such a creep. Call me if you want him flamed. Or at least a little singed around the edges."

I ended that conversation with a "will do" and went back to sipping my caffeine. I actually was at loose ends on a Sunday. I had all week to read up on my next magic lesson, no writing deadlines to adhere to, and the house was reasonably clean. Reading, the baseball game, and a long nap sounded ideal.

The following week saw me dealing with *all* the work – both mine and Ev's. Because he regularly took off for parts unknown, I was able to fend people off with "he's out of the office" without saying he'd been hurt and was in the hospital. Sally, my assistant, was even better at blowing folks off. I heard her more than once tell someone, "I don't know when he'll be back. If you want an immediate decision, I'll make one, but I don't know if it would be the same as Mr. Angelich would make." Perhaps not the most business-like response but if you knew our clients, you'd know that snark is sometimes the only way to handle them.

Ev finally returned to the office the next Monday. He looked like hell warmed over and didn't bellow nearly as much as usual. It probably hurt to draw in that much breath. Thank goodness.

Two weeks later, he was pretty much back to normal. And off on one of his crazy-train rides. Remember that movie investment? He decided to go watch it being filmed…and more than likely put his two cents' worth in. I felt sorry for the director and actors. But since he was an investor, there was really nothing they could do to stop him from observing.

So, he took off for New Orleans and that's when the shit hit the fan – again.

CHAPTER SEVEN

After that fateful call from John, Gregory and I had a brief conversation (argument) about whether I would accompany him to New Orleans. He insisted he could find Ev and bring him home on his own. I reminded him that I was the one who found him when he went missing in Atlanta and wasn't about to be left out of the hunt. He finally acquiesced and while I called Sally to fill her in and ask her to work full time for a bit, made his own calls to arrange a flight to New Orleans and someplace to stay.

That night, I had to have another argument with my cat.

*"You could be in some danger. Or you may get upset enough to lose control. You must take me with you."*

I had no carrier for my cat and doubted any airplane would let him wander around the cabin. On the other hand, he had a point. I knew he was in my head *wherever* I went but that his ability to help diminished with distance. It would be easier for him to tamp down my temper if he were close by. That way, I wouldn't have to worry about the Witches' Council lopping off my head for causing an earthquake or something. I called upstairs to my witch neighbors who had cats.

"I need to go out of town and Fudge needs to come with. Do you have a carrier I can borrow?" I asked Marge.

"Of course. I'll get one out of the closet and one of us will bring it right down." She hung up and in just a couple of minutes, there was a brief knock at my back door. Elinda didn't wait for me to answer but just came right on in.

"Here you are. I brought the large one so he has room to move around a little. Do we need to bring in your mail or anything?"

I shrugged. "I have no idea how long I'll be gone. Ev's gone missing again. So, yeah, probably. Just in case."

She gave me a hug. "Your ogre certainly does get himself into a world of trouble, doesn't he? You be careful, darlin'. We'll keep the home fires burning." She closed my door quietly behind her.

Fudge hopped off the sofa and inspected the carrier. "*Must I?*"

"You must. If you want to travel with me on an airplane, that is. They don't let any animals but service animals on a plane without a carrier."

"*You should look into that. I could be a seeing-eye cat.*"

"But I'm not blind. So, a carrier it is."

I started packing – after I'd checked the weather forecast. It honestly sounded much like I was accustomed to: hotter 'n Hades and enough humidity to make it soupy. Plus, afternoon thunderstorms but luckily, no tropical storms or hurricanes in the immediate forecast. Although I knew buildings had air conditioning, who knew where we'd end up? Sleeveless tops, a lightweight sweater and a raincoat all got crammed into my carryon.

Gregory picked us up at dark-thirty and much to my surprise, headed toward Minneapolis-St. Paul International rather than Flying Cloud where the charter service Ev used flew out of.

"Our normal company is fully-booked and I was able to get us on a commercial flight that would get us down there faster than waiting for them. We have a layover in Atlanta, but we'll still get to New Orleans three hours before they could. I have a feeling time is of the essence."

Six hours after leaving my place, we were checked into the Omni and ushered into a suite. Nice but it only had *one bed*. I looked at Gregory after the bellhop had collected his tip and left. "One bed? I like you but…"

The corners of his mouth quirked. "Last minute reservations? The sofa pulls out. You get the bed, I get the sofa."

"I've slept on my share. Sofa beds suck. Couldn't you have found accommodations with adjoining rooms or something?"

His mouth corners turned a little further up. "Sofa beds are heaven compared to cots or even the ground. It won't bother me in the least. Be thankful I was able to book a suite with two bathrooms. Now, while you unpack, I'm going to get Fudge's things. Then I have to see if I can home in on Ev."

(It always weirded me out that Gregory knew exactly where in my apartment everything was. He'd even retrieved a suit out of my closet once. The right one on the first try. Someday I'd have the gumption to ask him *exactly* how he knew all that.)

I'd let Fudge out of the carrier as soon as the bellhop had closed the door. In the time it took me to open the closet doors to unpack the few things I'd brought, I heard his belongings plop onto the bathroom floor.

*"Water and food would be welcome."*

Ignoring the cat for the moment, I went back into the sitting area to find it empty. The balcony doors were open, letting in the noise of the city plus the damp of hot, humid air. Gregory was out on the balcony with his eyes closed, turning this way and that. I joined him, closing the doors to preserve the comfort of our air-conditioned room.

"He's somewhere in the French Quarter. I think. Rather near, though. With so much magic floating around, it's difficult to get a fix. I need to call John. Order a late lunch from room service, will you? Whatever they have in the way of a muffeleta will do for me."

A what? I grabbed the room service menu from the desk. Ah. A sandwich. A sort of Italian sandwich. It actually sounded good, so I ordered two. While Gregory chatted quietly on his cell, I filled Fudge's litter box, put food and water in their dishes, and basically tried to make us at home.

We each ate half of our huge sandwiches and put the rest in the fridge for later. "Put your walking shoes on. Let's go find Ev," Gregory suggested.

"What did John say?" I asked as we made our way down the stairs.

"Nothing's changed since yesterday. I'm going to see if I can weed out Ev's signal from all the magical interference. Stay close so I don't lose you in these crowds."

As soon as we left the air-conditioned hotel, I longed to go back to the room. I'd been outside for less than a minute and was starting to melt in the heat and humidity. On the sidewalk in front of me, Gregory closed his eyes again, turning left and right. Opening them, he turned right and started walking. At the street corner, he turned right again. After trying to skip my way around people to keep up even in just a half block, I finally just grabbed his hand – it *was* a zoo!

I tried to sightsee a little while Gregory tugged me this way and that to avoid people. I'd never been to New Orleans and although the view from the taxi that transported us from the airport made it seem like any other city, the French Quarter was quite a sight. The buildings were much older than I was accustomed to seeing, most of them cheek-by-jowl but a few with tiny courtyards visible through gates, and a lot of lacy wrought iron balconies. Some of those balconies had gorgeous ferns draping over the railing. A lot of them were flying the French flag with plenty of red-white-and-blue bunting; many of them boasted flags with a black-and-gold fleur de lis. (For the New Orleans Saints – an American football team, if you didn't know.) Glancing in the shop windows as I walked by, I could see artwork and jewelry, as well as the menus for some restaurants. The strains of Dixieland jazz came from somewhere nearby. Over it all was the cacophony of a dozen languages from hundreds of tourists on this street alone.

After the fourth time tripping on an uneven sidewalk, I stopped gawking and started watching where I put my feet. Gregory stopped at each street corner to search but continued walking straight down…Royal Street, the sign said.

We walked several blocks, the crowds thinning somewhat the farther we went. Gregory suddenly turned right at a corner, pulling me with him. This area looked more like warehouses and not quite as prosperous as where we'd been earlier. Scaffolding covered the façades of a couple of buildings that, to my eye, looked like they were about to fall down. He halted in front of a door under an arch of pipes and boards so quickly that I ran into his back.

"Here. He's in here. Now, to get him out?" Gregory eyed the building up and down.

"Just go in, smack around whoever is guarding him and untie him?" I helpfully offered.

"The building is warded and it's elven magic. This is more complicated than Ev pissing off a wizard over a woman. I can't unravel the spell without it backfiring onto us. I need to make some calls. Let's go back to the hotel."

"But Ev," I protested as he dragged me down the street and around the corner.

"He's fine for the moment. They won't do anything to him until and unless whatever it is they want doesn't happen. And it wouldn't do for us to get hurt and *not* get him. Come on."

The crowds thickened up again as we walked back toward our hotel along a different route. I smelled coffee!

"Hey, I smell coffee! Where is it coming from and can we get some?"

Gregory slowed down but never stopped wending his way through the throngs. "You've never been to New Orleans? We will come back later, perhaps after dinner, and you can sample the famous coffee and beignets from Café du Monde. It will be less crowded then, anyways."

Ooh. I'd heard about Café du Monde and definitely wanted to pay it a visit. "Yes, but what about Ev?"

"It will be tomorrow at the earliest before I can figure out what is going on and how to extricate him from whatever he's gotten himself into. After I've made my calls, we will undoubtedly have the evening free. I will take you to dinner, we can do some night sightseeing, and have a cup of coffee. Will that suffice?"

It would. If he wasn't that worried about Ev at the moment then I wouldn't be either, although the "elven magic" comment concerned me. The handsome Perchaladon's face popped into my head. It had been a few weeks since he'd made an appearance and I thought we were done with him. Perhaps not? Or maybe it was some other issue. With Ev, one never knew.

Once back in our room, Gregory warded it from overly-large ears and made a few calls while I listened in on his side of the conversation. It consisted mostly of him trying nearly all his contacts to figure out how to break the magic surrounding the building Ev was in. Apparently, elven magic was completely different from how human-types went about things.

About halfway through one conversation, Gregory stifled a curse, looked at his phone with disgust, then jammed the charging plug into it.

"May I borrow your mobile, please? I've killed my battery once again and do not wish to use the hotel phone where listening in is easy."

I wordlessly handed my cell over. It was nice to know I wasn't the only one who drained cell phone batteries. Ever since my magic had manifested, I could only get about a half day of use before I had to plug it in – and that was with the ugly, rubberized case Gregory had given me, which was identical to the one covering his. That only prevented me from frying the delicate electronics.

Gregory finished his calls and plugged my phone in next to his on the desk. "Where would you like to go for dinner? New Orleans is full of good restaurants."

I opened my mouth to reply that I didn't care when there was a knock on the door. "Were you expecting someone?" I asked.

"No. Back away. I will answer it," came the terse reply. He moved toward the door, his right hand behind his back, a ball of carmine energy glowing in his palm. He looked through the peephole, gave me an odd look, then opened the door.

My jaw hit the floor. An elf stood there, decked out in not a custom-tailored suit but long, midnight blue robes embroidered in silver and gold. His long black hair had white streaks through it. Crows' feet crinkled the corners of his eyes, but no other wrinkles creased his face.

*"Close your mouth. You will attract flies."*

I closed my mouth with a gulp but couldn't help continuing to stare.

A baritone voice intoned, "You may release your energy, wizard. I mean you and the lady no harm."

"I will release it when you tell me who you are and what you are doing here," Gregory rejoined.

"My name is Nelion. I believe we have a common adversary in my son, Perchaladon. I have come to offer my help."

Gregory released his energy and with a wave, ushered Nelion into our room.

*"Offer him some refreshment. Women are supposed to do these things in his world."*

I mentally snorted. A misogynistic society?

*"No. Their women are artists and warriors, just like the men. However, they have a lower opinion of human women and in this setting your role is unknown, so he probably thinks you are just the wizard's woman. Better to keep on his right side."*

I decided to do things my way. Setting up the cup-at-a-time coffeemaker, I remarked that I wanted a cup of coffee and would anyone else like one while I was at it? Both men accepted a cup so after I'd made three, we got down to brass tacks.

"First," Gregory said, "How did you find us? Second, why do you think your son is involved in our business here?"

Nelion grimaced. "To the second: There are rumors in my world that Perchaladon has, once again, attempted to entice non-elven investors for one of his schemes. I will admit to you that he is a source of embarrassment to me. I also heard that an ogre of your acquaintance is or was involved with him and said ogre has disappeared. I believe the two may be related.

"As for how I found you, I own this hotel. The desk staff is well-trained. Any non-human guests are automatically catalogued. To be frank, most every hotel in this city does the same. Given the, shall we say, boisterous atmosphere, sometimes things can get out of control and it is helpful to know who is capable of what. It was a simple matter to discover your relationship to the ogre."

That did not sit well with me, but I could tell Gregory took the cataloguing with a grain of salt. I slid him a look and he just shrugged his shoulders.

"It is possible your son is mixed up in Evander's disappearance," Gregory told him. "I know where Ev is and the building is warded with elven enchantments which, as you know, I cannot break without consequences. Can you?"

Nelion shrugged his shoulders. "Possibly. If not me, then one of our senior mages. However, I would prefer to handle my son and have him release your ogre and whomever else he may be holding for whatever reason. If you will agree to give me twenty-four hours to find my son and bring him to heel."

Gregory stood. "I will give you that but no more. If Ev has not been released by tomorrow evening, you or one of your people will accompany me to the building and break the wards. Are we agreed?"

Nelion bowed. "We are. You will hear from me within a day's time one way or the other." He turned to me. "Thank you for the coffee, Miss McCollum," and strode out of the room.

After we'd heard the "click" of the door latching, Gregory let out a breath. "Well, wasn't that interesting?"

I fumed. "Cataloguing? They can do that? Isn't that a breach of privacy or something?"

"Ah, Amy," Gregory sighed. "You have much to learn of our world. Yes, they can do that and no, it's no more a breach of privacy than you ordering nothing but fruits and vegetables through room service and them determining you're a vegetarian. In a hotel like this, that would go in a file and if you stayed here again, the room service menu would probably be customized.

"And, as he pointed out, things *do* get out of control in New Orleans and it *does* help to know who's visiting your town. Not that the mundane police care but the paranormal enforcers want as much knowledge as they can get.

"Now, as I was saying before I was interrupted, where would you like to go for dinner?"

# CHAPTER EIGHT

After dinner (which was yummy), he did indeed take me on a nighttime tour of New Orleans where I learned the true meaning of sultry summer nights in the south. The air temperature was somewhat cooler than when the sun was out, but it was still hot and sticky. Even the slight breeze generated by the air flowing by as the horse pulled the carriage wasn't cooling enough. I used the carriage company's flyer as a fan.

The driver kept up a nonstop commentary as he navigated his way through the narrow streets of the French Quarter, dodging the already-drunk revelers, then down the wider boulevards in the Garden District with its antebellum houses, all lit up as if to welcome us to the city.

Gregory, who had seen it all before (some of it more than a century ago), seemed lost in thought during most of the ride. He finally turned toward me. "Would you like that coffee now, or perhaps a cocktail? There are some fine musicians in this city and I think you'd enjoy having a listen."

I don't drink iced coffee and something cold sounded wonderful, so I agreed to the music. Gregory tapped the driver's back, interrupting his narrative. "Drop us anywhere on Frenchman Street, if you would."

Paying little or no attention to tipsy pedestrians and impatient car drivers, our host double-parked his carriage on a street that rivaled Bourbon Street's reputation. Bars lined both sides of the street, with people walking in and out at will, many with cocktails in their hands. Strains of different types of music mingled with the boisterous tones of partiers. Sunday evening, when most people were winding down their weekend and getting ready for the workweek, held no meaning here.

Gregory shoved a wad of bills into the driver's hand and helped me down from the carriage. We stepped over to the sidewalk, but it was no less crowded than the street. "What's your preference? Jazz? Southern rock? Straight-up country?" He raised his voice to be heard over the noise.

"Southern rock. Somewhere with air conditioning?"

He tilted his head to listen for a moment, then grabbed my hand, pulling me along through the crowds as he had earlier in the day. "This way."

Putting a couple of bills into the hand of a bouncer at the door of one of the establishments, he took the lead as we made our way up a short flight of stairs. To our left, the bar stretched along one wall and it was three deep in places. Immediately in front of the door was a crowded dance floor with the band playing on a dais to our right. I spied a couple rising from a table in front of the window and, for a change, I was the one doing the dragging as I grabbed Gregory's hand.

"Are you leaving?" I yelled. The man nodded his head, so I plunked myself down on one of the chairs and pushed their glasses away. Gregory sat next to me.

"This was fortuitous," he said in my ear. "These places are usually standing-room only by this time of night."

I nodded as he craned his head, looking for a wait person. Spying someone in a T-shirt with the bar's logo on it, he raised his hand to catch her attention. She acknowledged his wave and after serving the drinks on her tray, made her way over to us.

"Tanqueray and tonic with extra limes for the lady; a Heineken for me," Gregory ordered.

I punched his shoulder. "How did you know what I wanted to drink?"

"Isn't that your usual?"

"Well, yes, but maybe I wanted a glass of wine instead."

"It's hot. Since you didn't want coffee I assumed you wanted something cold. Red wine isn't usually served cold. Was I wrong?"

"No, but you might have asked." I was only slightly put out. He was right, as he usually was.

The band was toe-tapping good, as evidenced by the number of people crowding the dance floor. Gregory's fingers drummed the table in time to the beat and I found myself chair-dancing. All of a sudden, he stood and held out his hand.

"May I have this dance, m'lady?" His eyes twinkled and the corners of his mouth twitched into a grin.

Once again, I sent gratitude to my mother as he pulled me onto the floor and started to jitterbug. Not that we could get very rambunctious with it due to the crowding but nonetheless, my feet moved in a remembered pattern as he swung me around. Like most practiced male dancers, he adroitly avoided crashing into anyone else but unlike anyone else I'd ever danced with, he seemed to have created a cushion of air surrounding us. Anyone who got within a foot gently bounced off the shield in another direction.

Two songs later, I was out of breath and pulled him back to the table where I finished my drink in a couple of gulps. "I haven't done that since I was a kid. That was fun," I told him.

He was just as flushed as I and drained his beer. "You should do it more often. I think it's much more fun than the way people dance today – mostly by themselves even if they supposedly have a partner." He held up two fingers to the waitress as she passed by.

A couple more drinks and several dances later, I was bushed. Once again, it was approaching midnight and my bed was calling. Well, the hotel bed, anyways.

Fudge greeted us at the door, winding his way between both our legs. *"I am glad you enjoyed yourself. You do not do that often enough."*

We said our goodnights and I heard the sounds of the sofabed being pulled out as I readied myself for sleep. The reason for our trip crashed its way back into my brain. I wondered how Ev was faring and what the next day would bring, what with the elves being involved and all. Why was Ev missing in the first place? If it was money, cooping him up somewhere wouldn't loosen the purse strings.

*"Why do you worry so much about something you cannot control? Tomorrow will come and whatever will happen will happen. Go to sleep!"*

The cat had a point. I snuggled down into the oversize bed and felt Fudge make his usual nest in my hair.

The next thing I knew, the sun was shining through the window. I'd forgotten to pull the drapes closed and it was bright! Looking at the clock, I could see I'd actually slept in because it was 6:30 a.m. The smell of coffee opened my eyes even farther, so I pulled on the fancy robe the hotel provided and made my way into the sitting area.

The sofabed was already put away and a single cup sat next to the coffeepot. I looked around and found Gregory sitting on the balcony, fully dressed, with a newspaper in one hand and a coffee cup in the other. He obviously heard me stirring because he glanced up and greeted me.

"I trust you slept well? I did not wake you when I rose, did I?"

I sipped my coffee. Gregory always traveled with the special roast he got from his Italian friend and I could understand why. It was so much better than what most hotels provided. "I didn't hear a thing. How long have you been up?"

"I do not require much sleep. I've been up since about five and have gone for a walk to scope things out a little more."

"You did? I didn't even hear the door. So, what did you find out?"

"Nothing has changed since yesterday afternoon. Ev is still in that building and the wards still surround it. As a matter of fact, there's another layer that wasn't there yesterday. Someone, I think, is getting nervous. I'm meeting John at his hotel at nine. Would you care to come with?"

What else was I going to do? I'd insinuated myself into the trip knowing full well Gregory could probably handle anything that came along. In for a penny, in for a pound.

"Yes, of course. I'm curious about how all the pieces of the puzzle fit together."

"As am I. John knows all the players in this movie and I want to know who they are. From there, I might be able to figure out who's involved and why Ev has disappeared. You might find this newspaper article interesting. It's about the movie being shot and some of the things that have happened during the shooting."

He passed me the newspaper and pointed to a headline. I quickly scanned the news item. The movie was being shot at one of those antebellum mansions we passed on our tour the previous evening. According to sources, equipment was moved overnight; other equipment shorted out; some of the antiques in the house also moved from one room to another; two cast members said they'd almost been pushed down the stairs; and a host of other "ghost-like" occurrences. New Orleans was used to hauntings (hell, they had tours about them) but this mansion had never exhibited signs before.

"It's either a real ghost that doesn't like the fact that their house has been invaded or someone doesn't want this movie to be produced," I commented. "Your thoughts?"

"The places that are haunted have been that way for years – sometimes a century or more. But given that everything we've heard thus far seems to point to a money issue, I suspect the latter. We'll find out more when we see John."

At eight-thirty, we climbed into a cab that took us to an address Gregory gave the driver. After fighting rush hour traffic, we ended up back in the Garden District, stopping in front of another mansion. To all outward appearances, it looked like any other. But if you looked closely, all the windows had been blacked out. "One of three vampire hotels in the city," Gregory whispered.

I nodded. Although humans knew vampires existed, they *really* didn't want any particulars. It would be difficult for the vamps to stay in a regular hotel so private homes where sunlight could easily be blocked made a lot of sense.

A human answered the doorbell. Which also made sense. Even with the porch roof, enough sunlight hit the front door that any vampire, even an old one, would start smoking.

"We're here to see John Minton," Gregory told him.

"Of course. You're expected. He'll meet you in the parlor in a few minutes, which is this way. May I offer you coffee, tea, or water?"

We were escorted into a room that was brightly lit with wall sconces and lamps, heavy velvet drapes were drawn to disguise the blacked-out windows, and it was lavishly decorated with antiques. Or at least really good reproductions. Not that I had a discerning eye, but some of them looked like Louis XIV – all ornately carved and gilded. Not my cup of tea but hey. Thinking about it, the furnishings probably were all authentic. Vamps were pretty much immortal and had a long time to collect things.

Coffee was served from an urn on a butler's table, in dainty porcelain cups and saucers. I immediately set mine down on a side table, gingerly took a seat in the flimsy-looking chair next to it, then picked up only the cup. I always had a difficult time balancing cups and saucers, and these looked like they'd shatter if you sneezed hard. Give me a sturdy ceramic mug any day!

John strode into the room with a "Hey, sorry to be delayed." He shook first Gregory's hand, then mine, being sure to avoid the bracelet dangling from my wrist. As soon as Ev had filled me in on the paranormal-type people I was most likely to meet working for him, I had my grandmother's silver cross mounted on a silver chain. John was old enough it wouldn't kill him, but it *hurt*. Although I was immune to them thanks to my witchy blood, it kept them all at a safe distance.

"I haven't been able to find out much from my end," he said as he poured himself a cup of coffee then turned and leaned against the table. "What do you know?"

Gregory filled him in on what we thought was the elves' involvement, the fact that he thought Ev was being held in one of the warehouses in the French Quarter, and that Nelion had asked us for twenty-four hours. Then he mentioned the newspaper article and asked John's opinion.

"I won't lie. There's something fishy going on with this movie. Abraham is one of the ones who felt himself nearly pushed down the stairs." (Abraham was John's client who had a supporting role in the film. He was also being watched by one of our dwarf guards.)

"There's also the financial side of things. I don't know of any elf involvement but that's not saying there isn't. Last I heard, all the strange goings-on were starting to push this thing over budget and the producers are asking the major investors to pony up some more cash."

I interrupted. "Why would someone not want this movie made?"

"I'm not certain," John told me. "There are some unpleasant undercurrents, though. Nothing I can put my finger on but there seems to be some animosity between the producers and about half of the crew.”

“How many paras in the crew and what are they?” Gregory asked.

“Umm…” John turned his eyes to the ceiling as he thought. “Perhaps a half dozen of my kind who, obviously, work only on the night scenes. They’re all either in props or costumes. Another handful of weres working the cameras, all wolves from the local clan; I’ve already told you about the wizard actor; and I think the script girl is a witch but I’m not certain. Probably a few others I’ve not yet run into.”

“I think we can rule out the actor,” Gregory said. “He has a contract to fulfill and the sooner it’s done, the sooner he can go onto the next project. You’d know if any of the vamps was pulling anything, wouldn’t you?”

John tapped his chin. “Possibly but perhaps not. The vampire population here is huge, second only to Las Vegas in the States, and more arrive or are made nearly every day. I don’t know any of them personally, but I can certainly ask my hostess here.”

“Do so, if you would. I’m curious as to who might involve themselves with this Perchaladon chap. He obviously goes outside his species for most anything. I will see if I can get anything out of the local werewolf clan leader, although I’ll have to make a few calls to find out who that is.”

John smiled. “That’s easy. His name is Vincent [pronounce that with a French accent, if you please] and he’s the key grip for the movie. Been in these parts for over a half century and knows everyone who’s anyone, especially in the film business. But as you know, we and weres don’t get along very well so yes, it’s perhaps best if you speak with him.”

Gregory rose from the settee. “I will do so immediately if they are filming today. Are they?”

John nodded. “As far as I know, yes.”

"I will let you know what I find out. Amy?" Gregory made his way to the door.

"And I, you," John said from the safety of the parlor. He would not emerge until the heavy wood front door had been closed again.

The human butler bade us a good day, closing the door behind us with a solid "thunk." Gregory stepped to the street, hailing one of the passing cabs.

"I will take you back to the hotel," he told me after he'd said "the Omni" to the cabbie. As I opened my mouth to protest, he held up his hand. "You know as well as I that most weres, especially the wolves, look at women as inferior. Since this Vincent doesn't know either of us, it's best if I approach him alone at first.

"I will scope the site out and if I think you can do some good, I will call you. Otherwise, I will see you back at the room in time for a late lunch?"

I sighed. He was right once again. Tony, my now-deceased werewolf boyfriend, had been an anomaly. He didn't mind my independence but others I'd encountered had used the epithet "little lady" when speaking to me. It grated. A lot. So, I acquiesced and as I exited the car in front of the hotel, heard Gregory give the driver an address not too far from where we'd just come. I'm sure the guy was more than a little exasperated.

Once back in the room, I fired up both the coffeepot and the laptop. May as well try to get some work done while I was waiting. I called Sally to check in.

"I'm so glad you called. I was about to call you," she told me.

Huh? Something she couldn't handle?

"What's up?"

"That damned elf. He left two messages over the weekend and has already been here this morning. I'll give him something for persistence. He's unhappy that Ev isn't available and when I told him you were out, too, he turned on his heel and left without so much as a goodbye. What do you want me to do?"

Perchaladon was back in the Twin Cities, not here? Things just got even more complicated.

"Continue just blowing him off. I'm not sure what's going on with him. Or down here, for that matter. Anything in the weekend reports?"

We talked business for a while with me telling her to forward certain emails to me so I could deal with them directly. A full page of calls for me to return later, I hung up with a sigh. I couldn't wait until Ev could return three-quarters of them himself.

But first, I called Gregory to tell him about the elf. "That's interesting," he said when I related Sally's frustrations. "That complicates things."

"Yeah, that's what I thought. If not him, then who?"

"I don't know. I'm meeting with this Vincent (he pronounced it correctly: *Veen-sahnt*) guy in a couple of minutes then I'll head back to the hotel. See you soon."

I poured a cup of coffee and started returning calls. One of the ones on my list was Marvin, the dwarf following Abraham around.

"What?" a gravelly voice asked.

"Marvin, it's Amy. You called Ev and he's not available. What's up?"

"Oh, man. I can't guard this guy against unseen things. He damned near fell down the stairs two days ago and it's all my fault because he was pushed, he says. I was standing out of camera range watching and nobody was behind him but it's still my fault. He's not the only one, either. Whaddya want me to do?"

"I saw the newspaper article," I replied.

"You did? You get the *Picayune Times* up there?"

"It's the *Times-Picayune*," I corrected, "and I'm in New Orleans. If you're on set you should be able to see Gregory hanging around there."

Silence. I could imagine Marvin craning his head to look around. At slightly under five feet tall, he was shorter even than me but one hell of a body-language reader. Or just body reader. He could tell you just about anything you wanted to know about a person by looking at them from their waist down. I never did figure out how. But as guards, dwarves were awesome. Bad guys never looked down and as a result, usually found themselves on their backs, disarmed if they were carrying anything, with an ugly, fierce face staring at them from above. They were about two hundred pounds of pure muscle and I'd seen a dwarf incapacitate a man twice his size.

"Got him. What're y'all doing down here? Are you and Gregory an item now?"

I winced. "Not that it's any of your business but of course not. As for Abraham's concerns, remind him you can't protect him against something neither of you can see. Ask if he wants a wizard. I can always swap you with Mario if he becomes insistent."

"Nah, don't think that'll be necessary. I think he just wigged out. That vamp agent of his said the same thing. Just thought I'd check to see what Ev wanted but you'll do."

No goodbyes. He just hung up on me. Dwarves weren't up on social niceties.

A half-pot of coffee, twenty emails and about the same number of phone calls later, Gregory walked in the door.

"We have a conundrum," he pronounced as he poured himself a cup.

"And that would be?"

"The wards on that building are elven yet the only elf who's given Ev difficulties is still back home. Vincent says there's been one hanging around the set but doesn't know who he is. And he's not ours because he's blond and Vincent says he smells like a local – something of a bayou scent, I gather."

He sighed and sat on the sofa. "So, we're stuck until Nelion gets back to us. And depending on what he says, I may want to take you back to the set this evening. They're on an extended lunch break now because yet another camera broke. Then they have to set up for a night shoot. There's more than one witch on set and it's possible you will be able to get more information than I could."

At last, I could do something! My stomach growled so I reached into the refrigerator for the other half of yesterday's lunch. Gregory held out his hand, so I grabbed his, too. We ate in silence.

# CHAPTER NINE

Just for grins (and to give myself something to do after lunch), I started googling the major players in this film: producers, director, stars. John was rarely wrong about his feelings, so who had it in for whom?

"Hey Gregory, I may have something," I yelled to the man who was back out on the balcony, people watching despite the heat. It sounded like the air conditioning labored from the warmth he let in during the time it took for him to come back into the room.

"What?"

"It says here that one of the producers just married the ex-wife of one of the assistant directors. It was a messy divorce followed by a lavish, in-your-face wedding just a couple of weeks after the divorce was final. And that said producer tried to nix the hiring of the AD only to be told he and the director came as a package deal. Perhaps some animosity there?"

Gregory tugged on his chin. "Possibly. I guess. If the contract was written properly, the AD would get paid at least a base regardless of whether the film actually made it to the screen. Are either of them paras?"

"Don't know. This is in *Variety* and they don't mention species in their articles."

"Something for us to investigate when we go back. If we have to go back. Keep reading. Perhaps you will come up with more information."

I nodded, and Gregory turned back toward the balcony. He didn't make it far before someone rapped on the door. Once again, I stayed in my chair and watched him hold an energy ball in the palm of his hand while looking through the peephole. The red sparkles disappeared almost immediately, and he opened the door to usher Nelion in. I stood, closing the laptop as I did.

"Good afternoon," he intoned. Today's robes were royal instead of midnight blue with all silver embroidery.

"Do you have news for us?" Gregory asked.

*"Offer him coffee again. I think he liked it yesterday and it never hurts to have an elven elder on your side."*

I mentally snorted again. My cat could be bossy, but it wasn't a bad idea. I turned toward the men. "Whatever it may be, I'd like coffee to accompany my news. Would anyone else care for some?"

Both declined, which surprised me. Gregory was usually as much of a coffeeholic as I. Nonetheless, I made myself a cup, listening while I did so.

"I really have nothing to tell you," Nelion started. Gregory opened his mouth to reply but a raised hand forestalled him. "My son is not in the city and I have yet to be able to tie him definitively to your ogre's disappearance. But something tells me he *is* tied to it. Therefore, I will continue to aid you.

"My most senior mage is waiting outside with my guards. He will accompany us to the building you say your ogre is in and dismantle the wards. Then we shall see what or who is inside and where that might lead us."

"Of course, and thank you," Gregory nodded as he rose from his chair. "Amy, would you care to accompany us?"

Nelion raised an eyebrow. "You would take your woman into a potentially dangerous situation?"

I was about to get all indignant when Gregory answered for me. "She is not my woman. I'm sure your research told you that she is Evander's assistant. She's also a rather strong witch and can take care of herself."

"As you wish. Shall we?" Nelion strode toward the door, his robes making a slight swishing sound as he walked. Somehow Gregory managed to beat him to it and opened the door, holding it for both of us. He winked at me as I passed him.

*"Do not turn your back on them. Especially his guards."*

"Why? Nelion does not appear to mean us harm."

*"Just a feeling. Keep your eyes open. I am watching with you."*

Okay, that was strange but if Fudge felt something was off, something probably was. Resolving to stay vigilant, I followed Gregory and Nelion to the elevators. Three other elves brought up the rear. One looked like an elven version of Dumbledore with bulky robes, long white hair, a long white beard, and bushy eyebrows; the other two were beefed-up versions of Perchaladon – and of course, drool-worthy. No one said a word until we were safely ensconced in a limo with tinted windows.

"Where is the building?" Nelion asked.

"On Barracks between Chartres and Decatur, about half way down the block on the west side of the street," Gregory replied.

"You heard that?" Nelion asked the driver, who nodded and raised the privacy screen as he pulled away from the curb.

I stared at my hands during the ride. The guards were seated at each door, both looking out their respective windows and I couldn't look out a window without it appearing I was staring at them. Nelion and Gregory were doing something on their cell phones and the older man had his eyes closed.

I was grateful someone else was doing the driving. Based on the slow-and-go I felt, traffic was a mess. Or perhaps he was avoiding pedestrians. Either way, I wouldn't have had the patience.

We'd pulled onto the street where Ev was being held when the old man yelled "Stop" without opening his eyes. He was obviously heard even with the privacy screen up because the driver slammed on the brakes, nearly throwing the rest of us onto the floor.

"What is it, my old friend?" Nelion asked.

Eyes still closed, the mage said, "There is a barrier just up ahead. If the witch and wizard approach, it will harm them."

Gregory and I looked at each other. This was just getting weirder and weirder.

"Drop us here and find a place to park," Nelion said to the driver after he'd lowered the privacy screen. Turning to us, "Please wait here until my friend has taken down all the wards. It's obvious someone does not want you around."

That was a 'duh.' If there was a barrier that would hurt me, I certainly wasn't going to walk into it. I surveyed the street after we'd all exited the car. I didn't see or feel anything, but that didn't mean there wasn't something there.

Gregory and I stood back as the four elves walked straight to the building in question. "Well, that tells us something," Gregory murmured.

"Oh?"

"That ward is keyed to allow elves through but, I think, no other species. Therefore, whoever we're dealing with has to be an elf. Otherwise, they'd have to key for other species, as well."

While he spoke, the mage turned, put his hand up, and pushed. I watched as his hand reacted as if he'd pushed on a piece of Spandex. He turned and whispered something to Nelion before reaching into the folds of his robes. He pulled out a small drawstring bag, opened it and sprinkled some dust onto his palm before pushing again. This time I heard a tinkling sound, as if glass had shattered and fallen on the ground.

"You may approach, now," he told us. We did so but kept our distance. The mage continued walking toward the building Gregory said had wards on it. Nelion, however, waited for us to catch up, his guards flanking him.

"I am told this barrier bears the signature of one of Perchaladon's friends. Therefore, I believe I was correct in assuming my son is somehow involved, despite the fact that he is still in Minnesota."

"He knows magical signatures?" I asked.

Nelion gave me a small smile. "Similar to the way you register with your Witches' Council, my friend knows the signature of every elf in the United States."

I noticed two things: first, that Nelion did not offer names for the mage or the guards, which made sense. Names have power – especially if you know exactly how the person in question pronounces it. Nelion probably did not pronounce his name correctly when he introduced himself although I suspected there were more magical protections around him and his name than water in the oceans.

Second, he knew about the Witches' Council and their rules. So, he wasn't just a high-powered dad with a wayward son but someone high up in the elven community. So was the mage. If Ev wasn't in trouble, I'd have been inclined to find out more. Not that Nelion would divulge anything to little ol' me but it would've been worth a try.

*Your elf is the* Head *of the elves in all of the United States. His mage is Alberon, who is also the Head of his class in the United States. Tread carefully. You do not want to anger him.*"

"How do you know this?"

*I asked Waldo* [the Head of the Familiars' Council] *yesterday.*"

"And you didn't tell me yesterday because…?"

*I did not know then if it would be important. It seems now that it might be.*"

Cats. Familiars or not, they're a close-mouthed bunch. But my assessment of the pickle Ev was in just went up a notch or two.

"I have dismantled the wards surrounding the building. You may enter," Alberon called.

"Prepare an energy ball," Gregory told me. "We do not know what we will encounter, so be ready."

I duly formed a ball in my hand and held it at the ready. I wasn't really trained for magical combat but had learned – quite by accident – that I could throw the magical equivalent of a stun gun. I thought it would work on anyone but an ogre. Then again, I didn't have a lot of experience with this sort of thing. I could feel Fudge's presence at the back of my mind, ready to give me a magical boost if I needed it.

One of Nelion's guards put his hand to the doorknob. I saw a slight shimmer and the guard twisted it, opening the door with a very rusty creeeeaaakkk of the hinges. It was loud enough to announce our entry to anyone who might be inside. Given the scaffolding, I'd thought the building was being worked on. Oiling door hinges to spare my ears would've been first on my list. Obviously not theirs.

We followed the first guard in, Gregory behind him and me behind Gregory. The other guard stayed on the sidewalk with Nelion and Alberon, who had their heads together in conversation.

The interior wasn't quite pitch black – light shone between the slats boarding up broken windows on the second floor. It was still dim and oh, the musty smell! Fudge would've had a case of the sneezes immediately. More scaffolding was along the walls inside, as if they weren't there for work but to shore the walls up. We all looked around, trying to see if there were any humanoid forms on the floor.

Gregory tapped the guard's shoulder and pointed at a staircase toward the back and then at himself, indicating he was going up. He looked at me and made a gesture indicating I should stay with the guard. Not certain how I could help, I did stay.

Watching where he walked, Gregory made his way over to the stairs on silent feet. Pausing a moment to look at the treads, he sidled up the stairs, testing each step before he put his weight down.

*"Breathe."*

I hadn't realized I was holding my breath. But I was so nervous! Exhaling and inhaling as quietly as I could, I checked my palm to ensure the energy ball was still there – my hands were sweaty from the stress. Thankfully, energy doesn't dissipate with water the same way fire would. Gregory reached the landing and disappeared around a corner.

"Bugger all!" Gregory's roar echoed through the empty building. He reappeared at the top of the stairs, holding what appeared to be a piece of cloth with writing on it. He stomped back down the stairs, still keeping to the side of the treads rather than the middle. His expression was one of those "if looks could kill."

I released the energy I was holding, watching the green sparkles float away and disappear into the air. I also heaved a huge sigh of relief. I wasn't sure I was ready to get into a magical fight with anyone.

Gregory stormed past me and out the door. I looked at the guard, who shrugged his shoulders and followed. I did, too.

"Mage, can you tell whose signature *this* is?" Gregory demanded as he held out the cloth to Alberon.

"What's going on?" I asked.

"Someone figured out my beacon spell on Ev and duplicated it on this fabric, somehow masking what I'd put into the tattoo on his shoulder. I have no bloody idea where he is now."

"It is the same person who put up the wards both on the street and this building," Alberon told us.

"This person is known to us but not his exact location," Nelion said. "I suggest we take you back to the hotel where you can wait in comfort while we locate him. Once we have him in custody and have spoken with him, I will let you know where your ogre is. Will that be acceptable?"

"It will have to be since I cannot track Evander. I do appreciate your assistance in all this," Gregory said, somewhat quieted after his outburst.

"It is best if we cooperate with one another. This person is a known associate of my son's and I do not wish to embroil my family's name in any further embarrassing situations. Once I have the friend, I can find out what Perchaladon is up to *this* time and, hopefully, stop whatever he is doing. *Then* I will take my son in hand. At least I know where he is – at the moment, in any event."

We all climbed back in the limo for the quick ride back to the hotel where we were dropped off with only an "I'll be in touch" from Nelion. Gregory fumed all the way to the room and once inside, practically ran to the balcony. He threw the door open and with a "whoosh" that blew my hair back and scattered some papers I'd left on the desk, released what felt like a megaton of Air energy up into the sky.

*"Is it safe to come out?"*

I took a peek at Gregory who was standing on the balcony, gripping the railing and staring without seeing. "Where the fuck could he be?" I heard him say to himself.

"I think so. He's pissed and rightly so, but I think he's blown off the worst of it."

Fudge emerged from the bedroom and instead of twining himself around my legs, went immediately to the balcony and did it to Gregory. I almost felt a little jealous until I saw Gregory's shoulders relax a little as he bent down to pick Fudge up.

"Thanks, Fudge. I know you'll help any way you can."

# CHAPTER TEN

"I need coffee. Would you care for a cup?" Gregory was attempting to get himself back to normal.

"Of course. Have you come up with a next step?"

He busied himself at the bar, pouring water and measuring coffee into the machine. "Go back to the set this evening to talk with more people. The elves have their own agenda and while it *appears* to coincide with ours, I do not trust them and prefer to do my own investigation. You can come with or not."

"Well of course I'll come with. I want my boss back just as badly as you do and anything I can do to help that along…"

"All right then. We'll have an early dinner here and then head back. Last I heard they were going to restart about seven-thirty."

When we arrived at the mansion, we had to clear security. RVs and trucks lined the street, fat wires running from many through the fence in a pattern I swear was specifically designed to make you trip. There were a lot of people hanging around on the sidewalk, probably trying to get a glimpse of someone famous. The help must have come from John because Gregory produced two badges that got us waved through the gate.

Gregory immediately headed around back to the garden, me in his wake. At the corner of the house, he turned and handed me one of the badges. "Wear this while we're here so no one questions your presence. I need to speak with the weres again. How about you check out the ladies manning the catering tent? At least one of them is a witch and I suspect they'd be more inclined to talk girl-to-girl."

I put the lanyard around my neck, looking at the badge. It had my name and photo on it. My driver's license photo. I wondered who, in this convoluted world I was working in, had access to DMV files. It concerned me, but I'd figure that out later. I still had to find my boss.

Gregory disappeared into the mass of people milling about. After locating the caterers (not difficult – two tents toward the back of the property), I tried to appear as if I were just meandering around rather than making a beeline for them. As I approached my target, a man carrying a camera on his shoulder hurried past me. He gave off a werewolf vibe which meant he was probably connected somehow to the clan leader Gregory had met.

"What a lovely view," one of the ladies behind the tables sighed. I agreed. If he looked as good from the front as he did the rear, he was calendar model material. The Universe had granted me an opening.

"Yes, isn't it," I said, appreciatively watching him walk away. I perused the choices on the table as if I were going to get something to eat. "I haven't seen him before. Does anyone know if he's single?"

"Wouldn't do you any good if he was," an older lady told me. "He's a were and they always stick to their own species."

I knew better but that wasn't germane to what I wanted to know. I let out a sigh that rivaled the one I'd heard. "Such a shame, really." I craned my neck, looking around. "Not a lot of choice and when the best-looking one doesn't go outside his species…"

"Oh, there's choice if you're not that picky," a blonde about my size and age with a witch vibe said. "There are all sorts of men around here who aren't weres or vampires."

"Is that so? My name's Amy, by the way, and may I have a cup of coffee?"

She reached for a disposable cup and held it under the urn's spigot. "Do you need cream or sugar? I'm Anne. And yes, the pickings are good at this shoot if you're just looking to get laid. I haven't seen you around before. What do you do here?"

I had to think fast. "Snoop" probably wasn't a job description that would endear me to anyone. A variant on the truth was probably my best bet.

"My boss is an investor and came to look in on his money. I go where he goes."

"*Niiicce.* Do you get to go a lot of different places?"

I shrugged. "Not really. It's usually the same places. This is the first time I've ever been to a movie set, though. Is it always this crowded and hectic-feeling?"

"Yup," she grinned. "I believe the phrase is controlled chaos. Even when they're actually shooting and it's quiet, people are scurrying around out of camera shot doing stuff. Excuse me for a moment."

She went to help someone else and I turned to survey my surroundings. Although the sun had almost set, you wouldn't have been able to tell. Lights on poles made it appear to be mid-afternoon. Cameramen were placed strategically, some operating from crane-like contraptions, a couple on ladders of varying heights. As I watched, a hole opened up underneath one of them, tilting the ladder and throwing both camera and operator to the ground.

"Shit!" came from more than one person. People scurried over to the man lying on the ground with the camera in pieces next to him. He hadn't fallen from much of a height and appeared to be okay, just a little shaken up. The camera, on the other hand, wouldn't be recording anything for a while.

"Wow. That's like the fifth time something like this has happened," Anne said from behind me. "And every time it has to be something magical, but I didn't feel a thing. Did you?"

I shook my head. "No, but I'm far enough away that I wouldn't have picked up on anything subtle and it doesn't take a lot just to move some dirt. I read in the paper they think it's ghosts. If that's the case, there wouldn't be anything to pick up on, would there?"

"No, but I honestly don't think it's ghosts. I've lived in New Orleans all my life and this house has never been haunted. I doubt they'd start now. You must be Earth. I couldn't move dirt without attracting attention to save my life. Unless I just created a mudslide or something."

So she was probably Water. In a way, that made sense. My "textbook" said most Water element folks tended to be really sensitive to emotions, meaning they'd pick up on sexual vibes. And…anger and animosities.

"So, if this has been happening and you think it's got something to do with magic, who do you think is responsible for it?" I asked.

"Oh, hell. Any number of them. Probably a third of the crew are witches or wizards and I saw at least one elf hanging around which, by the way, was weird. And just like any workplace, there are romances, broken romances, jockeying for positions. Except for the main players, we're all local and have worked together more than once.

"Why are you so interested?"

I shrugged. "This whole movie thing fascinates me. There are so many people behind the scenes that you just don't think about when you're watching a film, you know? And there's all the problems this one has encountered. I read the entertainment magazines and haven't ever read of a movie being cursed like this one seems to be."

At that moment, Gregory touched my shoulder from behind. "May I have a cup of coffee, black, please?" he said to Anne.

After he'd been served, he gently turned me around. "Take a walk with me."

"What's up?" I asked after he'd guided me to a secluded spot, away from the hubbub of the latest catastrophe.

"Vincent saw our mysterious elf hanging around just a few minutes ago. Shortly before the camera accident. And although it's not publicly known nor does he look like it, the assistant director who was mentioned in that article you read is half elf. I think we may have found our connection to the incidents here but that still doesn't explain what happened to Ev."

"So now what do we do?"

"*We* don't do anything. Since I can't track Ev, I'm not able to do anything here. I'm going to call Nelion when we get back to the hotel and tomorrow morning, we're headed home until someone tells me something I can work with."

"But…"

"But what? No one here that I can find knows anything about his disappearance. Until someone, probably Alberon, gets close enough to remove the masking spell, I can't find him. And if they're that close, *they've* found him. We're just spinning our wheels. Unless you have other ideas?"

I didn't. I felt so helpless. I'd had no dreams that could help someone with *way* more experience than me bring my boss home. I sighed.

"I guess you're right. I just don't like leaving finding Ev in someone else's hands, you know?"

"I feel the same. His safety is my responsibility and even though this solo trip was his idea, I feel as if I've let him down. But the elves are involved and they are nothing if not resourceful, with a magic much more powerful than mine.

"Come. I've called for a taxi to take us back to the hotel. It should be out front shortly."

I waved at Anne as we hurried past the catering tent. Perhaps if we'd been able to stay longer I would have made a new friend, but such is life.

Back at the hotel, Gregory once again warded the room and I listened in on his side of the conversation as he told Nelion his suspicions.

"There is nothing more we can do here so I am leaving it in your hands and returning home. Please do call me with any updates," he closed, hit the "end" button and immediately dialed other numbers to arrange for our flight home and then hotel checkout.

The following morning was a flurry of activity. Gregory gave Fudge a shove through the ether to send him home and immediately followed with Fudge's accoutrements. We hurriedly packed everything else, checked out of the hotel and climbed into a cab for the relatively short ride to Lakefront Airport where we boarded one of those teensy jets that scared the bejeezus out of me for the flight home.

Fudge stayed in my mind the whole trip, keeping me from wigging out. His "voice" did not diminish with distance. *I do not understand why you seem calm during some flights and not others,"* he complained.

"You've never flown in an airplane before yesterday, have you?" I asked.

*"No. When I have needed to travel long distances in a short period of time, which has only been during this lifetime, there has been a suitable Air element to help. Why?"*

"I don't know if I can explain it, then."

*"Try."* He was making an effort to distract me, but it wasn't working. I was still making a conscious effort to ignore my stomach.

"Large planes, what we usually call jumbo jets, fly higher and don't encounter as much turbulence. These small jets don't have that advantage."

*"I understand they tell you this turbulence is just potholes in the air. You do not have difficulty driving on uneven roads. What is the difference?"*

I heaved a sigh, which got Gregory's attention.

"Are you okay?" he asked me.

"As okay as I can be in a small jet, yes," I replied with a grimace. "I'm trying to explain the difference between flying in a jumbo jet and one of these deathtraps to Fudge."

Gregory chuckled. "Good luck with that! We'll be safely on the ground in less than an hour. I know you can hang on until then."

I turned my attention back to Fudge with another sigh. "I know it's irrational. I *know* it. But I haven't been able to convince myself there's nothing to fear."

*"Meditate? I hear humans love to do that. Ommmm…"*

I snorted. To myself – and Fudge, that is. Out loud would have brought stares from the other five passengers. "When have you ever known me to meditate?"

Fudge continued. *"Or how about mad, passionate sex? That would definitely distract you."*

"With whom? And in front of everyone else on this contraption? I don't think so. Next idea?"

*"You like the wizard, do you not? And you have read stories about sex in those tiny bathrooms, so that would give you privacy."*

I'm ninety-eight percent certain I turned beet red. "FUDGE! This is not a conversation I want to have with you!"

*"I am just trying to help."*

"Well, sex, especially with Gregory, isn't on the agenda. Think of something else."

*"Word games? I will say something, and you say the first thing you think of. I'll start. κάνω σεξ."*

"What? What the hell was that?"

*"I am sorry. I forgot you do not speak Greek. At least not yet. In English. To have sex…"*

Gregory nudged me. "What are you two talking about? You're blushing."

I elbowed him back.

"Fudge, what the hell got you on this subject? And drop it!" I thought back and immediately said "Nothing" to Gregory. This was a conversation I had no intention of repeating.

I felt the plane lose altitude and the flight attendant told us to prepare for landing.

*"You were distracted, were you not? Your irrational fear did not upset your stomach any further. I believe I can count myself a success."*

I'm sure he was preening himself back in the apartment. "Yes, okay. You're right. But next time, can you pick a different subject, please?"

I heard a snicker and felt him withdraw as the wheels hit the tarmac. Now that his job was done, it was more than likely naptime.

# CHAPTER ELEVEN

"Two cabs," Gregory said as we left the plane. "You go back to the office. I have to go to MSP to get the car."

I left my suitcase at the bottom of the stairs to the office. If we had a visitor who wondered about it, so be it. I couldn't think of a single reason to haul it up and back down again.

"What are you doing back? Did you find Ev?" Sally asked as I walked in the door. Shit. I'd forgotten to call her to tell her we were coming home.

"Hang on. I need more coffee," I said over my shoulder on the way to the kitchen. I emptied the pot into a mug and started a fresh batch before walking back into the reception area and sinking into one of the ogre-sized guest chairs. Feeling somewhat dwarfed, I scooted my butt forward so I was sitting on the edge and proceeded to recount what had happened over the last few days.

"Wow. That's all I can think of to say," she told me.

"Yeah. I'm not feeling too good about the situation, but I don't know what else to do. So, anything earth-shattering happen?"

"Nothing you don't know about. I was just going to send you an email about starting payroll but since you're here…"

"You go ahead and do it. I'm sure you left a huge pile of crap on my desk and I may as well start whittling it down. But once you're done, go home for a couple of days. You've earned it."

She grimaced. "Nah. Jack's out of town again and I'd just be bored to tears sitting at home. I'll see you again tomorrow. I can at least catch the phones for you."

I once again thanked the Universe for sending Sally to me. She was good enough to completely take over my job if needed but didn't want or have to work full time. It was a perfect arrangement.

The afternoon passed swiftly as I started getting caught up. By four-forty-five, I'd signed off on the payroll, cut the to-do pile in half and was yawning. I was thinking about calling it a day when I heard the outer door open and a dreamy baritone voice intone, "Good afternoon, Mrs. Morgens. I understand Miss McCollum is back. Might I have word with her?"

How the hell did Perchaladon know I was back? Did he have a bug planted in the office or something? And what did he want with me? Time to find out.

I rose from my desk and walked into the reception area. "I heard my name," I said. "Is there something I can do for you?"

"Why, yes!" he turned to me with a smile. "I was wondering if you would accompany me to dinner tonight."

What the actual fuck! Dinner with him? Why?

My confusion must have shown on my face because he continued, "I enjoyed our dance the other evening and thought we might get to know one another better."

"Dance?" Sally mouthed at me from behind him, her eyebrows nearly up to her hairline. I was reminded I'd forgotten to tell her about that evening.

"Ummm," I spluttered.

"*I cannot protect you against elven magic,*" Fudge said, obviously awake from whatever naps he had taken.

"Not now," I thought back. "I can't have two conversations at once."

"Please." Perchaladon said.

What the hell. Maybe I'd be able to find out something useful. "Of course. That sounds lovely. Just let me shut it down for the night and get my purse."

He smiled and leaned against the wall, obviously ready to wait for me.

*"I repeat. I cannot protect you against elven magic from a distance."*

"I understand," I said as I powered my computer off. On an impulse, I quickly sent Gregory a text as the screen told me it was shutting down.

"Elf P here. Wants to take me to dinner. I said yes. Any suggestions?"

I turned the phone to vibrate only, slid it in the back pocket of the jeans I was wearing, grabbed my purse and walked back out to the uncomfortable silence between Sally and Perchaladon.

"As always, forward the phones to me when you leave," I told Sally and with a grimace, "Sorry, but with Ev out of town, I have to be on call," to Perchaladon.

She still had a quizzical look on her face but nodded. He said, "I understand. Shall we?" and opened the door for me.

On the way down the stairs, I said, "I'm sorry I'm not dressed for going out. I came directly from the airport."

"Don't worry about your attire," he said, and "I presume this is yours?" as we passed my suitcase.

"Yes. There was no time to go home so I just left it there. There's nothing I need in it, so I'll get it later."

A liveried chauffeur was standing with the limo door open as we exited. The guy obviously wasn't an elf – he wasn't drop-dead gorgeous and I could see the rounded ear tops sticking out of the sides of his head. No long, silky hair, either. Just a buzz-cut under the uniform cap. Once we were ensconced inside, he returned to the driver's seat with his shoulders held in an expectant pose and his head cocked toward the passenger compartment.

"I confess I do not know your food preferences. Is there something in particular you crave, or something you abhor?"

I tried to at least *look* relaxed. "I really am a basic-food kind of girl. Nothing fancy, nothing really too spicy. I'm the type that eats to live rather than lives to eat. If that helps."

"Excellent. I concur," he exclaimed, then gave the driver instructions to drive to Lord Fletcher's, a restaurant on Lake Minnetonka known for its relaxed atmosphere and good food. The privacy glass slid closed.

Perchaladon leaned against the window and stretched his long legs out. "So, Miss McCollum, Amy, if I might, why are you, an attractive witch, working for an ogre?"

"You asked me that question once before, remember? My answered hasn't changed. It's a good job. Why are you, an elf, so interested in me, a witch? I was told elves don't normally go outside their own species."

"And I answered that question, too. I find other species interesting and don't feel the need to be as insular as many of my kind do."

Okay. Another tack. "Why are you still hanging around? Ev told you he wasn't interested in investing in your company. Most people *do* take 'no' for an answer."

He chuckled. "That company has been fully-funded. I do not need your ogre's money. But is not the fact I find you attractive reason enough to keep 'hanging around,' as you put it?" He used air quotes so really was up on the latest human(ish) things.

Well, shit. That didn't work, either, except to make me blush. Just at that moment, my butt buzzed. "Excuse me," I said, trying to hide my discomfort. I pulled my phone out to see I had two text messages.

"Do not bring up father. Or New Orleans. Have a good time?" said the first, Gregory's reply to my earlier.

"Charlie said you got into a limo with an elf? Call me when you can!" This from Cassandra. *That* one I would answer later.

"Sorry. Business," I said as I slid my phone back into my pocket.

"Of course. By the way, where is your employer? And did you enjoy your days off?"

"He is out of town on business and my trip was also business, so no, it really wasn't enjoyable."

Perchaladon seemed to muse on this last. "But you were seen dancing in New Orleans with that wizard, your boss' guard. Wasn't that fun?"

I got even more uncomfortable. First, he knew I was back. And now this. "Are you keeping tabs on me? I hadn't announced my arrival home to anyone and now you knew I was in New Orleans. That's kind of creepy, you know?"

He lowered his eyes. "My apologies but I am not watching you. A business associate saw you in New Orleans. I happened to be at Flying Cloud to meet another associate when you disembarked from your flight."

"And how did your business associate know it was me?"

Perchaladon cleared his throat. "He is more than an associate, he's also a good friend. We keep each other updated on our personal as well as professional lives so he knew of my interest in you and your connection to Evander. Both you and the wizard were known to us from our research on Evander prior to my approaching him. My friend put two and two together. Nothing more."

So, there was no keeping New Orleans under wraps as Gregory had hoped. "This friend of yours wouldn't happen to be blond, would he?"

His eyes widened. "Why yes, he is. How did you know? He said you didn't see him while he was in the bar."

Before I could answer, the car stopped and the chauffeur opened the door for me. Phew. That would give me time to think.

My thoughts were diverted. It may have been mid-week, but it was the height of summer. How were we going to get a table at such a popular spot? I needn't have worried.

"Good evening, Perchaladon. Your table is waiting," the maître d' greeted us. "This way, please."

We followed him through the dining room, where His Handsomeness turned a few ladies' heads, out to a screened-in porch with seating. I sat in the chair held for me and Perchaladon seated himself across the table. The view of the lake was spectacular and the music drifting in from their completely-outdoor seating area was pleasant but not deafening.

Admiring the view and ordering drinks gave me a little more time to get my thoughts together. He appeared to be genuinely surprised I knew his friend was blond. Therefore, he probably didn't know of Ev's connection to the movie. Perhaps not even of his friend's involvement there.

*"Do not trust him."*

"Well, duh," I thought back. "I don't know him that well and you know I don't trust easily anyways. Take a chill pill."

*"Why would I take a pill? Is there something wrong with me I am not aware of? Tell me. I can fix this body easily."*

"It's an expression. It means 'relax'."

*"Oh, of course. I have heard you use this phrase before. Still, elves outside their own race is too unusual to not be of concern."*

"I am aware. That said, I think he may be of help. So, I will trust him with Ev's disappearance and see what happens."

*"Remember, it is not just your neck but mine…"*

Our drinks arrived and Perchaladon leaned across the table, holding his goblet up. "A toast. To getting to know one another better."

I clinked glasses with him and after we'd both sipped our wine, he asked again how I knew his friend was blond.

"We visited a movie set while we were in New Orleans. The presence of a male elf was noted as strange and I was told he was blond. Given your race's penchant for not mixing with others, and the fact I'd not seen any other elves while I was there, I made an assumption."

"You assumed correctly. My friend *is* involved in a film currently being shot in the Garden District and I know he was there, looking into things."

Looking into things. As in ensuring everything was screwed up? I wondered if Perchaladon knew his friend as well as he thought he did.

"Were you aware that there are all sorts of accidents happening on that set? I even saw one myself; a hole opened up underneath a ladder, spilling the camera and its operator."

Perchaladon squirmed in his seat. Had I hit a nerve?

"May I ask what, exactly, you were doing in New Orleans? Unless my information is incorrect, you are not romantically involved with Mr. Tremayne so it wasn't a weekend getaway for lovers."

*"Elves cannot tell a lie. They can, however, misdirect or choose not to answer at all."*

"You didn't answer my question. Were you aware of the accidents?"

"They've been reporting them in the human tabloids, haven't they? Anyone who follows the movie industry, as do I, would know about them."

That didn't exactly answer my question, but I couldn't rephrase without sounding suspicious. Oh, hell. Did I care? Not really. I wanted to know what happened to my boss.

I sipped more wine. I was going all in and damn the consequences. "Let me ask it another way. Is your friend responsible for the accidents?"

Perchaladon's eyes narrowed. "Your question makes it sound as if my friend and by extension, I am an unsavory character. Is that what you think? If so, why are you here with me, in this glorious setting, knowing my magic is stronger than your own?"

More misdirection. But he knew something, and I wanted answers. "My boss invested in that movie, went down to check on his investment and, at the same time as those accidents were happening on the set, disappeared. My gut tells me the two are connected and you are my only connection to the unusual appearance of an elf on that set. I will go to almost, *almost* any lengths to find out what happened to my boss. That includes dinner with an elf I do not know well."

Perchaladon leaned back in his chair and let out a guffaw loud enough to draw attention from the other diners. "Your red hair does you justice. You are a feisty one, aren't you?"

We were interrupted by the waiter, asking if we'd made our dinner selections. Fresh-caught fish with rice pilaf for both of us had him nodding and scurrying away.

Perchaladon leaned forward once again and as he did so, I felt a bubble of air form around our table. Unlike anyone I knew who could ward a space, he didn't wave his hands or do anything to indicate he'd cast a spell. And I didn't feel any energy expended, either. Impressive!

"All right, Miss McCollum, I will answer as best I am able. Yes, my friend is disrupting progress on that film. He is being paid handsomely to do so. As you probably know, our magic is undetectable to other species so he's perfect for the job.

"As to your ogre's disappearance, I know nothing. I have no reason to want him gone. On the contrary, should I need funding for another company, I would want him hale and hearty to put some of his money into it.

"Now that I have answered your questions, may we get down to the business of a nice dinner?"

My butt buzzed again. "Excuse me," I said as I pulled it out and saw another text message.

"Want your boss back? Call when you are alone." This with the sending number noted as "private." How had whoever sent this gotten my cell phone number? And how was I supposed to call someone when they blocked their number? This wasn't sounding good. I quickly forwarded it to Gregory then sat staring at the screen.

"Is something amiss?" Perchaladon asked.

Wordlessly, I turned the phone so he could see it. His face creased in a frown.

"I believe this takes precedence over a nice meal. We will get ours to go and return to your office." He raised his hand to summon the waiter and gave instructions to package everything up in a hurry. Pulling out his own phone, he hit a speed dial number. I heard him tell his driver to get the picnic supplies out of the trunk and prepare the limo. We would be leaving for the city shortly.

"Picnic supplies?" I asked.

"One never knows when one must eat on the run. I prefer to *dine* rather than just eat so yes, picnic supplies. China, silver, and crystal for two, all in a lovely little basket that I carry just in case."

My phone buzzed again. It was a reply from Gregory. "Do not call. I will handle."

"I'm on my way to office. Meet you there?"

"One hour."

The waiter returned with a large bag. Perchaladon exchanged it for a wad of bills and we made our way back out to the parking lot where the driver stood with the door open. I crawled inside to find a small table dropped from the center backrest, covered with a white linen tablecloth and settings for two laid out.

Perchaladon proceeded to unload the bag, serving up the fish and rice pilaf with a practiced hand. He reached inside another compartment and after a little bit of clinking bottles around, pulled out a bottle of pinot grigio, held it between his hands for a moment, then pulled out the cork and poured each of us a glass.

"Do not worry. We will find your ogre and put this behind us so I can take you out properly. Now, enjoy."

I sipped my wine, which was nicely chilled. I raised my eyebrows over the glass.

"Another perk of being an elf and having our magic. We can chill or heat objects with our hands. I am glad you are a wine drinker, though. I can only chill, not freeze, so I can't make ice cubes for cocktails."

I laughed. "Nonetheless, it's a nice ability."

We both dug into our food. The driver was a good one. Despite sometimes curvy roads and the vagaries of traffic, I didn't spill a drop of wine or miss my mouth with the fork.

Forty minutes later, we'd finished eating and the limo was just sliding into the curb in front of the office. Gregory's Hummer was already there.

"Please allow me to accompany you. I don't know how but I may be able to help." Perchaladon looked at me with what seemed like pleading in his eyes.

I sighed. "I don't know how Gregory will take your presence but okay, come on."

We sprinted up the stairs. Well, I did. Perchaladon's long legs allowed him to easily walk up, taking two stairs at a time. Gregory must have heard the noise because he greeted us at the door.

"What is he doing here?" Gregory demanded of me.

"Perchaladon, this is Gregory. Gregory, Perchaladon. He seems to think he can help."

Gregory gave Perchaladon a gimlet eye as he ushered us into the office. "Yes? And how?"

Gregory leaned against the wall. I perched on the corner of Sally's desk. Perchaladon seated himself in one of the ogre-sized chairs, leaned back and crossed his legs. Unlike me, he didn't sink into its depths. "Amy tells me you suspect a friend of mine has something to do with your employer's disappearance. While I know nothing about it, I have contacts you may find useful in locating him."

Gregory turned to me. "You told him?"

I nodded. "It seemed the thing to do at the time. And he appeared genuinely surprised when I told him." I shrugged my shoulders. "I don't know about you but any help I can get finding Ev is welcome."

Gregory blew out a breath. It sounded more like a snort. "Okay. Fine. The number that sent the text message is from southwestern Louisiana. The ID of the phone's owner is masked, even to law enforcement, which suggests magical interference."

"How did you get it? My phone said whoever sent the text blocked their ID," I asked.

"The call can still be traced, *if* you have the right connections, which I do," he replied.

He did. He not only knew mundane law enforcement folks but was rather cozy with the paranormal enforcers. Not just the enforcers but council members, too. Gregory was *very* well-connected. It was one of the reasons Ev liked him so much and paid him rather handsomely, to boot.

"There is an enclave in that area of Louisiana," Perchaladon offered. "My father heads it. If you will give me the number, I will ask him to investigate."

"I have already done so," Gregory retorted.

Perchaladon's eyes opened to the size of saucers. "You know my father? How? He does not normally mix with non-elves."

This time Gregory did indeed snort. "He is already involved in the investigation. He approached us while we were in New Orleans, thinking perhaps you were involved. I have been in contact with him and through him, Alberon."

Hey, did you know? Elves blush! At least this one does. He turned a beautiful shade of pink at Gregory's statement.

"I will admit my father and I haven't always seen eye-to-eye on some things. But in this, he is wrong. I know nothing about the ogre. But if you have already spoken with him, I don't know how else I can help."

Gregory's phone rang. He held up a hand to forestall any conversation as he answered it.

"Yes? Yes. No, he is sitting right in front of me and claims to know nothing. Yes. He apparently took Evander's assistant out to dinner and decided to accompany her after the text message. I see. Yes, of course. I will await your call."

Hitting the 'end' button, Gregory turned his attention back to Perchaladon.

"It appears your friend, Obrist, is up to his eyeballs in this. The number that texted Amy belongs to him. That said, your father does not know where he is, nor can Alberon trace him."

Perchaladon chuckled. "It is a game we played when we were young and wanted to get out of schooling. 'How to hide from the mage?' We got rather good at it by the time we were teenagers. I thought Alberon had figured out all our tricks by now but apparently, Obrist has come up with some new ones."

"So, how do we find your friend and by extension, my boss?" I asked.

"I don't know. Alberon is the strongest mage I've ever heard of. If he can't find Obrist, I don't know who can. Perhaps you should call him as instructed?"

"But I'm not supposed to know the number, am I? He hit star-sixty-seven before texting me, so I wouldn't see the number. Is he really that dumb?"

Perchaladon sighed. "Dumb? No. Impetuous? Unfortunately, yes. He doesn't always think things all the way through. I guess you will just have to wait until he texts again. I will be curious to know what he wants."

"As will I. I suggest we all return home until the next text arrives," Gregory moved toward the door. "May I drop you at home, Amy?"

"I would like to see the lady home if it's okay with you," Perchaladon said.

"Guys. Guys. I'm fine and I don't need a ride home, but thank you. Gregory, I'll call you when I hear something, okay? Perchaladon, thank you for what probably would have been a lovely evening. I'm sorry it was cut short." I dropped off the corner of the desk and, picking up my purse, motioned everyone out so I could lock up.

At the foot of the stairs, Perchaladon put his hand on my arm. "I really would like to see you home. I think that's the chivalrous thing to do, isn't it? I would also like to see you again, hopefully when our evening won't be cut short. I find you intriguing."

"Thank you for the thought but I really would prefer it if you didn't see me home. And yes, once things calm down, dinner without interruption would be nice."

We exchanged phone numbers and I watched as he climbed into his limo and drove away. I also noticed that the Hummer had only traveled a half block. Gregory was undoubtedly looking through the rearview mirror to ensure my safety. I turned towards home.

CHAPTER TWELVE

*"Now what are you going to do?"*

I only had one foot in the door. I finished entering my apartment, kicked the door closed behind me and threw my purse down on the desk. "Wait for the next call, I guess."

*"You seem to like the elf. Why? In my experience, elves are untrustworthy."*

"Perhaps your experience has skewed your perception. He seems nice enough and now that I know he's not involved in Ev's disappearance, I don't see the harm in perhaps getting to know him a little better. He's definitely handsome enough!"

Fudge grunted. *"Humans and their fascination with physical appearance. It is what is inside that counts."*

"I know. And if you will recall, I have dated men who do not live up to fashion standards. But having something nice to look at while you're discovering what's inside is no bad thing."

*"If you say so. By the way, you have a lesson to prepare for."*

I groaned. "Don't remind me. I got off this last week because we were out of town. Gregory told me on the plane I now have two weeks' lessons to learn."

*"So you should study."*

I made a cup of coffee, picked up *The Big Book of Potions and Philtres*, heard Professor Snape drone in my head, "Turn to page four hundred twenty-two," and began to read about protection potions. It reminded me of the one Gregory had made just a couple of days earlier. Now that I thought about it, some of these things could come in handy. Like the recipe a couple of pages after the introduction. It was for making you *un*interesting to the opposite sex. Something like that would come in handy when shopping at the discount store. "Hey baby, how's about you and me…" gets old after a while.

It wasn't long, though, before I started yawning. I never did sleep well anywhere but my own bed and the trip was starting to catch up with me. I put the studying aside, fed Fudge and crawled into bed.

I was positive I'd have dreams of a certain elf. After all, I'd just spent a couple of hours trying not to drool all over myself while still maintaining the eye contact expected during a date. I was wrong in this regard.

I found myself in a stand of trees. It was night, the sky was clear, and the almost-full moon was a stark contrast to the dark shadows made by the trees. The ground below my feet was soft and the longer I stood there, the wetter my toes felt. The smell of trees in full leaf and wet grass was strong.

As I observed my surroundings, bird-like shadows flitted this way and that, back-lit by the moon. They were so fast I almost thought I was seeing things until I saw another and yet another. High-pitched squeaks, so faint I thought my ears were deceiving me, came from somewhere to my right.

I heard a familiar hum and slapped at a mosquito. No bite, no itch, though. I wasn't physically wherever I was. Over the last year, I'd grown accustomed to "true dreams" – not something my subconscious was trying to work out or my imagination had cooked up but that I was dreaming about something that was really happening, somewhere, in the here and now. I sighed. So much for a pleasant dream about a handsome elf.

More shadows silently glided across my vision.

*"Bats,"* I heard in my head.

Bats? Logic told me there was nothing to be afraid of but some inner demon that had listened to children's bedtime stories set my heart to racing in fear. The thumping ratcheted up a notch when something stirred the air just above my head. That something flew away then whirled around and I saw a shadow aiming directly for me at breakneck speed. I instinctively ducked as it neared me and I'm certain I heard a hiss, as if a steam radiator had sprung a leak, when it passed overhead.

I was so focused on my pounding heart that I almost missed the tingling feeling I get when magic is in use nearby. Magic? In the middle of a forest – or wherever I was?

I crouched down, trying to make myself less of a target for bats, slapped at yet another imaginary biting insect, and took a good look at my surroundings. There. One of the bats swooping this way and that just below the treetops had a small patch of glitter on it. I continued to watch the sparkles do dizzying aerobatics, sometimes so far over my head I almost got a crick in my neck, sometimes skimming the ground or brushing against a tree trunk. The moon gradually went on her path, making the forest darker and the sky to my right started to lighten. It was getting toward dawn.

*"Time to wake up."* A soft paw batted my nose. I opened my eyes to find Fudge sitting on my chest, staring down at me. The light outside my window told me dawn – and my alarm clock – wasn't long in coming.

"Why did you wake me? I could've slept another…" I looked at the clock. "…half hour!"

*"So you would not stand there staring like an idiot when there was nothing else to see. The bats would be roosting in a few minutes. Also, so you could write down any details you need to remember to tell the wizard."*

I grumbled, swung my legs over the side of the bed and padded into the kitchen to start my coffee, Fudge following. I preferred my *normal* routine of the coffeepot timer going off ten minutes before my alarm. That way I could guzzle down a cup immediately. While I waited for my morning elixir, I made my way to the bathroom and scooped the litterbox.

My morning routine usually consisted of guzzling multiple cups of coffee, checking social media and personal email before a round of stretching then a shower. This morning, however, I called Gregory after my first cup.

"I'm up but why are you calling this early?" He sounded grumpy, even for a morning person.

"Because I had a true dream and you said to always tell you as soon as I'd had one so I wouldn't lose details. I'm calling to tell you."

That got his attention. "I'm listening."

I related everything I could remember – with a couple of prompts from Fudge, naturally. The line was silent for a minute, but I could hear the sounds of Gregory moving around the cottage. He was undoubtedly pacing as he thought about what I'd said.

"My guess is that, once again, you saw Ev. That single patch of magic could be my beacon spell tattoo. But as a bat? Transmogrification is highly-advanced spellwork and only a few can do it. I can't."

"Trans-what?"

A sigh escaped him. "You haven't gotten that far in your studies yet. Transmogrification is transforming something – or someone – into something else. Like the proverbial turning someone into a toad."

"That's *possible?* I thought it was just a myth!"

"No, it's not a myth. As I said, it's highly advanced magic and not everyone is capable of such a spell." He paused. "But elves might be. Go to work. I'll call Nelion and let you know what he says."

He hung up. I turned my attention back to the mundane. Social media was boring and there was nothing interesting in email. I quickly paid some bills then turned my attention to Mahjong for a few minutes before resuming my routine.

I found it difficult to concentrate on work. I stared at the phone, willing Gregory to call back and tell me what he'd found. I ate the lunch Cassandra brought without really tasting it. As she sat in my guest chair watching me eat, I quickly relating what had happened in New Orleans and in my dream.

"Your boss gets himself into the worst predicaments, doesn't he?" she said when I finished. She took my plate. "I have to go back down but let me know if there's anything we can do to help."

Sally came in promptly at one. "Any word?" she said as she stuck her head in my door.

"Nothing yet."

"So I guess we just keep on keeping on, huh? By the way, there's an invitation to a party sitting in the stack of mail I have for Ev. Should I RSVP yes or no?"

"When?"

"Next Friday night. I don't know who it is – they're not in his address book – but it's hand-lettered and has gilt edges."

I snorted. "In his circles, *everyone's* invitation is hand-lettered and has gilt edges. That way you look like you're someone, don'tcha know. Decline. Even if we have him back by then, I don't know if he's going to be in any shape to go to a party. Even if he thinks he is."

She laughed. "You got it, boss. You want me to run AP this afternoon?"

"No, I've got it. I'd rather you pull the contracts that renew in September. Compare them to notes and let me know what you think."

The afternoon dragged. I finished my work, attempted to do some of Ev's marketing (at which he excelled and I sucked), and finally started to button up my office for the day. Just as I was about to grab my purse and head for the door, Sally put a call through to me.

"Good afternoon, Amy," Perchaladon's voice oozed through the phone.

"Hello, Perchaladon. What can I do for you?"

"It's what I can do for you, I think," he replied. "Have dinner with me tonight."

"Things are still up in the air," I told him. "I don't think I'd be the best company right now. Give me a few days?"

"Obviously, you still don't have your employer back. Perhaps I can take your mind off matters."

"Oh, honestly." I was already on edge and his attention wasn't helping. "Thank you, but no. As I said, give me a while. I have other things to do, anyways."

"As you wish." He hung up without a proper goodbye. Did I piss him off? Probably. But too bad. I snatched my things and waved to Sally as I stomped out the door.

My head was spinning with "what-if" scenarios pending a call from Gregory and I knew I wouldn't be able to take a nap. As always when I was full of nervous energy, I cleaned.

*"It is a good thing you have nothing decorated with spots. You would have scrubbed them all off by now."*

"Shut up," I growled. "It's better than just pacing up and down the hallway and around the living room."

*"You have studying to do. You could throw your energy into that."*

"I can't concentrate. You should know by now I worry."

Before Fudge could get in yet another wry observation, my phone rang. Without looking at it, I hit the answer button.

"Hello?" I'm sure I sounded out of breath, perhaps even nervous. I definitely wasn't a calm, cool, and collected person.

"Calm yourself." Gregory had read my mood correctly. "I just got off the phone with Nelion."

"And?"

"Yes, elves can perform transmogrification spells. Quite easily, although it is a practice that is frowned upon for rather obvious reasons. I described your dream environment and he thinks it's an undeveloped area in their enclave in western Louisiana. One of his lieutenants will be checking it out this evening. We should know something tomorrow.

"Get a good night's sleep. I will call you when I hear something." Uncharacteristically, he hung up without saying goodbye. That made me nervous. He was hiding something.

*"So now that you have had your telephone call, you should be able to concentrate on your studies, correct?"*

I sighed. That cat was, in one regard, correct. I did have to study. Just like regular school, I'd have a test on two chapters in just three days. It was time to buckle down. I put the cleaning supplies away, sat at my desk and pulled the tome toward me.

Page four hundred fifty-five of the chapter on protection potions was more of the same. Not that I'd be expected to remember all these recipes (after all, isn't that what a reference book is for?) but the methodology and ingredients were similar. Just a minor twist here and there, depending on the person who wrote the recipe. Gregory had been teaching me that customizing each potion to the individual situation was more effective. In other words, don't rely on someone else; come up with your own shit.

Dinner came and went, and I was nose to the parchment. Fudge was curled up on the couch, ostensibly asleep.

The next chapter was on cleansing. Negative energy was a real thing – as I'd discovered when a vampire trashed my apartment a little over a year back. At the time, I hadn't a clue about all this magical stuff. Cassandra had come by to smoke it out – literally. She burned so much white sage my apartment looked like it was shrouded in fog.

But there were times you couldn't cleanse with smoke. In an office, for instance. In that case, you made a potion and either wiped everything down with it or used a sprayer. More recipes, all of which Gregory would tell me were starting points for my own concoctions.

"If I'm supposed to come up with my own recipes, why am I studying all this?" I mused to myself. Or, at least, I thought to myself.

"*Because if you look at them, you will notice patterns in ingredients and methods of use. I believe the wizard means for you to absorb which are most common, so you do not always need to look up things in a book. Which you may not have at hand.*"

"Hell, Fudge, I won't have most of the ingredients at hand, much less the book."

"*Yes, you do and probably would. Look in your kitchen. I would wager many of the ingredients you are looking at are in there. I believe the same would be true in most human houses.*"

I looked at the recipes in this section again. Sage. Not necessarily white sage but the kind you cook with. Lemon. Parsley. Thyme. Aw, crap. He was right. I pulled out my notebook and started making a list of everything in this chapter I knew would be in a well-stocked kitchen (not necessarily mine). It was pretty long by the time I was done.

I heard a whispered "I told you so" in my head as I closed my books and prepared for bed. Damn, smug cat.

One of the things I hated about taking over for Ev was I couldn't turn my phone off when I went to bed. Clients, for the most part, were night owls and Ev handled problems at all hours of the day and night. I regretted that fact when, at around 3:00 a.m., I was jolted awake by the shrill sound of my ringtone.

Heart racing from being woken so abruptly, I looked to see who was calling me. The notification simply read, "Private." I stabbed the "answer" button and hoped the grumpiness sounded in my voice when I said, "Hello."

"You must not want your boss back too badly. You didn't call after my text," said an unknown voice. It wasn't a deep voice but definitely male, and the words were slightly slurred as if the caller were inebriated.

"What?" I almost shouted into the phone. Then got my shit together. "If this is the person who texted me last night, you used star-sixty-seven, you idiot. I can't even return a text to a blocked number, much less call it."

"Oh. Well, now that I have you…"

"What do you want?" I interrupted. "And what did Ev ever do to you?"

There was a pause on the other end. A throat cleared. "Your boss got in my way. You should be thankful he's still alive. As to what I want? Money would be helpful. Say, a quarter million."

I was ninety percent positive Ev was still alive and was the bat I'd seen in my dream. But this guy wouldn't know that.

"And how do I know he's still alive? Put him on the phone so I can confirm for myself. Once I know he's okay, we can talk about the money."

Silence. He'd put himself into something of a pickle by changing Ev. Last I knew, bats couldn't talk. At least not any language I'd understand.

"Your boss is just fine but he's not able to come to the phone right now. Make arrangements for the money and I'll return him unharmed."

This guy obviously didn't know any kidnapping rules. "Nuh-uh. I don't pay until I speak with him. Call me back when he can talk." I hung up and immediately hit speed-dial for Gregory.

"Mmmpf. Hello?" I'd obviously woken him.

"Hey, it's me. I think Perchaladon's friend just called."

"Is that so?" Gregory was now awake. "And what did he say?"

"Told me Ev was fine and asked for a quarter-million ransom. I asked to speak to Ev and he said Ev couldn't come to the phone. Told him I wouldn't pay anything until I'd spoken with Ev, hung up and called you. By the way, he sounded sort of drunk."

The sound of movement and water running came through the phone. The next words were a little muffled as Gregory cradled the phone on his shoulder. I was betting he was making coffee. He chuckled.

"Somewhat difficult to put a bat on the telephone, isn't it?"

"That's what I thought," I giggled.

"This guy really is an amateur, isn't he? You did right. I'll tell Nelion what happened when he calls sometime later this morning. Go back to sleep."

"'Night," I said, hung up, threw the phone on my bedside table and snuggled back down under the covers. I could get a couple more hours' sleep before the alarm went off.

I spent the next several minutes snickering as visions of a bat holding a cell phone to its ear floated around my brain. First, it was a normal-sized bat holding a normal-sized cell phone by wrapping its wing around the phone. Then the cartoons kicked in, with a bat-sized phone.

Fudge got up from his spot on the spare pillow, turned a circle, and plopped back down again.

*"I am never going to get back to sleep if you keep thinking of these things. Neither will you."*

"Sorry," I replied. "But after dealing with an idiot, it's hard not to."

"*Ommm…*" Fudge's chest rumbled, as well.

Between the nondescript sound and Fudge's purring, the images finally left my head and I drifted back off to sleep.

# CHAPTER THIRTEEN

At eleven the next morning, the office door opened. I sighed as I put my pencil down. Who, now? I slipped on my shoes and went out into the reception area.

To find Perchaladon holding a huge bouquet of roses. There must have been three dozen. He smiled over the flowers and held them out toward me. "For you."

"Why, thank you," I said. "Let me find a vase for these. I'll be right back."

I rummaged through the cupboards and finally decided I was going to have to divide the bouquet in two. I just didn't have anything large enough. I carried two vases out to reception and set them both on Sally's desk.

"They're beautiful," I told him. "But for what?"

"Can I not give a beautiful woman some beautiful flowers?" he asked.

"Well, yes," I blushed. "But…"

"I did have an ulterior motive." He looked at me slyly.

It figured. He probably wanted something. My face must have reflected my thoughts. "What?"

He frowned. "Nothing untoward. I wanted to know if I could take you to lunch."

Not as bad as I'd thought but his attention was beginning to get annoying. I tried to be polite. "I'm sorry but no. There's too much happening with Ev gone. Perhaps a rain check?"

"Despite the stress you must feel, you have to take care of yourself, too. A nice, relaxed lunch would help keep you calm."

I heaved a very audible sigh. "I'm sure it would be very pleasant but once again, no."

"What must I do to convince you?"

"Ask again another time. Thank you for the flowers; they really are gorgeous. I do hate to be rude but I have work to do so if you don't mind…" My statement was punctuated by the phone ringing.

"I understand. Of course. I'll call again at another time, then." With a wink, he turned and left the office as I picked up the phone on Sally's desk.

"Angelich Security, how may I help you?"

"Good morning, Amy," Gregory's voice sounded more awake than I probably did after an interrupted night.

"Hey, Gregory. I'm on Sally's phone. Let me go back to my office." I put him on hold, walked back to my desk, and kicked off my shoes while picking up the receiver. "You have news?"

"In a way, yes." I heard a slurp on the other end as he took a sip of his coffee. He probably heard the same thing on his end as I sipped mine. "Nelion's lieutenant scouted the area in question last night. He didn't see any bats or any evidence of them. No sign of any active magic, either. They are expanding their search tonight to include the national park that abuts the enclave. The lieutenant is friends with one of the park rangers, who may help narrow down the search area.

"In addition, their brand of law enforcement now has an all-points-bulletin for the Obrist character. If he's found, they have ways of finding out what he knows, regardless of what he wishes to divulge."

"So we're still in a holding pattern, is that what you're saying?"

"Yes. There's really nothing we can do until Ev is located and the elves are the best ones to do that."

That wasn't what I wanted to hear. "Lovely. Okay. Fine."

"I will call again when I hear something. I've told Nelion not to hold off calling me until morning if he has news so I may call you in the middle of the night."

My fists clenched but I unclenched them. There was nothing I could do but wait. "Fine. I'll wait for your call. Bye."

I turned my attention back to my work. Cassandra brought my lunch in about an hour later and after answering her query with "no news," I absentmindedly ate my sandwich while going over insurance quotes. The agent wanted an answer in another two days so if Ev wasn't found, I'd have to make the decision myself. I preferred to coach him which way I wanted him to go and let *him* make the choice. That way I got no grief and he still felt in control.

"Oooh, who loves me?" Sally's voice interrupted my thoughts. I had to think for a moment, then remembered I'd totally forgotten about the flowers.

"I do. Actually, Perchaladon does. He brought those for me this morning and I forgot them on your desk."

She stood in my office doorway, one vase in her hand, the other hand on her hip and eyebrows raised to her hairline.

"The elf brought you flowers? And this many? Man, he must have the hots for you! Can I at least keep one vase on my desk? They smell lovely."

"You can keep both," I told her. "I'd undoubtedly knock it off." I waved my hand around the piles of paper covering my desk.

"Take a break and talk to me. What's up with the elf? And what's the news on Ev?"

I put my pencil down and looked at her. "No news on Ev yet. And Perchaladon? I have no clue. I told him Tuesday night to wait until things had calmed down with Ev, yet he bothered me both yesterday and this morning. It's getting irritating."

"You have a drop-dead gorgeous man interested in you and you're irritated? What's wrong with you?"

"Ev. That's what's wrong with me. Gregory is leaving everything in the elves' hands. Which is so unlike him it's not even funny. That worries me. And I can't think of anything to do, either. I'm stuck waiting. Which I don't like. Then to have someone I really don't know want me to act like nothing's wrong and go on a date with him, even after I've told him the truth, that Ev's disappeared, probably kidnapped? Sorry, he's not looking out for me; he's looking out for himself. Not my idea of a great guy."

She frowned. "When you put it that way, I guess I understand. But damn!"

"Yeah, damn. Have you finished going through the contracts?"

"Not yet. Should be done with them this time tomorrow. Anything else I need to do?"

"Nope. Just keep me off the phone the rest of the day, if you can. I'm trying to sort out the workers' comp insurance and it's no fun. Fewer interruptions means I can get through this today, I hope."

She stuck her nose in the flowers, inhaling deeply as she headed back to her desk, then raised her head long enough to say, "I'll try."

By Sunday, I'd had enough. I paced my apartment. Gregory wouldn't talk to me, wouldn't give me a reason why he didn't go after Ev himself, when I knew approximately where he was. What was so special about the elves, anyways? On a normal basis, he'd have charged in like a bull moose, taking control of the situation and getting our boss back.

I looked up the area I thought Ev was in on the internet. It looked like an easy drive from New Orleans. I could fly down, rent a car, and go get him myself. Then I'd have to figure out how to turn him back into his ogre self and probably deal with the accompanying anger. It wouldn't be the first time. But how does one catch a bat? I started researching that, too.

*"I know what you are thinking. It is not a good plan."*

"Why not? No one else is doing anything."

Fudge cocked his head. *"What makes you think you, a barely-trained witch, can do something a wizard with much more experience cannot? You are being foolish. I believe the current phrase for such a venture would be hare-brained."*

"But I have to do *something*. We can't just leave Ev down there, flying around forever! Why is Gregory not doing something himself?"

Like an internet meme, Fudge lay down and put his paws over his face. *"You know nothing of elves, do you?"*

I shook my head. "Only what I have experienced so far."

He removed his paws from his face and glared at me. *"Then allow me to give you a lesson.*

*"You know the magical energy you can see around you, correct? I believe you call it 'sparkles.'"*

I nodded.

*"Elves* are *that magic. It infuses their entire being. There is nothing you, or any other witch or wizard, for that matter, can do to them. If you cast a spell in their direction, they simply absorb it.*

*"I will allow you this, however. You know that you use plants, stones and other things as helpers in your spells, to allow them to continue without refreshment."*

I nodded again.

*"Elves do not do such. They use their inherent magic when casting spells. As such, the spells either need to be refreshed, or they will degrade with each sunrise. What does that tell you?"*

I had to calm myself down to think rationally. Fudge followed me with his eyes as I paced around the living room, into the kitchen, and back again.

"That either someone needs to go back to refresh the spell on occasion, or at some point, Ev will turn back into himself?"

*"Very good. Think some more. The wiz…Gregory's spells are generally stronger than yours at this point, correct?"*

I paced some more. "So what you're saying is just like with us, the stronger the elf, the stronger his magic. I presume with some, age indicates strength? As in, Alberon's magic would be stronger than, say, Perchaladon's?"

*"Correct. There is a reason Alberon is senior mage to someone who not only heads his enclave but the entire United States.*

*"Your friend, Perchaladon…"*

I glared. "He's not my friend."

*"Indeed. Your acquaintance, then, and his friend, are young and presumably, have not immersed themselves in study, as evidenced by their entry into the human world. Therefore, their magic would not be as strong.*

*"Although it is wrong to assume anything, it is quite possible both the wiz…Gregory and the elder elves are waiting either for the spell to degrade and produce a very angry ogre, or that one of the others will arrive at this area to refresh the spell. Either way, they will have a way to retrieve your employer."*

"Why do you have such difficulty with names? Twice now, you have had to refrain from calling Gregory 'the wizard.'"

*"Are you trying to change the subject?"*

"No. It's just something that struck me."

Fudge sighed. *"As I have told you before, names are not something I am accustomed to using. In the past, people were referred to by their relationship to our witch or wizard. It has only been a few months since I started calling you by your name, has it not? May we return to the subject of your employer?"*

I resumed my pacing. "If Alberon is as strong as you suggest, why have they not traveled to the area, found the bat with the magic stuck to him, and reversed the spell? They know approximately where Ev is."

*"That I cannot tell you. It may have something to do with internal politics."*

Fudge turned his head toward the door just as a knock sounded. I looked through the peephole to see Cassandra standing there, a quizzical yet angry look on her face.

"What's up?" I asked as I opened the door.

She stalked in. "I don't know. You tell me. Merlin wouldn't leave me alone, projecting feelings of anxiety, finally knocking the picture of the two of us at the handfasting onto the floor to get my attention."

She looked down at Fudge. "You sent a message, didn't you?"

I looked down with her. "Well?"

*"I did. I thought perhaps she would be able to talk sense to you if I could not."*

I sighed. "I'm sorry, Cassandra. It appears my cat thinks I am incapable of logical thinking or something."

She walked into the kitchen and helped herself to a cup of coffee. "So, what are you thinking about that is illogical?"

"I was thinking about going down to Louisiana and getting my boss back, since neither the elves nor Gregory appear to want to do that."

To my surprise, she let out a loud guffaw. "And once you got your bat, how were you going to change him back into an ogre?"

"I hadn't gotten to that part."

"You *do* know you have no power to reverse an elf's spell, right?"

"Well, yes, but Fudge was just telling me that if the spells aren't renewed, they degrade over time. So, if I had the bat and no one renewed it, he'd eventually turn back into himself, yes?"

That earned me a glare. "Probably. But then you'd have a pissed-off elf coming after you. And how were you planning on protecting yourself?"

"I hadn't thought that far."

"Of course not. You're thinking with your heart, not your head." She looked from Fudge to me and back again. "How much do you know about elves? I admit our knowledge is scanty due to lack of interaction."

*"Please relay what I have told you."*

I filled Cassandra in on what we'd already discussed and added, "I will admit that the few times Perchaladon has done magic around me that I've felt *nothing*. I usually get a tingly feeling when there's magic being done but his didn't register at all."

"I'll repeat myself. How were you planning on protecting yourself against a pissed-off elf, especially now that I know their magic isn't tangible to us?"

"Okay." I looked at both of them. "It was a bad idea. But it's been a week, I don't have my boss back, no one's given me a timetable, and you know how I hate to feel helpless!"

Cassandra put her arm around me, and Fudge wove his way between our legs.

"Something will happen sooner or later. Those high-falutin' elves you've been talking to won't let it go on forever. They like to keep their problems to themselves and if it continues, word will get out that they can't handle their own people. That would be an embarrassment, I would think, wouldn't you?"

I heaved a sigh and nodded. "Yeah. I guess. I just don't like sitting on my hands."

"Good. Then I'm going back to my Sunday and my husband. As they say, keep calm. Things will work out."

She gave me a squeeze, put her coffee cup in the kitchen sink and let herself out the door. I was left alone with my thoughts – and my familiar.

*"You are no longer thinking of getting your employer yourself, correct?"*

I nodded my acquiescence.

*"Good. Because it is time for a nap."*

Fudge curled up in a corner of the sofa, apparently purposely turning his back to me, and within minutes, was asleep. I wished I could sleep as easily.

Knowing I wasn't in a frame of mind to study but also knowing I had to keep myself occupied with something related to my anxiety, I searched the Witches' Web (a handy online resource only recently started by Delilah Emerson, the secretary of the Midwest Witches' Council but available to anyone who had a password) for what information was available on elves.

It wasn't much.

"Elves are a humanoid race but they are in no fashion human. They look very much like the *Star Trek* characters known as Vulcans. They have sharp features, highly arched eyebrows and the top cartilage of their ears forms a point. The few elves encountered by our kind have always been described as 'perfect' with no discernible physical flaws.

"They consider themselves to be superior to every other life form. Their reasoning may be that although they look somewhat like us, they are completely magical creatures. It is believed they have the capability to transform their appearance to any sort of animal they choose with a simple thought. Spells, as well, are performed only by thought.

"It is for this reason their magic is fleeting. Without anchors such as herbs, stones, and the like, their spells degrade a little with every sunrise and as such, must be renewed on a regular basis to maintain them.

"Elves live in settlements akin to our cities called 'enclaves.' These are always located in rural areas, preferably forested. (We know of no enclave outside an area heavily populated by trees.) No witch or wizard has ever been allowed into an enclave, so we have no further description.

"They have a hierarchy, and it is believed the strongest and eldest hold the highest positions. Each geographic area has, for lack of a better term, a governor and a senior mage. The governor oversees both economic and political activities. The senior mage is someone who is versed in every aspect of their magic, is the strongest magic user in the area, and assists in the governing, as well as overseeing their healers.

"That is the extent of our knowledge of elves. If anyone has further information to add, please contact the webmaster, delilah@witchesweb.org."

I opened my email and composed a note to Delilah, telling her that the elves' magic wasn't palpable. At least to me. I could at least do that much. I closed my laptop and curled up next to Fudge, hoping to sleep at least part of the day away.

Fifteen minutes later, my phone rang.

"Miss McCollum, this is Althea Fitzsimmons. We met a few months ago."

Oh, shit. The Head of the Midwest Witches' Council was calling me. What the hell did I do? I took what I hoped was an inaudible deep breath.

"Yes, ma'am. I remember. What can I do for you?"

"Delilah just forwarded your email to me. May I ask how you know about elven magic?"

I thought she and Gregory were friends, and that he would have informed her, or at least the Wizards' Council guy, about what was happening, and that guy – I couldn't remember his name – would have shared. Obviously not. So, I had to spill the beans about Ev, Perchaladon, and everything. Holding back information from the Witches' Council would have just gotten me in deeper shit and since I was already on their radar due to my temper, I felt it wise to let her know what was going on.

"This is an interesting development," she said when I'd finished. "And once again, it involves your boss."

I sighed. "Yeah, I know. It seems that recently, he can't keep himself out of trouble. Do you have any suggestions?"

The line was silent for a moment. "Not right now. This really doesn't involve witches, per se. It's between your boss and whatever elf he got in the way of. However, this Perchaladon's interest in you may be an opportunity to learn more about elves. Please do keep me informed if he persists in his attentions toward you."

I squirmed in my seat. "Ms. Fitzsimmons, he may be handsome as all get-out, but he gives me the creeps and I'm trying to discourage him. And what you just said makes me feel like a lab experiment or something. Exactly what are you asking?"

"I'm not asking you to do anything which would make you feel uncomfortable. But we know so little about them that *anything* you can tell us, such as the fact their magic isn't palpable, could go a long way toward helping us to understand them more. Any little tidbit you may think helpful, please pass on. It may help someone else, somewhere down the road, you know?"

I did know. I just didn't like playing spy or whatever it was she wanted me to do. It also made my blip on the Council's radar even brighter, which I also didn't like.

"I assume your phone will save my number, yes?" She interrupted my thoughts. "Please do call if you have any more useful information. Goodbye."

And…I was listening to dead air. It was time to get out of the house and work off some of this frustration. I grabbed my ID and keys, hauled my bike up the stairs and hightailed it for the paths around the lakes.

Sunny Sunday afternoons aren't the best times for pushing yourself by working up a good pace. It seemed every bike rider and rollerblader had the same idea as me. The paths were crowded so I could only ride at a leisurely pace along with everyone else. The ambient heat meant the aroma of sunscreen and sweat permeated the air. I had made one circuit around Lake Bde Maka Ska and was contemplating chucking it all and riding home when I heard a familiar voice call my name.

Swiveling my head this way and that, all while trying not to crash into the riders ahead and to either side of me, I finally spotted the culprit. It was that damned elf, riding what appeared to be a brand-new racing bike, hurrying through the crowd to catch up with me. Can you say stalker?

I pulled over and stopped. Within a second or two, he was standing by my side. "What a pleasant surprise!" he exclaimed.

I frowned at him. "An elf riding a bike? This is an unusual sight."

"I had heard it was a favored pastime of many people at this time of year. I thought I would give it a try. Not to mention the people-watching is fabulous. What brings you out on such a fine afternoon?"

"What else?" I dully responded. "Riding my bike, getting some fresh air and exercise, just like everyone else. May I ask how this *coincidental* meeting happened?"

While I was talking, I noticed several women turn their heads to look at the handsome elf. One didn't pay enough attention to what she was doing and plowed into her friend, who was also rubber-necking. The ensuing crash had a domino effect and took out about a half-dozen other riders. The elf paid absolutely no attention to the accident.

He shrugged. "It is known you ride on nice days, so I took a chance. I thought perhaps instead of that lunch you turned down a couple of days ago, that I could persuade you to partake of an afternoon tea with me on a blanket, like so many other couples do."

My legendary Irish temper flared. *"Couples?* We are not a *couple.* Are you familiar with the human term, 'last straw'? If not, please do look it up. And leave me the fuck alone. I have no desire to see you again. Do I make myself clear?"

*"Calm yourself."*

"Calm? With a stalker?" I shot back.

*"You must. If not, I will. You know what happens when you get very angry."*

Shit. I did. I took a deep breath then glared at Perchaladon. "I am leaving now. Do not attempt to follow me or I will call the authorities."

He smirked. "You know the human authorities can do nothing to me."

"Oh, yes. I'm well aware. But they can certainly inconvenience you. And you would *hate* to be inconvenienced, I'm sure."

I turned my bike for home but thought to take a very circuitous route. I wasn't sure if he knew where I lived and on the off-chance he didn't, I didn't want to lead him directly to my apartment.

On second thought…I grabbed my cell phone out of my pocket and called Gregory.

"Hey," I said when he answered. "I need a favor."

"If I can, certainly."

"Can you pick me up in the Hummer? I went for a bike ride, that damned elf accosted me on the bike path, and I don't want him following me home."

"Can you keep him busy for an hour? I have something simmering that can't be left alone. Then I can come. I will track you by your phone so don't turn it off."

My patience was nearly at an end, but I realized I had to wait for the favor. "Of course. I'll continue riding, heading toward the southern shore of Lake Harriet. That will be closer for you and the opposite direction of home. And thank you."

I hung up, tucked my phone back in my pocket, and turned my bike around. I rode with the crowd, trying not to be in a hurry, and trying very hard not to look over my shoulder. It was difficult to maintain an air of nonchalance when all I wanted to do was find the asshole I was certain was behind me and fling an energy ball at his handsome-yet-unwelcome face.

Two circuits of Lake Harriet later, I heard the familiar horn of the HumVee. Gregory had managed to snag a rare-as-hens-teeth parking spot right on the parkway. As I approached, the gate lifted open. I put my bike in the back (not without a few grunts – the floor came up to my waist) then clambered into the front.

"I took a momentary detour I thought you might appreciate," Gregory said as he handed me a cup of Starbucks. "Now, tell me what's going on."

As he pulled into traffic and headed, not for my apartment but in the direction of his cottage behind Ev's house, I filled him in on the last few days since our return from New Orleans.

"I'm not certain of Althea's motives," he said. "Although yes, we'd certainly like as much information as possible on the elves, asking you to put up with his attention isn't her normal style. Something else is going on."

"Why are we headed toward your place rather than mine?" I asked.

"Because I can better protect you there *and* if he is indeed following you somehow, he'll think you live with me. And Fudge showed up just as I was about ready to leave so I figured this was somehow his idea."

"How did you get to Gregory's and why?" I asked in my head.

*"The witch above us came down with a treat for you, letting herself into the house when you did not answer the door. It did not have any tuna in it, by*

*the way. I just nudged her enough so she would give me a boost. You know I can travel on my own through the ether.*

*"The wizard has the right of it. You must not be at your own home at the moment to protect what little privacy you seem to have left. The elf is acting strangely and I would not want a repeat of the vampire incident.*

*"Please do ask the wiz…Gregory to get my things. Some of yours, as well. You generally need a shower after riding that contraption you call a bicycle."*

I should probably explain. About a year ago, a young vampire went off the deep end, thinking he was in love with me, and got very insistent, even breaking into my house and trashing it. He has since, I am told, greeted the dawn. Good riddance! Now, if there was some elven equivalent to getting fried by sunlight…

"Okay," I sighed. "I'll stay with you, at least overnight. But we need to figure out what's going on, not only with him but with Ev, too. It's been a week and I'm at my wits' end!"

"I am trying very hard to be diplomatic with Nelion," Gregory replied. "But I, too, am starting to lose patience. The initial spell on Ev should have dissipated by now with a week's worth of sunrises. If their transmogrification spell does not transform clothing, similar to a werewolf's transformation, an angry, bare-assed ogre running around that state park would have drawn attention. Hell, even a fully-clothed one would. Yet we've heard nothing, which means this Obrist character is somehow slipping around to renew it. Then the question begs, why?

"Nelion is being very close-mouthed and very uncommunicative. Perchaladon seems to be infatuated with you but I doubt it has anything to do with romance. I'd also like to know how he's finding you. Then there's Althea's request of you. Something larger than just Ev's disappearance is happening and I'd like to know what."

I took a large gulp of my venti latte. "Me, too. In the meantime, what do we do?"

"Keep you off the magical radar as much as possible, for starters. Someone, for some reason, has decided to involve you in whatever is happening. So, you stay at my place for a bit. I'll take you to and from work. While you're working, I'm going to have a chat with people higher up the food chain to see if I can find out what the machinations are all about."

So, for at least one evening, I got to partake of someone else's good cooking. Once again, I curled up on the couch with the handmade quilt draped over me for modesty's sake, Fudge making a nest of my hair behind me. It wasn't my queen-sized bed, but it was comfortable enough.

# CHAPTER FOURTEEN

Gregory accompanied into the office the next morning, explaining that he'd use Ev's phone to make his calls. Due to demand, Cassandra had started opening the deli on Monday, so I was able to get my usual latte. His presence raised Cassandra's eyebrows, but she said nothing. I knew she'd ask when she brought my lunch. I tried to get into my usual Monday routine but thoughts of Ev's (and my) current predicament swirled in my head.

About an hour later, Gregory poked his head in my office. "I'm going down to Council headquarters to have a talk with Althea and Howard." I mentally slapped my forehead. *That's* the Wizard Council guy's name! "I should be back in a couple of hours. Will you be all right alone?"

I nodded. "I'm not expecting anyone to visit so I'll lock the door. Sally has her own key and I'll let Cassandra know to knock when she brings lunch. I'll be fine. You'll let me know what you find out?"

I followed him out and locked the door behind him. Then texted Cassandra to tell her I was on lockdown, to text me before she brought lunch, and a full explanation would be given in between bites. Then I turned my attention back to my work, which was almost doubled with Ev's absence.

Shortly before noon, my phone buzzed with a text message. "Can't bring lunch up. The elf is here, wanting to know if we know why you're not at work because the door is locked. He's got the female customers in a tizzy and the males are glaring at him. <grin> Will let you know when he leaves."

That told me one thing. He didn't have some sort of tracking spell on me, otherwise he'd know I was right upstairs, locked door or not. Which was a relief, but I still wanted to know how he kept tracking me down.

My phone buzzed again. "You are not at work. Are you ill? May I bring you anything? ~P"

Grr. "I am just a little under the weather. Perhaps a summer cold. Thank you for asking. Now please remember what I told you yesterday and lose this number." I may not be able to lie well in person but in print? I'm *good*. I patted myself on the back for even being fairly polite.

A few minutes later I got yet another text but this one was welcome. "He's gone. On my way up."

I unlocked the door, ushered her in, and re-locked it. She handed me a plate of what looked like a BLT sandwich and homemade chips. "So, what's the calamity? I mean, besides Ev's problem."

In between mouthfuls of sandwich, I explained what had happened at the lake the previous day and what both Gregory and Fudge had to say about it.

"Okay, that's a little more than creepy. What is it with you and stalkers? First a vampire and now an elf. Sheesh!"

I nodded. "I know, right? I'm just a nobody, even for the first eight years of working for an ogre and all of a sudden, everyone's clamoring for my attention. I'd very much like to go back to anonymity. Because I'm not all that important, I'm putting it down to Ev's stupidity. He's gotten himself – and me – into some situations lately, hasn't he?"

"Ain't that the truth. Hopefully, Gregory can get some answers. I've noticed he's pretty good at that. Are you done? I have to get back."

I handed her my empty plate and walked her out the door. "I'll keep you posted."

Since Cassandra got married, a brief chat at lunch four or five days a week and an occasional girls' night out was our only chance to catch up. I missed our Friday night pizza-and-gab fests.

A key turned the lock a short while later and Sally's voice announced her arrival. "Why's the door locked?"

"Lock it back up and come on in. I'll catch you up."

Once again, I had to go through the entire weekend story. I was getting to the point I was just going to write it down in a blog somewhere and tell people to check that so I didn't have to keep repeating myself.

"You and men, I swear! At the rate things are going with other species, you should probably stick to fully-human ones."

"As if I pick these guys! Okay, yes, I did pick Tony but it wasn't my fault he got killed. The others were – or are – just plain crazy which, I believe, has nothing to do with me. Although, if Perchaladon doesn't go away soon, I may consider entering a convent."

Sally laughed. "He may be able to track you there, but I'll bet he won't like the location! What do you have for me today?"

"Not a lot. Sort the mail. Decline any party invitations Ev might get, and continue doing what you do so well – avoiding answering questions as to where Ev is."

"I'll be glad when he's back and I don't have to do that anymore. I'm running out of creative excuses."

An hour later, I was sorting through contracts, trying to figure out how Ev might match up guards and clients, when Sally buzzed me with a phone call.

"Can you take the rest of the afternoon off?" Gregory asked.

"Ummm. Probably. What's up?"

"Do you remember Ed Bartz, the security guy?"

I had to think for a moment, then it came to me. "He heads up the Council's investigative arm, right? Looks sort of like a pumped Michael Chiklis?"

"That's the man. He has an interesting theory I think you ought to hear. We'll meet you at Cork's in a half hour?"

"Okay. I might be a few minutes late, but I'll be there."

He hung up and I went back to reviewing contracts, noting which pairings I thought would work, and making myself notes as to which needed to be decided almost immediately and which could wait a few days, in the hopes we got Ev back and I wouldn't get blamed for a mismatch.

Grabbing my purse, I waved goodbye to Sally and headed across the street. Cork's was my favorite watering hole and at this time of day, it would be fairly quiet. Cork would ensure we had whatever privacy we needed.

I had to let my eyes adjust after the bright sunlight but that was okay. Just that brief jaunt in the summertime heat and humidity had me sweating. Standing there, apparently letting my eyes adjust, allowed the air conditioning to dry me out a little. I saw Gregory wave at me from a booth in the far corner.

Ed stood and extended his hand as I approached the table. "It's nice to see you again, Ms. McCollum, and under perhaps slightly better circumstances?"

I shook his hand, blew a kiss at Gregory, and told him, "Please, call me Amy. And I'm not certain if these are better circumstances or not. Just as weird, anyways."

The men nodded their agreement as Cork set a glass of merlot in front of me. You see why it's one of my favorite spots? I don't have to order or anything.

After Cork returned to the bar, Gregory said, "I'm casting a privacy spell. Although Cork is as discreet as they come, who knows what ears are listening?" I felt my standard magic-being-done tingle then my ears popped as the dome of privacy covered us.

Ed cleared his throat. "As strange as it may sound, based on what Gregory has told me and certain information I have uncovered, I believe there is a conspiracy between some of the younger elves in the Louisiana enclave and some younger witches and wizards."

My eyebrows hit my hairline. "To what end?"

"I'm not entirely certain. As you probably have noticed, some young elves are making themselves known in the human world, which in this day and age is extremely odd. The elves have more or less kept themselves hidden for the last, oh, five hundred years or so. Yes, they participate in human commerce – that's where the majority of their money comes from, but up to now, it has always been through human agents who thought they were working for humans."

I looked at Gregory. "But Nelion and Alberon came right to our hotel door and were walking in the streets with us."

"You probably did not notice because it's so subtle, but they had glamoured themselves to look human. I saw it as an overlay to their real appearance. You're magical, so the glamour wouldn't have affected your sight."

I shook my head. "No, I saw no "humans." (I used air quotes.) Or a 'human overlay.' Just normal elven appearance, complete with pointy ears and flowing robes."

"You are a young witch, Ms. Mc…Amy. While we generally can't tell they're casting, sometimes we can see the results of their casting, but that takes practice," Ed interjected.

"So what do you think the conspiracy is?" I asked.

"As I said, I'm not certain. But as you know, although paranormals are generally accepted in society, it's more of a 'don't ask, don't tell' scenario. It's my belief some of the younger set is tired of being in the closet, so to speak, and wants to do something about it. I'm not sure what, but I've been seeing signs of discontent."

"And what does this have to do with me?" I was majorly perplexed.

"You are one of those younger witches. It's possible you're being felt out to join their, um, movement."

"And Ev's disappearance?"

Gregory answered that one. "To get to you. It's well-known you're protective of Ev, no matter how odd some might think it. And, you've just come into your powers. If he disappeared mysteriously, you might be willing to do something in the open to get him back. At least, that's a theory."

"Is this why Ms. Fitzsimmons wanted me to stay in touch with that creepy elf?"

Ed nodded. "None of us are able to get close to a younger elf and it was thought you might relay news of this movement back to the Elders. However, based on what Gregory told me this morning, that idea has been taken off the table. Your peace of mind, and perhaps your safety, are more important."

I sighed in relief. But on the other hand…

"May I ask what sort of dangers bringing the paranormals more out into the open would pose? It seems to me it wouldn't be such a bad thing."

"Violence, for one thing," Ed replied. "Things haven't changed *that* much in the course of human history. People fear what they don't understand or what is out of their sphere of normalcy. Weres would be killed because they *might* harm someone. Magic users, too, because you *might* cast a spell to harm someone who couldn't retaliate."

"Your circle of friends is accepting of almost anyone," Gregory added. "But trust us, there are people out there who would fear you just because you use magic. That's one of the reasons I have always taught you away from where people could see what was happening. I don't want any unfortunate incidents to hamper your learning."

"But what of the obvious paranormals, like Ev? Or Cork? They can't hide themselves or their nature, y'know?"

"And if you notice, Ev keeps to the paranormal crowd in his social endeavors. Business is either with paranormals or those accepting of them. He doesn't even go to the grocery store on his own. He keeps as low a profile as possible to avoid confrontations. Even still, there have been times when his feelings have been hurt because someone's said something derogatory within his hearing or have shunned him just because of who he is. Cork is probably pretty much the same. We *look* human. For those who do not, it can be difficult."

"Okay, I'll buy that. So what am I supposed to do about all this?"

"Althea and Nelion are working together to try to smoke out the instigators. Nelion believes his son and friend are two prime suspects. I have my eyes on a couple of young wizards at the University of Minnesota who make frequent trips to Chicago and New Orleans.

"So, apart from cozying up to Perchaladon, I repeat. What am I supposed to do? Dating a college kid isn't exactly in my playbook."

"We'd like you to go get your boss back," Ed said.

Huh? Hadn't I been discouraged from doing exactly that?

"And how am I supposed to accomplish that? And if he's still a bat, how do I change him back?"

Gregory gave me one of his "teaching moment" looks. "I will accompany you. For one thing, it's probable Obrist is watching the area. We have no idea exactly what they're up to, but we might be able to draw him out into the open. We obviously don't trust him, so I will be there to watch your back.

"Alberon and some of his trusted people will be nearby. They hope to be able to catch Obrist doing something he's been forbidden to do. As well, once we have the bat, Alberon *should* be able to unravel the spell and give us our ogre back."

"I don't get it. Why didn't they just go get Ev and snatch Obrist while they're at it?"

"Because they haven't been able to find either one. Unfortunately, I am unable to effectively describe the area you saw in your dream. Without knowing exactly where to look, they're incapable of doing much. You, on the other hand, should be able to pinpoint the location once we're walking around, yes?"

This was a lot to handle. Yes, I could still see the area vividly in my mind but that was a lot of walking to do. However, it seemed to be the only solution.

"Get my boss back. Check. But how does this help with your conspiracy?"

"Nelion assured Althea once they have Obrist in custody, they'll be able to find out exactly what is going on," Ed answered. "She did not ask further, nor would he tell us anything else, anyways. We just have to trust that they can get some information *and* that they will share it."

"You listening to all this?" I mentally asked.

*"Of course. If I understand correctly, you are to go retrieve your employer and help capture rabble-rousers?"*

I chuckled. Sometimes my familiar used some antiquated words. I think the last time I heard 'rabble-rousers' was from one of my elderly college history professors. But I knew what he meant.

I turned my attention back to the table. "Okay. When?"

"We will leave Wednesday morning," Gregory said. "There are some things that need to be put into place. I will pick you – and Fudge – up at your apartment. Pack hiking clothes, including some waterproof shoes."

*"I will have to travel in one of those flying contraptions?"*

"Fudge wants to know if he will have to fly."

Ed raised his eyebrows. "You have a talking familiar?"

I nodded but before Ed could say anything else, Gregory answered.

"Unfortunately, yes, he will have to fly with us. I do not know what accommodations we will have, and I would like to use him as a scout, if possible. He has a better nose than any humanoid."

I heard a grumble in my mind, then, *"Very well. I will assist in retrieving your employer. But I demand extra tuna as payment."*

I finished my wine, headed home, and called Sally to see if she could work full-time for a few days starting Wednesday.

"After rearranging some things, yes, I can. What's up?"

Without going into detail, I told her Gregory and I were going to find and retrieve Ev.

"Okaaay…and once you get him, then what?"

I sighed. "It seems there's a lot of political bullshit going on, but the elves have agreed to turn him back to his irascible self. Of course, I'll probably get to deal with the fallout."

"Politics. It figures. I thought the human political system was bad but paranormals seem to be worse."

"Yep. I thought what with being minorities in the greater scheme of things, that would make pulling together easy, but apparently not. I have some things to do to get ready. I'll see you tomorrow afternoon."

I hung up and immediately called Elinda, one of the witches upstairs, to ask if I could borrow a cat carrier again. Fudge usually walked beside me wherever we needed to go so I never bothered buying one. If things continued, I should probably rectify that.

"Of course, darlin'," she replied. "I assume he hates those things, so I'll bring the larger one down. Can we do anything else?"

"Nah. Hopefully, I won't be gone that long. But thanks."

Then I had some shopping to do. Hiking clothes? Waterproof shoes? Not in my city-girl wardrobe. I let my fingers do the walking on the internet, first to figure out what exactly was meant by "hiking clothes." It seemed my normal jeans would be fine and with the heat and humidity I expected, just a lightweight jacket to protect my arms would suffice. Then there was the issue of shoes. Well, boots. I found what I thought would work on a sporting goods website, heaved a sigh and paid for overnight shipping.

Tuesday was hectic, trying to clean up as much as possible, not knowing how long I would be gone from the office. Thankfully, there was a lot I could put on Sally's desk. It would certainly keep her busy!

Wednesday morning, Gregory picked us up in the Hummer and we headed to Flying Cloud Airport, Fudge grumbling in my head the entire way.

*"There is no room in this thing! How am I supposed to see out?"*

"Quitcherbitchin'. You're in a carrier meant for a medium-sized dog, which means you have plenty of room. There's nothing to see but road and traffic. Once we're in the plane, there will be even less to see. And it's only for a few hours."

"We will be landing in Lake Charles," Gregory told us, "which is only about a half hour from the wildlife refuge we think Ev is in. Since we will need to be able to see bats, Nelion has used his influence to allow us access after the park closes. There's a lot of ground to cover so I hope you're up for a lot of walking."

"And a hotel for sleeping and such?" I asked.

"We will figure that out later. I am more concerned with getting down there and getting Ev. We have to meet with the elves before anything else happens."

*"I have to be near elves? This gets worse and worse."*

I privately agreed with him but there was no helping it.

"Wait. I just had a thought," I blurted out.

"And that would be?"

"What do you need me for? You can track Ev's beacon spell if there's no masking on it, right?"

As he navigated us to a parking spot, he frowned. "And what makes you think there is no masking? If Obrist is indeed in the area and is aware of the search, why would he not continue to hide my spell?"

Duh. But… "I still don't understand what Ev has to do with any of this. If there *is* some conspiracy or insurgency going on, I don't think Ev would know about it."

"Nor do I. It's not his style. But he must have seen or heard something to make someone uncomfortable. Now, no more discussion until we land."

# CHAPTER FIFTEEEN

Two-plus hours of flying in a small plane later, we finally landed. My stomach was grateful. Smaller jets don't plow through air currents as well as the larger ones. Fudge expressed relief, as well.

*"When we are able to return home, please ask Gregory just to give me a boost. That was an unpleasant experience I would not care to repeat."*

"Yeah, well. I have to fly and misery loves company, so I may just make you return with me."

Gregory left us for a few moments and returned with a bundle of paper. He glanced once at it, then stuffed it in his back pocket.

"Come on. We have a meeting to get to." He grabbed Fudge's carrier in one hand and his overnight bag in another, leaving me to haul my stuff in his wake. He was in a hurry!

Once ensconced in the rented SUV, he reached around and opened the carrier door for Fudge, who immediately clambered into my lap and put his front paws on the dashboard. *"Freedom!"*

A half hour later, we were in the main parking lot of Cameron Prairie National Wildlife Refuge. As we pulled in, four elves emerged from a black SUV parked near the entrance. One raised his hand in greeting. I recognized Nelion, Alberon and the two guards who were with them in New Orleans. "No limo this time," I mused to myself.

Gregory maneuvered the car over near them and parked. Fudge nearly flew out the door as I opened it, making for the other side of a nearby tree.

Alberon followed his progress with interest. "Do you always travel with your cat, Ms. McCollum?" he asked.

"Only if I think it necessary," I replied with a smirk. "In this case, his nose is better than even yours for finding my boss."

Alberon grunted and muttered something to himself.

*"Please do not antagonize them on my account,"* Fudge pleaded. *"That one can do nasty things to both of us."*

"Do they not like cats?"

*"I do not know. But I do not like them."*

"It's a short-term association, probably for a good cause. So, pull up your big girl panties and deal with them."

*"I am no female, nor do I wear panties."*

"I know. It's another figure of speech. It means…"

*"I can deduce its meaning, thank you."*

Nelion waited for us to walk over to their vehicle, rather than advance toward us. [Such arrogance!] He addressed Gregory: "It will be easier for us to determine the necessary area in daylight hours. I have a map of the refuge from the ranger we know. The refuge is over nine thousand acres. Perhaps we can narrow it down somewhat?"

He reached a hand back and one of the guards put a roll of paper in his hand. He and Gregory spread it out on their car's hood. "It was woody, so the grasslands and wetlands are probably out. Amy, give us an opinion, please?" Gregory said.

I wandered over, Fudge at my heels, having completed his business. Nelion glared down at him. Ignoring that, I looked at the map.

"The ground was sort of squishy, so maybe here?" I pointed to an area marked "gallery forest" which, I'd learned in my research, meant forested wetlands. "Or, here's another place marked the same. And here's yet a third. Until I see it, I don't know which."

Nelion nodded. "We will drive to each area and walk around. Will that be sufficient? Unfortunately, we do not have room in our vehicle for all of us. Mr. Tremayne, perhaps it would be best to follow us. Our driver knows the area."

We all piled back in our respective cars. Fudge settled himself with his rear in my lap and front paws on the dash, ears twitching this way and that. Gregory followed the elves out the parking lot, down the main road and onto a side road. Ten minutes later, we pulled over to the side, alongside what appeared to be pasture with trees in the distance.

The four elves emerged from their car. Nelion waved at the trees. "This is the first of the wet forests marked on the map. We will have to walk across the grassland to get to it."

Gregory looked at my feet. "You may want to change your shoes," he said. "There can be snakes…"

I shuddered. Although logically, I know they're more afraid of me than I am of them, the thought of one slithering over my feet gave me the willies. I hurriedly grabbed my expensive hiking boots from my bag in the back seat and changed.

*"I can hear them before you see them. I will warn you."*

"Thanks."

And so the six (*"seven"*) of us started walking toward the trees, most of us keeping an eye on our feet. Fudge ranged hither and thither, nose to the ground just like a good bloodhound, sometimes startling a bird out of taller grass, which he half-heartedly chased before going back to his search.

As we approached the trees, Fudge slowed, then stopped. *"Please tell everyone to stop walking. There is elven spoor here, and it does not belong to any of these."*

I stopped in my tracks and cleared my throat. "Fudge has asked us to stop here. He smells something."

Everyone stopped. "Arrogant familiar," Alberon grumbled.

My cat had disappeared from sight. "You okay, bud?" I thought.

*"I will rejoin you in a moment. The spoor stops a few yards in, so this is not the place."*

He came trotting out of the trees and, uncharacteristically, jumped into my arms. I was so startled I barely caught him. Once he'd settled himself, he turned to look at the elves and, I kid you not, put his nose up in the air.

*"Please relay what I tell you. Elves have been here, and recently — since the last rainfall. Two that I can smell, and one werewolf. However, they only went a few yards into the trees, then returned. Therefore, I do not believe this is the place for which you search."*

Nelion's eyebrows raised. "I'm told it rained three nights ago. Werewolves? With elves? What are they up to? Very well. We will return to the vehicles and continue our search."

Meanwhile, Alberon was glaring at Fudge, who returned his own stare. I *would* find out what was between elves and familiars at some point!

As we made our way back to the cars, Fudge yelled, *"HALT!"* and since I must have screamed when my brain hurt from the shriek no one else could hear, everyone else stopped, too.

*"There is a cottonmouth three yards in front of the elf in the blue robe."*

"Nelion, there's a cottonmouth three yards in front of you."

"How…? Oh. Of course."

Alberon stared at the spot in question and a moment later, we saw the grass sway ninety degrees away from us. "It is safe to proceed."

"Could you not yell? That hurt! Literally!" I thought.

*"My apologies. I did not mean to hurt but it was imperative to stop everyone immediately before the snake was trod on."*

"Hold one moment," Gregory said. "Do you have a headache from that?" he asked me.

I nodded. The section of my head right inside my ears really did hurt, just like that sharp ache you get after attending a rock concert without earplugs.

Gregory waved both hands over the sides of my head and, just like magic (heh), my headache was gone. He looked down at Fudge, still cradled in my arms. "You know better," was all he said before motioning everyone forward again.

We piled back into the cars again, Fudge once more perched so he could see outside the windshield. As he followed the other car, Gregory asked Fudge, "What's up with you and the elves?"

"I'd like to know that same answer," I said.

"*Ask the Head Witch to ask Waldo. It is not my story to tell,*" was all he would say.

"I will definitely do that. There's something here that witches and wizards probably need to know," Gregory said when I relayed the reply.

"*Probably not, but he is welcome to the information if Waldo deems it appropriate.*"

Familiars. Who can tell what goes on with a species as long-lived as them? (Is species the word? They changed species, genus, even taxonomic family, dependent on their witch or wizard, so what are they called?)

"*Species will do.*"

We stopped once more at the side of another gravel road, this time closer to trees. Once more, Fudge hopped out quickly and started sniffing around. This time, he honed in on a scent quickly and started moving in almost a straight line into the trees. "*Wait here. I believe I may have found your spot.*"

After I relayed Fudge's command, everyone leaned against the cars. One of the guard elves even lit what appeared to be a cigarette but put it out quickly at Alberon's glare.

Ten minutes later, Fudge came back out of the trees. "*This is your area. The elves and werewolf went about a hundred yards into the trees, where there is a clearing similar to what you saw in your dream. But it is still too bright for the bats to be out and about. Shall I find their nests?"*

After I'd told everyone what Fudge found, Alberon cleared his throat. "I believe we would be better served to come back at twilight, about," he looked up at the sky, "three hours hence. Shall we repair to our respective homes and meet back here?"

Gregory pulled his cell phone out, did something on an app, closed it and looked at the elves. "That will give us enough time to get back to Lake Charles, find a hotel and get a bite to eat. We will see you back here?"

The elves got into their car and pulled away in the direction we'd been headed. Gregory did some searching on his phone, then plugged it into the car. "Make a U-turn," Siri told us.

Three hours later, we'd found a pet-friendly hotel, eaten a delivered pizza, and were back on the deserted road, waiting for the elves to arrive. Fudge, taking advantage of the opportunity for unrestricted outdoors, had gone roaming. The longer we waited, the lower the sun got, and the more I fidgeted.

"Calm yourself," Gregory told me while handing me a small spray bottle. "They will be here shortly, I'm sure. In the meantime, spritz yourself with this."

"What's this?" I asked as I followed his instructions, then handed the bottle back and watched as he did the same to himself.

"Insect repellant of my own making. We are in a damp area so there are undoubtedly gnats and mosquitos."

I picked at the hem of my shirt. "Why do we have to wait for them? It's nearly twilight out here in the open. It should be dark enough among the trees for the bats to come out. Can't we just go find Ev ourselves?"

Gregory sighed. "Politics. Because of whatever is happening with these youngsters, I have instructions from both Howard and Althea to cooperate with the elves. Actually, I have been told to let them take the lead. And do remember that my beacon spell has been masked. I cannot find him on my own."

"But I can," I reminded him. "Remember in my dream? I felt the tingle I always feel when magic is being used around me and saw the sparkle of your magic in the tattoo."

"Perhaps. Or perhaps it was just in your dream. Nonetheless, we will wait."

And wait we did. It was nearly full dark before we saw headlights barreling in our direction. Headlights that swerved toward us, making me think we were going to be run down. At the last moment, brakes squealed, and the car came to a skidding stop three feet in front of us.

The two guards nearly knocked each other to the ground in their hurry to get out of the car. Nelion and Alberon descended with all their dignity intact but you could tell there was a sense of urgency with them, too. Still inside the car, the driver killed the ignition and sat stoically in his seat.

"My apologies for our tardiness," Nelion said as he came around to us. "There was a crisis at the enclave. Thirty young elves, approximately the same age as my son and his friend, stormed into our meeting, demanding elves take our place in the outer world. It took some time to restrain them. The unrest is growing."

Gregory just nodded. "I believe we will need torches. Amy, please call Fudge back because we will need him, too."

As I put out a mental call to Fudge, Alberon cleared his throat. "No torches will be needed. We can see in the dark well enough. If you like, I am able to enhance your eyesight to match ours."

I think a growl escaped my throat. I didn't want anyone, especially an elf, messing with my physiology.

Fudge stood in front of me, hackles raised. *"Do not let them perform any magic on you."*

"No shit?" I thought. I was about to open my mouth to say that out loud, but Gregory beat me to it, albeit much more politely than I would have done.

"Thank you, but no. We have torches, which we will keep pointed at the ground to avoid scaring the bats. Fudge, if you will lead the way, the elves can follow you, and we will follow them." He reached into the pocket of the light jacket he was wearing and handed me one of two small flashlights he pulled out. The man must have been a Boy Scout because he was always prepared.

So our little parade trooped through the grass and into the woods, me bringing up the rear because, of course, women had to be last in everything. Fudge daintily trotted ahead, lowering his nose on occasion and making slight course corrections.

Once we were actually inside the woods, it was slower going. (Not really *woods,* per se. More like a stand of trees. But a big one.) We had to watch where we put our feet, to avoid tripping on exposed roots and fallen branches. It had been quiet, out here in the middle of nowhere, but now the silence seemed oppressive. I expected to hear night critters, as I did in the woods of northern Minnesota, but nothing stirred.

*"Another three minutes walking at this pace will bring us to the clearing. Someone is there before us, although I am not close enough to determine who, what, or how many."*

I reached ahead of me and tugged on Gregory's jacket to get his attention. I whispered what Fudge had told me and he, in turn, touched the shoulder of the guard in front of him to repeat what I'd said. I expected the pattern to continue all the way to the guard in front, but a second later, everyone had stopped. Elves had telepathy?

Nelion beckoned Gregory forward. Being the nosy type, I followed.

"Please wait here while we investigate. If whoever the familiar says are there are elves, there will be nothing you can do."

He didn't whisper but spoke so quietly I barely heard him from behind Gregory.

"I disagree," Gregory retorted in the same low voice. "Elves are not immune to physical acts. And if they are *not* elves, then I *can* be of assistance. I will remind you that it is my employer we are here to rescue."

Nelion shrugged his shoulders. "If you insist."

Gregory and I shut off our flashlights, hoping to rely on the elves' sight. Once again, we moved forward, this time with more stealth. I know Fudge and the elves made absolutely no noise as they walked. Gregory and I, despite our care, snapped the occasional twig. The noise seemed to echo in the quiet.

True to Fudge's prediction, about three minutes later we came to the edge of a clearing. It was indeed the same one I'd seen in my dream, complete with the fallen logs and moonlight casting shadows. The ground seemed soft beneath my feet, although it didn't feel too squishy. I squinted up at the sky and saw small shapes flitting around, although I saw no magical sparkles.

The front guard moved to his left, the one between Nelion and Gregory to his right, in a flanking motion. Gregory positioned himself between Nelion and Alberon, with me directly behind him, Fudge at my feet on my left side.

The clearing appeared to be deserted but Fudge had been certain someone or something was there, so we waited. A moment, two, then a crashing sound on the left side of the clearing. Nelion spoke quietly.

"One of the guards has subdued a werewolf. They are searching for others. Please wait."

But waiting was out of the question. The noise had disturbed nesting birds – and bats. With a frightened cry, birds took to the air, mixing with the bats already there and the ones that had joined them. At the same time, Alberon held up his hand and I felt an explosion in front of him. Gregory instinctively dropped to the ground, pulling me with him.

"There is at least one elf here because that was a magical attack Alberon just thwarted. We *are* helpless against that, even with our shields. Stay down until it's over."

"Come out and face us," Nelion said. He didn't shout but his voice was authoritative in its tone.

"And if I don't?" a voice said from somewhere to the right.

"The consequences will be worse. Surrendering yourself will ensure a trial. *Not* surrendering will ensure your death." Alberon was confident in his abilities.

A laugh, then, "What have I done? Nothing outside our laws. I have simply worked to ensure we can take our rightful place in the world *as elves* without using glamour to keep the puny humans comfortable."

"I disagree," Nelion replied, all the while scanning the sides of the clearing. "I believe you have performed transmogrification. *That* is against our laws."

"*I* didn't and no, it's not. It's discouraged but there is nothing in the laws prohibiting it. Pffft. It was just an ogre. They are stupid and count for nothing, anyways."

I bristled at that, and I felt Gregory tense up. Ev may not be the brightest bulb in the chandelier in some respects but he was far from "counting for nothing."

I started to tune out the argument. It sounded like every generational spat I'd ever heard of and, at the moment, was less concerning than getting my boss back in one piece. I scanned the skies once again. Nothing was flying overhead. Our noise had scared everything off. It was then I noticed Fudge's warmth had disappeared from my side.

"Where are you?"

"*Scouting to find where the bats have gone. Are the elves done arguing yet?*"

I tuned back in. "No. Obrist, or whoever it is, is still pleading his case. Nelion is trying to reason with him. It doesn't appear to be working. I'm not certain what will happen next."

A sigh touched my mind. *"The birds and bats will not return until the clearing is empty and has been so for a while. That make take some time if they insist on diplomacy rather than action. Therefore, I need to find them for you."*

Gregory, too, left my side, crouching down and making his way through the trees around the right of the clearing. My guess was he thought the younger elf might be distracted during his conversation with Nelion and could be taken by surprise. I was stuck lying on my stomach behind Nelion and Alberon. I hoped neither of them backed up without looking first.

The arguments continued, the younger one arguing for his position and Nelion refuting him. Alberon simply stood quietly, his hand extended, palm out, presumably maintaining a shield of some sort.

All of a sudden, I heard a crashing through the trees, coming our direction. Not certain if it was friend or foe, I put my head down and tried to make myself as small as I could.

Then I heard, *"Get this out of my mouth before my instincts take over and I kill it!"*

I raised my head to see Fudge bounding toward us through the clearing, oblivious to whatever may be happening with the elves, holding something as gingerly as he could in his mouth. Ignoring whatever danger there might be from the rogue elf (or the senior ones, for that matter), I sat up and cupped my hands. As he came to a crashing halt, skidding between the legs of Nelion and Alberon, he opened his mouth and dropped something warm and furry. *"Close your hands, quick, before it flies away!"*

I obeyed, barely able to contain whatever was struggling to get out. Fudge's sides were heaving and his tail was twitching wildly.

*"I am fairly certain that is your employer. It does not smell like any of the other bats."*

Nelion had broken off his parlay to see what was going on behind him. "What is that?" he asked.

"Fudge says he thinks it's Ev. Hey Gregory," I called, "I think we have him!"

Nelion gave a short nod to Alberon who, with his free hand, traced a pattern in the air, then shoved that hand toward where the voice had been coming from. I heard a loud intake of breath, then another. Then Gregory's voice saying, "shit." All the while, the furry thing in my hand squirmed.

*"We must contain it somehow. You will be unable to hold it long, and it may bite you."*

Well, wasn't that a comfort! If it was indeed Ev and he bit me, I'd never let him live it down. Especially if I had to go through that series of rabies shots.

*"I will return when you have restored him,"* Fudge said as he trotted off. Fighting the natural instincts of the body you inhabited must be a real pain.

"Anyone happen to have a pillowcase on them?" I asked. I'd read that was the best way to trap a bat that had gotten inside a house and it was the only thing I could think of on the spur of the moment.

"If this oaf will let me down and Alberon remove his binding, you may use my jacket," Gregory said. He was slung over one shoulder of the guard who'd gone off to the right and was now walking toward Nelion and Alberon. An elf with long blond hair nearly trailing on the ground hung off the other. The guard was impressive. He was carrying two full-sized men and didn't appear bothered by it. However, he leaned over and unceremoniously dumped his charges at Alberon's feet, both grunting with the impact.

Alberon looked down at Gregory. "You must have been directly behind him to have received the full brunt of the spell."

"I was. I was about to jump him when you hit us. Would you kindly unbind me, please, so I can help Amy?"

"Unbind me as well, you ancient hunk of mistletoe," the elf said, attempting to right himself while blowing his hair out of his face.

"Ancient hunk of mistletoe?" I asked.

"It is unflattering to be compared to a parasitic plant, is it not?" Alberon calmly replied, while pointing his right index finger at Gregory, who finally flexed his limbs and stood to remove his jacket.

"I will hold it over your hands. When I say 'now,' open them," Gregory said. He held his jacket open, ensuring the sleeves were caught in his hands, then lowered it over my hands. "Now," he said. As soon as I released the little fella, he half-flew straight into the material, which Gregory gathered together to form a small pocket.

"We will not be able to contain him long this way. There's little air in there," Gregory told the elves. "Alberon, I would appreciate you restoring my employer sooner rather than later."

"Of course. Just a moment more," Nelion answered.

"Where is Obrist?" he asked the elf, who was still laying on the ground, hair partially covering his face.

Oho. So this wasn't "our man." The plot thickens, as they say.

"I don't know and even if I did, I wouldn't tell you," he spat out.

Nelion signaled the guard who, once again, picked up the blond, slung him over a shoulder and headed toward the cars.

He sighed. "This one will prove difficult, I am afraid."

"He is not the one who cast the transmogrification spell, I will say that," Alberon said. "Let me have a look at your prize."

"I cannot open the jacket without losing him," Gregory said.

"Do not worry. I will convince him to stay quiet. Give me a moment."

Alberon stared at the pile of material in Gregory's hands as he had stared at the snake earlier in the day. "You may untangle him from your jacket and re-don it if, you wish. He will stay with you now."

First a snake, then a bat. I was going to start referring to him as Doctor Doolittle in my head. I almost snickered out loud at the thought but caught myself. This was a serious situation!

Gregory gently peeled back the layers of fabric to expose a brown bat in his hand, sitting quietly but breathing heavily, and with big, black eyes darting all around. One wing didn't completely tuck into his side, suggesting an injury.

Alberon peered down at him, then squatted to get a look from the side. With a wave of his hand, I felt the tingle of magic that had been missing and saw a bit of sparkle on the bat's shoulder. It was indeed Ev!

"Hmm," Alberon mused. "The cloaking spell was easy enough, but I have never seen a transmogrification spell like this. I have made it visible to your eyes, wizard, in the hopes you see something I do not."

Gregory stared with him. "Is that black thread a trigger?"

I looked myself. I could actually see the spell woven around the bat! It looked like a very fine mesh that followed the contours of the bat's body, including around the injured wing. Most of it was a sickly green, but one black thread twisted in and out of the design. But that was all I could see. Spells such as these were beyond my abilities.

"I believe you are correct," Alberon replied to Gregory. "If I attempt to dismantle it as I would any other spell, the black thread would kill your employer. It is a failsafe, knowing we revere all life. Well, most elves do. Whoever cast this one certainly does not."

"Other than that, is it a typical spell, one that will degrade with time?"

"I believe so. At least, I see nothing that would make me think otherwise. The strength of the binding tells me it will be seven, perhaps ten days before it weakens enough to fall apart.

"I would suggest we take him with us to our enclave. A healer can see to that wing and we have areas where he could feed and still be safe. With your permission, of course."

Gregory frowned. "He is irascible on a normal basis. Are you sure you want to deal with him when the spell does disintegrate? On the other hand, I'm not certain how we would care for him until it does. Amy, do you have any suggestions?"

I didn't. Keeping him in a cage was out of the question, much less finding bugs for him to eat until whatever was going to happen, happened. On the other hand, a familiar face needed to be on hand to attempt to calm him when he did come out of it.

"Will he remember what happened?" I asked.

"Undoubtedly," Alberon told me. "His ogre mind is in there, somewhere, although it does not have control of the body in this form."

That was *so* not good! "Ev will blow a gasket when he's back. One of us, probably Gregory, needs to be around to be a calming influence when he comes to himself. Otherwise, your enclave could sustain some major damage."

"That's true," Gregory nodded. "He's been known to be violent over smaller things than being turned into a bat. If he knows it was an elf who changed him, any of your kind anywhere near would bear the brunt of his anger."

Alberon mused a moment. "While we could bind him to prevent damage, I do not think that to be a wise course of action in such a volatile person. A compromise, then. We will care for him until I see it's almost time for the spell to break. Then we will bring him to you in Minneapolis. That way, we can all be present at the appropriate time. I know you will want to calm him, if you can, and Nelion will have questions regarding what he saw.”

Gregory shook his head. “Remember? Violence? I can think of nowhere to allow him to vent his frustrations that would not cause someone to call the authorities. Perhaps here, again? This seems remote enough and there isn’t much for him to destroy.”

A nod, then, “Very well. Nelion has your mobile number, I believe? He will call you when I think there is about a day left. Specific arrangements can be made at that time. If I may?”

He held out his hand and Gregory gently transferred the bat over, trying not to jostle the wing. Alberon cradled it, and, making cooing sounds, started off toward the cars. We followed.

“I don’t like leaving Ev with them, but I don’t see much of a choice, do you?” I asked.

“No. And that bothers me. Logically I know they are the best ones to care for him – they can fix the wing *and* they live out-of-doors, which is good for a bat and its diet. I’d have to locate a wildlife veterinarian and try to explain why I had a bat not indigenous to Minnesota with a broken wing, whereas their healers can have that bat flying again in a couple of days. I also wouldn’t relish crawling around on the ground, trying to find enough bugs to feed it. On the other hand, I feel like I’m abandoning him.”

“Me, too,” I sighed. “Do we go home or wait here for a week or more?”

“We go home. You back to work and me on the phone. I need to let Howard and Althea know what’s happened and get their instructions. I also need to put our charter service on standby. It’ll cost but I want to ensure I can fly directly to Lake Charles with an hour’s notice.”

I punched his arm. “So *we* can fly directly to Lake Charles.”

“*So* we *can fly directly to Lake Charles. I will not leave you to face that ogre alone.*”

"We'll talk about it later. No need to discuss this until we're alone," Gregory said quietly as we approached the cars.

Nelion and the two guards were standing at the back of their SUV with the hatch up. Out of curiosity, I walked around. Two men, one the blond elf and another, scruffy looking sort who was probably the werewolf, lay on the floor, looking as if they were bound with invisible ropes. It didn't look comfortable.

"What did you have against my boss?" I asked.

The werewolf snarled but the blond elf smiled. "Boss? What boss? Why in the world would I have anything to do with a witch's boss?"

Nelion put his hand on my shoulder. "These are just lowly soldiers and probably know little. I will tell Miss Fitzsimmons anything we are able to discover."

"Hey, little witch. Why are you with the old man? Wouldn't you rather be with someone closer to your own age?" The blond elf didn't seem to mind that he was trussed like a turkey, even if the bindings were invisible.

"Perhaps I would. But not you. I don't date men with dirt on their face and leaves stuck in their hair." I turned my back to him and walked over to our car.

"Nicely put," Gregory said as he opened my door for Fudge to jump in. "You *do* know male elves are rather vain?"

"I figured as much from Perchaladon. I don't know what his role is but bringing him down a peg or two seemed like the thing to do."

*"Ask the wiz…Gregory if he will send me home. I see no reason for me to fly in that machine again since he knows where we are going."*

I relayed the request.

"Before we leave, yes, I will send him home."

We drove back to Lake Charles, grabbed our things from the hotel and checked out (much to the consternation of the desk clerk, who'd just checked us in a few hours earlier) and headed toward the airport. About five minutes away, Gregory pulled to the side of the road, held his cell phone to his ear as if making a call, and gave Fudge the boost he needed to go home. No matter how many times I saw it, to watch my cat just fade away to nothing still bothered me.

Then there were the odd looks from the flight crew as we carried an empty pet carrier onto the plane along with our overnight bags…

"Have you heard anything from the elf?" Gregory asked me as we made our way from the plane to the Hummer.

"No. Maybe he got my message to leave me alone," I replied.

"Then, if you are comfortable, I will take you home rather than to my place."

I couldn't think of a reason not to go home and sleeping in my own bed would be blissful, so I agreed. Fudge greeted me at the door and, after ensuring his food and water bowls were full, I dropped everything and crawled into bed.

# CHAPTER SIXTEEN

Thursday, thankfully, wasn't too bad. I'd only been out of the office one day and Sally, the sweetheart, had handled just about everything that came in. A good thing, too. It had been well after midnight when I hit the sack and the summer sun woke me early, as always. I yawned my way through the day.

On Friday, I got another call from Marvin, who informed me that the location movie shoot was wrapping up and they were scheduled to return to Atlanta that night to finish on a soundstage. More odd things had happened but nothing to our client, thank goodness.

Louise and Elsa got me out of the house on Saturday for a bike ride around the lake and more people watching at the ice cream parlor. Had they not, I probably would have spent the entire time pacing my apartment – or cleaning. I was counting sunrises, you see.

Monday was more of the same but at least I had the usual weekend catch-up to keep me occupied. I heard the outer door open shortly before noon and chided myself for forgetting to lock the door but since it was only Cassandra bringing my lunch…

"I brought lunch for you," a baritone voice announced.

*That* had me shooting out of my chair. "I thought I told you to go far, far away!" I yelled. "Do I need to call the authorities?"

Perchaladon came around the corner and into my office, bearing a silver tray laden with food, china, cutlery, everything you would need for a fancy picnic.

He chuckled, then said, "Come, come, Amy. There is no need. I have no desire to harm you. Remember, we revere life. Especially female life."

"Enh. Yeah. Right. There are different kinds of harm. Inflicting your presence on someone who does not want it is one of them."

My phone chimed with a text. Ignoring the elf for the moment, I looked to see it was from Cassandra. "I saw the elf going upstairs. You okay?"

"Excuse me a moment," I said, then sent a reply, "Keep the line open." That was our clue to each other that if the other's phone rang with no one on the other end of the line, things had gone haywire and to come immediately.

"I wish merely to have lunch with a lovely lady. Is that so bad?" he said after I put my phone down.

I remembered Ms. Fitzsimmon's admonishment to find out anything I could. Despite the fact that I didn't appreciate being stalked, perhaps this was a prime opportunity.

"Okay, fine. You win. Lunch it is. But let's go out into the reception area. There's more room."

And I could stomp on the floor, if necessary.

"Wonderful. I have a variety of sandwiches, not knowing what you preferred. Plus crackers, hummus, crudités, and iced tea. All organic, of course."

Of course. Things were quiet as we ate, and I really couldn't complain about the food. It was as good as anything Cassandra brought – and I still wouldn't have to clean up.

As we relaxed after eating, Perchaladon sat forward in his chair. "Are you happy in your life?"

I opened, then closed my mouth. "What sort of a question is that?"

"An honest one, I think," he said. "I am very curious. As I have asked before, why do you work for an ogre? And why do I see you at human clubs, not at Club Tread, where you could be yourself?"

So I *was* being felt out for something! "I've answered the first question before. It's a good job, I am well compensated, and I enjoy the challenge. As to the second, be myself? I'm always myself, wherever I am."

"Perhaps I phrased it incorrectly. At Club Tread, you could use your magical abilities whereas in human clubs, you must keep them under wraps."

"It may be different for elves, although I have noticed *you* have no difficulty showing yourself to the world, but I do not have any difficulty *not* using my magic, or using it, depending on the situation. Nor do any of my friends. Why do you ask?"

He leaned forward, in a conspiratorial manner. "There are some of us who are tired of coddling the humans. We feel it is time for them to accept the entire world, not just their limited view of it. That is why I do not glamour myself in public. It is also why others, of my kind, yours, and the were community, do not hide, either."

"I *don't* hide," I told him. "I just don't see a need to advertise."

"But you *have* heard of problems when others *advertise*, as you phrase it?"

"Actually, no, not directly. I've been told there have been instances of violence but haven't seen or heard of anything myself."

"Allow me to assure you such things have happened. Even here in your beloved, relatively open-minded Twin Cities. It may not have made the news but just last week, a were-bear was ambushed outside a bar in St. Paul by ruffians who did not want *his type* in their favored establishment. Before he could change to protect himself, they'd damaged him enough to put him in hospital."

"And…?"

"As I said, there are those of us who feel it's time to come out into the open. Fight back, if necessary."

"You're advocating violence?"

"It's not preferred, but if necessary, yes."

I didn't like the sound of that. "And what am I supposed to do about it? Wear a sign that says, 'witch', and hope someone takes offense?"

"No. Nothing like that. But be seen with me, as I am, in public. With my friends, also as they are, both unglamoured elves and weres. There are weres, you know, who are obviously more than human, without resorting to the change."

I did know. Most of the weres I knew, while human in appearance, also had something predatory, or otherworldly, about them. Even if their nature was unknown, people were uncomfortable around them without knowing why. It's why *most* weres kept to their own kind, or places like Club Tread. That seemed to be changing, if what he said about the bar in St. Paul was any indication.

"While I agree with you in some respects, I have no wish to *be seen* with you, as you put it, and your friends. I like my life just the way it is, thank you. That includes showing, or *not* showing my magical abilities, according to the situation. Not going out of my way to make people uncomfortable."

Perchaladon sighed as he gathered up the remains of the lunch. "I am sorry you feel that way. I had hopes that, as young as you are, you might think differently."

"Obviously, you were wrong. And now, it's time for me to go back to work. Thank you for the lunch. And unless you know something about my boss's disappearance that you are willing to share, I would prefer we not meet again."

Sally opened the door just as I was about to show Perchaladon out. She only raised an eyebrow as she went to her desk, but I knew there would be questions once he left.

Although I wanted to slam it, I quietly closed the door behind him and turned to Sally. "Well, wasn't that a surprise?" she said.

"Yeah. And not a good one. Although, I got a nice lunch out of it."

"China, silver, and everything. The man goes in style. I'm assuming, since you've already told him to bugger off, that there was something more than just lunch."

Cassandra came barreling through the door. "What'd he want?"

This time, thankfully, I only had to relate the story once. "I've heard of the discontent," Cassandra said. "It's being discussed, both sides of the subject, quietly, in many circles."

"You haven't said anything to me." I was somewhat put out.

"No, because I didn't think it would affect you. Our mutual friends aren't involved, and you're pretty set in your ways, you know. It didn't sound like anything you'd care about."

"Care? Yes. Go out of my way to provoke people like Perchaladon wants? No. I prefer to be who I am all the time and if a difference of opinion arises somewhere, *discuss* it then. He's trying to *incite* adverse reactions publicly. Not my style, nor do I think it's the best course of action."

"I agree with you there. But we have it easier than elves or weres. Unless we do something overt, most people think we're human. It's different."

I sighed. "I know. And it does bother me. But right now, I'm not so concerned with that as I am sun-watching. Only three to six days and Ev will be back. I can't wait. And I can't believe I just said that."

Sally laughed. "It will be good to have him back, although I'm getting rather fond of quiet and fresh air. However, I'll finally be able to stop putting people off. That will be nice."

"I'll leave you two to your subterfuge on Ev's behalf. I still have a deli to run. See ya!" Cassandra skipped out the door and I heard her trotting down the stairs, even forgetting about the one stair that creaked loudly if you stepped on it too hard.

Gregory finally got the call from Nelion on Wednesday. We had about twenty-four hours to get to Lake Charles and thence to the spot in the Reserve where we'd let Ev become himself and, quite probably, go on a rampage.

Because the call was expected, arrangements weren't quite so hurried this time. I already had my overnight bag packed and Elinda's large carrier was waiting by the door. Once again, we boarded the private jet, Fudge complaining all the while.

"If you keep it up, I'll put a tranquilizer down your throat," I told him.

He grumbled but finally quieted down so the plane ride was peaceful, if nerve-wracking for me. Every time I had to fly on one of these things, I seriously considered retiring from my job with Ev, living off my writing royalties.

Second verse, almost the same as the first. Once in the rental car, Gregory opened the carrier door so Fudge could sit in my lap and look out the windshield. Forty-five minutes later, we pulled up to that same stand of trees where we'd originally found Ev and waited for the elves to show.

It was almost full dark when a car appeared in the distance. As it closed, the headlights almost blinded us. As if he purposely wanted to scare us, the driver again screeched to a halt just a couple of feet in front of our car. The guards got out first, followed by Nelion and Alberon. Alberon was holding his hand close to his body, obviously cradling something in it.

"My apologies for the tardiness," Nelion said to Gregory. "We once again had some younglings to deal with."

Gregory nodded in acknowledgement. "How long?" he asked Alberon.

"A few minutes. No more," he said as he walked a ways into the grass and very gently let the bat down. Then sat on the ground next to it, in an attitude of complete repose. Me? I was nearly holding my breath and the only thing that kept me from pacing was the thought that I didn't want to look *too* anxious in front of the elves. Instead, my hands clenched and unclenched in my pockets.

All of a sudden, a large bird quietly swooped down and, ignoring the elf just a pace or two away, picked up the bat in its claws. It quickly flew away, over the stand of trees in front of us. The outcry from everyone was loud.

"*Dinnudac!*" came out of both Nelion and Alberon. I assumed it was an elvish curse because both Gregory and I said, "Fuck."

"Was that a real owl?" Gregory asked the elves as the guards came running from the cars while Alberon picked himself off the ground and stared off into the distance.

"I do not believe so," Nelion answered. "One of the forms Perchaladon favors is a great horned owl. While they are found in this area, a natural owl would avoid all these humanoids."

"Now what?" I asked.

"I removed the masking from Mr. Tremaine's beacon spell last week," Alberon answered. "I do not believe they will have time to reapply it if we act quickly."

I looked to Gregory, who nodded his head. His eyes went blank for a moment, then, "Approximately a mile west of here, I believe."

"That will take some time for us to walk," I said. "The ground isn't exactly a running track."

"Beyond the trees is also quite swampy ground," one of the guards added. Nelion fixed him with a stare. The elf simply shrugged his shoulders and said, "I like to go hiking away from the bustle of the enclave."

*"I can cover that distance in a shorter period of time than you. Follow."*

"Fudge is going on ahead," I told everyone else as he sprinted into the trees in a straight line westward.

The six of us started walking, first wading through the grass then picking our way through the stand of trees, which was probably a couple of football fields in diameter. Beyond the trees, just as the guard said, the ground became squishy, then mucky. Walking slowed as we felt our way on each step, ensuring there was something resembling a solid spot under our foot. In addition, the mosquitoes thickened. Although I didn't get bit thanks to Gregory's spray stuff, their whine became an irritant.

As I picked my way through the mire, I vowed that Ev was going to replace my boots. I'd never be able to get them clean after this.

*"Hurry. There are three elves doing something magical around the bat which would not bode well for your employer."*

"Fudge has said to hurry," I told everyone. "And he says there are three elves."

Nelion muttered under his breath as we all attempted to pick up our pace, becoming heedless of the mud and gunk splashing our legs – or the noise we were making. There would be no sneaking up on anyone this night.

About ten minutes later, we were on firmer ground and our pace picked up even more. I jogged next to Gregory in silence, mentally thanking my friends for getting me into shape by riding bikes, alternating with being worried about what we might find when we arrived wherever it was we were going.

"Veer ten degrees south," Gregory said just loud enough for everyone to hear. "About a quarter mile, probably in that small clump of trees."

I couldn't see much of anything except the elven bodies in front of me and was surprised Gregory could. Then, as I looked a little harder, I made out a large black shape against a slightly grayer night sky. That must be a clump of trees, I thought.

The yowl of a spitting-mad cat split the air. "Fudge!" I yelled, uncaring about stealth if my cat was in trouble. I ran even faster, outpacing the guard in front, who managed to catch up and pass me once again.

As we approached the dark spot, the individual shapes of trees became apparent. And within the trees, the distinct sparkle of magic. We made a beeline toward it.

The second guard also ran in front of me and the two together crashed into the trees, heedless of noise. I was on their heels and skidded to a halt, Nelion nearly plowing into me.

The scene in front of us was chaos. The two guards were grappling with two other figures, while on the ground, my cat sat on top of a mound of something desperately trying to escape. A green, sparkling net of magic flew over my head, dropped onto the four fighting figures, and cinched up at their ankles, just like those images you see of fishermen casting a net and drawing it closed. As it closed, the net faded from my sight. Alberon and Nelion walked toward the now-immobile figures.

Gregory's flashlight illuminated Fudge and his victim. It was indeed a great horned owl, on its back with Fudge's claws embedded in its face. Both were breathing heavily.

*Your bat is on the tree stump behind me. When I attempted to interfere with their spell, this one batted me aside, changed, and tried to fly off. He apparently forgot that cats are quite adept at catching birds, even large ones.*

"Are you okay?" I asked him as I turned my own flashlight to the tree stump. A bat huddled there, unmoving, the sparkle of

Gregory's beacon spell on its shoulder. Gregory moved next to me, picked the bat up and cradled it in his free hand.

*"I am effectively unharmed. Some talon scratches, which I will be able to heal quickly. This one, however, may be blinded. I think I caught an eye with a claw."*

Nelion walked over toward us. "Alberon will deal with the others. I will deal with this one. Mister Familiar, if you will please release my son?"

Fudge retracted his claws and with a growl, walked away to start grooming himself. Nelion cast his own net of magic over the owl which, after a few moments, morphed into Perchaladon, who was quite the worse for wear. His left eye was bleeding profusely, along with various other deep scratches on his face. Fudge had done a number on him. He was no longer the handsomest man I'd ever seen.

"Although this is a matter for the enclave council, I would ask you now for your reasoning behind kidnapping another paranormal being and casting an illegal transmogrification spell."

Perchaladon said nothing, just glared at his father. At the same time, loud grunts came from behind us, where Alberon had effectively hog-tied the other two miscreants, freeing the two guards to stand and do what guards do – guard.

Nelion motioned Alberon over to where we were standing. "The condition of the bat?" he asked.

Gregory held out his hand, where the bat cowered, its sides heaving in apparent anxiety. Alberon stared at it.

"The transmogrification spell has been renewed and it still has the failsafe woven in. Apart from that, it appears unharmed, although frightened. The calming spell I put on a week ago is still in place, although wearing thin. It could fly soon."

Gregory sighed. "Can you convince whoever performed the spell on him to reverse it?"

Nelion also sighed. "We can try. The enclave council will convene tomorrow to try these three. The penalties will be harsh. One can hope that in exchange for some leniency, Obrist will reverse the spell but from what I have seen thus far, it is doubtful."

"Then I will take him with us. You will pardon me, Nelion, if I do not wish to entrust him to you again with these three in close proximity to him."

"Unfortunately, I must insist on taking the bat with us, at least until after the council meeting. It is evidence. Once the meeting has concluded, it can be returned to you to do with as you see fit."

Now that I'd been reassured about Fudge's condition, I was getting pissed. "Supposedly you're the most powerful elves in the country. You high and mighty elves with all your *natural* magic should be able to do something. My boss has been stuck in a bat's body for almost two weeks."

"Amy…" Gregory cautioned.

"No, Gregory, I'm going to have my say. Now you want to take him as *evidence* as if he's nothing but an object," I continued. "That's a *person* in there and you might make a little more effort to return him to himself. Or at least recognize that fact and quit referring to him as 'it'."

"Now see here young lady," Alberon started.

"She is correct," Nelion interrupted him. "We have been unfeeling where her employer is concerned. However," he addressed me directly, "as has been stated before, the only one who can usually remove such a spell is the one who cast it, regardless of the apparent strength of anyone else. While our magic is *natural*, as you put it, it is very individualized. Alberon, given time, could unwind it but there is also that failsafe woven in. Hence his reluctance to undo the spell."

Shit. I'd forgotten about that. What the hell was so important they'd risk killing Ev?

"So. Now what?" I tried to keep the blush from my face.

Nelion eyed us. "I would like to break with precedent. Mr. Tremaine can attest to the beacon spell. Your familiar can attest to the fact that this is, in fact, not a true bat. You would be needed to convey his remarks. Therefore, I would invite you to our enclave until after the council meeting tomorrow."

The two guards turned away from their charges and I swore their jaws dropped. I know mine did and Gregory at least opened his eyes about as wide as they could get.

"Nelion…" Alberon started.

"No, Alberon, they are necessary to the proceedings. Not that I would permit them to know the exact location. With your permission, Mr. Tremaine, Miss McCollum, one of our guards would drive you in your car with a blindfold spell on you."

"No spell," Gregory said before I could. "Real blindfolds, if you please."

"And Fudge?" I asked.

Nelion considered my cat, who was still sitting about six feet away, finishing getting all the mud off his legs. "Will he, too, wear a covering over his eyes?"

"Fudge?" I asked.

*"Of course he may blindfold me. I will still know where I am, but you need not tell him that."*

"He says yes," I relayed.

"In that case, may I suggest we make our way back to the vehicles? The guards will have to transport the prisoners first, then come back for us. I can prepare a slight repast while we wait."

*"I am* not *walking through that again. You will carry me."* Fudge walked over and hopped into my arms.

"So I have to slog through the mud carrying an additional fifteen pounds. Thanks a lot."

Gregory chuckled. "I take it he doesn't want to get dirty again?"

"Apparently not. But it's a small price to pay for his actions tonight, don't you think?" I nuzzled Fudge, who preened.

"Yes, I suppose so. Well done, Fudge."

"And my thanks as well," Nelion added. "Your deeds have helped uncover at least part of what we believe to be a conspiracy of some sort and caught my wayward son for me."

If possible, Fudge became even more smug. *"Ask if he can magic up some tuna for his repast. I deserve a big treat."*

"I will. Now get over yourself."

We made a U-turn and started our way back to the cars. I silently thanked the powers that be for the elves' night sight and sense of direction. I'm not sure I'd have been able to find my way back, otherwise.

This trip took longer than the first. The prisoners were, unsurprisingly, reluctant to cooperate and, at least to my eyes, purposely stumbled every now and again, forcing the guards to haul them to their feet. But based on the way they held their arms straight down at their sides, I assumed they were still "tied up," although I could not see the bindings.

It took almost a half hour to make it back. The driver had been lounging against their car but came to attention as we emerged from the trees. He rushed to open all the doors, then reached inside and did something. It took me a minute, but I realized he'd pulled up a third row of seats. One guard clambered in back, then the driver and second guard shoved the three prisoners in the second row. They weren't gentle about it, either. Finally, the driver and second guard climbed into the front, the engine started up, and they pulled away in a cloud of dust.

"We may as well be comfortable while we wait," Nelion said. "They will be approximately an hour and a half returning. If I recall correctly, you enjoy coffee. Would you like some?"

Coffee was just the thing I needed. It was getting on my bedtime and now that all the excitement had worn off, I was beginning to get tired. "Yes, please. That would be lovely."

Without even a wave of his hands, a coffee table and four wing chairs appeared on the grass near our car. A carafe, four mugs, a sugar and creamer set, and a bowl of fruit sat on a silver tray in the middle. Four blazing torches stood a few feet away from the setting, nicely illuminating the area for human eyes. Nelion considered Fudge, still nestled in my arms which, by the way, were starting to get tired. A heartbeat later, two small bowls materialized next to one of the chairs.

"*He knew! Tuna!*" Fudge hopped out of my arms and streaked to the bowls, first lapping at the water in one bowl, then chowing down on the contents of the second.

Gregory was the first to sit, still cradling Ev-the-bat in his hands. "Allow me," Alberon said. He took the bat from Gregory, stared at it a moment, then loosed it. It flew off toward the trees. I opened my mouth to protest.

Alberon smiled. "Please do not worry. It – he – is on what I believe you would call a leash. I have simply allowed him to go get something to eat. He will return when he is finished feeding."

Taking my cue from what Fudge had told me in the hotel, I poured four cups of coffee. Surprisingly, the pot felt just as heavy when I set it down as when I picked it up. I looked at it, then at Nelion who was sitting across from me. "Magically refilling?"

He chuckled. "Yes. It is much easier than creating a new one from scratch each time someone wants more."

I would almost have given my eye teeth to be able to perform that spell! Imagine: unlimited coffee! Then again, maybe not. I'd probably never sleep.

Gregory sipped his coffee. "So, what happens next?"

"Tonight, you will be our guests. Tomorrow at the highest point of the sun, the council will meet. You will give your testimony then be driven to wherever you wish to go."

"Although it has no bearing on their – transgressions – I would like to know how Perchaladon has been able to track me. He has appeared at various places I have been, almost as if I had the same sort of tracking spell on me that Ev has. It hasn't been perfect because he didn't know I was in the office when I was, but I'm finding even the hint of it unnerving."

"I can answer that," Alberon said. I raised my eyebrow at him.

"It is an obscure spell, one that was used when we were still in the wider world to track our children. It is no longer needed as children are not allowed out of the enclave until they reach their majority. I assume Perchaladon – or Obrist – found it in my books when I was teaching them. All we need is something with your DNA. A strand of hair plucked from your clothing, perhaps, gives us what we need and works similarly to Mr. Tremaine's beacon spell. That person can be found wherever they are. The fact that it hasn't been a perfect solution is suggested by the fact that he is lazy and does not pay close attention to what he is doing all the time."

"Rest assured, that spell will be removed tomorrow," Nelion assured me. "My son is, unfortunately, a coward at heart. Under threat, he *will* dispel it."

"Thank you," I replied, not really knowing what else to say. Calling Perchaladon a coward probably meant he knew his son was a creep. Then I let out a very undignified grunt as Fudge hopped back into my lap, turned a few times as cats do, then settled in for a nap.

We all sat drinking coffee, lost in our own thoughts. Without conversation, it became quiet; the only sound was the drone of the pesky mosquitoes. Fudge was overly warm in my lap; the night was warm and humid but not too uncomfortably so. I thought I might be able to sneak in forty winks while waiting. I put my now-empty coffee mug on the table, leaned back, and closed my eyes.

Only to immediately open them again when my butt vibrated. My cell phone. I pulled it out and looked at it, first shocked that I had service out here in the boonies and second, that it was Cassandra calling me after ten at night.

"Where are you? You need to come home!" she said after I answered.

"Calm down. What's wrong?"

"The building's on fire!"

"What?" I yelled. "How bad? What happened?" I stood up, dumping Fudge, and started pacing.

That made Gregory and the other two sit up and take notice. "What's going on?" Gregory asked. I waved him off.

"I don't know how bad it is or how it started. Flames are coming out the windows on all three stories. The fire department is here now, and they're hosing down my house to ensure it doesn't catch. We're standing across the street in front of Cork's, watching."

"We're in BFE, Louisiana. Hang on. Let me tell Gregory." I relayed what Cassandra had said.

"You need to go back," he told me.

"*Someone* has to be there and since Ev can't, I guess I'm elected. But what about Ev?"

"Allow me a suggestion?" Nelion interjected. I nodded.

"Although your familiar's testimony would be helpful, it is not absolutely necessary. I understand this emergency. Please, as soon as we arrive at the enclave, allow me to give you the use of our airplane to get you home as soon as possible." (He pronounced it "air-o-plane," proving again they weren't quite as up with the times as the younger generation.)

"That would be most welcome, thank you," Gregory said. He turned to me. "That's the fastest you will get home. I'm guessing…" He looked at his own phone for the time, "you'll be home by about three. You'll have time for some shuteye before dawn and assessing the damage."

I put the phone back to my ear. "You heard that?"

"I did. I'll see you at the building at seven?"

"I'll be there. See you then." I disconnected. "Shit. This could be disastrous."

"The building itself is brick, everything is insured, and all company data is backed up to the cloud. It will all work out." Gregory checked the time on his phone again. "The guards should be back quite soon, and you'll be in the air an hour after that. There's not much you can do until then."

I knew that but. Shit again. And damn.

# CHAPTER SEVENTEEN

The elves' vehicle returned about ten minutes after I'd hung up with Cassandra. I'd spent those ten minutes wearing a path in the grass, unable to sit still, Fudge trailing behind me with every back-and-forth.

*"You should calm yourself. Your heart rate is increased which is not good."*

"It's tough to be calm when a disaster has struck."

*"I do not understand everything Gregory said about insurance and the clouds but I believe he was reassuring you. And there is nothing you can do until we arrive home. Stop and breathe."*

When the car pulled up, Nelion murmured something and our fancy picnic disappeared. One of the guards emerged, approached Gregory and held out his hand for the keys to our car. Gregory reluctantly released them. We clambered into the back seat, Fudge on my lap. The guard handed three blindfolds over the seat, one small enough to fit over a cat's face.

"Please put these on. Nelion has said to trust that you will wear them correctly and not watch our progress. We will arrive at the enclave in about forty minutes."

We dutifully donned the masks, Fudge snickering as I put one on him. Our car started moving.

As tired as I was, forty minutes would have been a nice nap, but I was too keyed up. In addition, we weren't on a smooth interstate. Even if I'd dozed off, the occasional pothole would have jarred me awake. So I contented myself with thinking up all sorts of horrid scenarios I might encounter when I saw what remained of the office the next morning.

*"What is that epithet you humans use? Gloomy Gus? Things may not be as bad as you are imagining."*

"Perhaps. Perhaps not. But even if the building is still structurally sound, contents will have to be replaced and, criminy, the smoke smell!"

*"But there is nothing you can do until tomorrow. So why are you worrying about it now?"*

"You know I worry things over until I can actually do something about them. It's my nature."

Fudge sighed. *"I will never understand that."* I felt him retreat from my mind as he slipped into his usual doze.

Forty minutes wasn't really a long time and soon, I felt the car travelling much smoother roads and finally slowing to a stop.

"We are here. You may remove your blindfolds," the guard said.

I removed my blindfold and then Fudge's. We were alongside an airstrip with a corporate-sized jet waiting with its stairs down. Gregory gave a low whistle as we climbed out of the car. "That is one of the most expensive private jets on the market. These elves don't stint, do they? You will be at Flying Cloud in about an hour and a half."

"And Fudge?" I asked.

"I will send him home for you. That way he won't have to endure the flight and the elves won't have to endure his presence."

Nelion approached us. "The plane is fueled, a flight plan has been filed, and the pilot is ready whenever you are," he told me.

He turned to Gregory. "If you will join me in my vehicle, we will convey you to our guest quarters where you may freshen up and rest."

"Our vehicle and belongings?" Gregory asked.

"Will follow you. After the council meeting today, the same guard will convey you wherever you wish."

Gregory nodded, then turned to Fudge, who stood at my feet. "Ready? My place, if you please."

Fudge just looked up at him and his tail twitched once. Gregory gave Fudge a hard stare, then pushed both hands outward. One moment Fudge was there; the next, he wasn't. I'll admit: that was just a little freaky.

"On your way, Amy. Call me as soon as you've seen the office and we'll decide what to do."

"Miss McCollum," Nelion interjected. "Please accept my apologies for my son's behavior and my condolences on your current predicament. Mr. Tremaine will be able to confirm when Perchaladon's tracking spell has been removed from you. If we have anything further to tell you, I will ensure Mr. Tremaine knows all the details." He held out his hand. "I believe humans shake hands at this point."

"Yes, we normally do," I replied with a chuckle, grasping his hand in a firm grip. "And thank you very much for the use of your plane. It really is very kind of you." Even though I wasn't looking forward to yet another ride in a small plane, I tried to be polite.

I ascended the stairs and another handsome-as-all-get-out elf greeted me, indicating I could take a seat anywhere I wished, and please do use the seatbelts. I sat in the first row of seats and watched him pull up the stairs, secure the door, then sit in the co-pilot's seat.

"Miss McCollum," a different voice said over the intercom, "we will be airborne shortly. As soon as I have turned off the seatbelt sign, you will find refreshments in the galley at the back. Please help yourself to anything there. Our flight time is one hour, twenty minutes once we hit our cruising altitude of forty thousand feet. It should be a smooth ride. There are no weather disturbances along our path.”

I tried not to get nervous as the thrust of the engines pushed me back into my seat and I felt the plane tilt as we left the ground. A small plane flying higher than commercial jets normally flew. What could go wrong?

*“Nothing. You are flying with elves who have the ability to command the elements. Take a nap.”* Fudge’s voice sounded like he was across the aisle instead of a thousand miles away. He also sounded irritated with me.

*“I am. Should something mechanically go wrong with the machine, they can cushion it with Air. Should it start to come apart, they can hold it together. It is nothing more than metal, which is made from Earth elements. There is less to worry about than if the pilots were human. Go to sleep or at least stop worrying so I can take a nap.”*

Okay. So. I’m safe and should relax. Says the cat who is probably curled up on my pillow instead of sitting in a small, metal, flying contraption. I gritted my teeth, waiting for the plane to level out.

When it finally did, I unbuckled the seat belt and made my way back to the galley. Someone had been very thoughtful – a pot of coffee had been brewed. As well, there was a spigot for hot water, a selection of loose teas in marked bins, a bowl of fruit, some finger-type sandwiches, and chocolate chip cookies. Seems elves had some human-type food preferences. I opted for caffeine, chocolate, and sugar.

Once I was seated again, I had to find a way to distract myself. I couldn’t study – *The Big Book of Philtres and Potions* had not been converted to e-book format. So I pulled up a romance novel on the reading app on my phone and tried to settle in.

As we made our descent, the pilot came over the intercom. “Miss McCollum, we have been informed by flight control there is a car waiting for you. We will taxi to the terminal and you can meet your driver there.”

A car? At – I looked at my phone – nearly two in the morning? Who in the world…? I started getting nervous.

Once we landed, I disabled airplane mode on my phone and a moment later, it pinged with a text message. “Still concerned about security. Omar will meet you at Flying Cloud and take you to the cottage rather than your apartment. Get some sleep. He will wake you at six and take you to the office. G”

I may have mentioned him before but if you’ve forgotten, Omar was an ogre, a retired guard, and one of Ev’s best friends. He still helped out when needed and I guess Gregory decided he was needed. I heaved a sigh of relief. No stranger, thank goodness.

Omar rushed to me as I stepped off the stairs and enveloped me in a big hug. (His hugs were no more pleasant than Ev’s. He smelled just as bad.) “I wish Gregory had called me sooner. Once he told me what was going on…oh my god, elves! And Ev!”

I extricated myself from his embrace, took a big breath of fresh air, then said, “Yeah, I know. It’s a mess.”

“I’m supposed to take you to Gregory’s and watch the place while you get a couple hours’ shuteye. Do we need to stop for anything?”

“No,” I yawned. “I’ll shower at home after I’ve seen the office.”

“And a fire at the office, too!” Omar yammered nonstop about Ev, the elves, and the fire for the entire twenty-minute drive. After the first ten minutes, I tuned him out and simply spaced out.

We pulled into Ev’s driveway and headed around back to Gregory’s cottage. Lights were already on. “Gregory told me to change the linens on his bed for you. I’m also supposed to ensure there’s coffee ready when you wake. Go on to bed. I’ll wake you in a little over three hours.”

I stumbled through the door, made my way to the only bedroom in the house, stripped off my jeans and shirt and crawled under the covers. A cat hopped onto the bed and started to make a nest in my hair.

As exhausted as I was, I couldn't help but turn recent events over in my mind. Then the tears started flowing.

Fudge paused in his nest-making. *"Why are you crying?"*

"Anger. Frustration. Burnout, maybe? I'm tired of being the one that has to hold everything together. Just once I'd like it if Ev wouldn't get himself into…situations…and *he* could handle emergencies. Or disasters."

*"Your sense of duty and your affection for the ogre make you the ideal person to take up these responsibilities. It is not the first time he has taxed your emotions and probably will not be the last. Perhaps it is time to seek other employment?"*

I sniffed. "No. I'm just blowing off steam. Crying is better than punching a hole in the wall, isn't it?"

*"Less damaging, both to the wall and your hand. Get some sleep if you can. As you say, things will work out."*

I knew he was right, but I felt better after releasing some of the tension. The tears subsided and I drifted off.

It seemed I'd just closed my eyes when I heard Omar calling my name. "Amy, I'm sorry but it's six. You need to get up."

It didn't take long to pull my clothes back on and pull my hair into a ponytail. I found a spare toothbrush in the medicine chest and freshened up a little. Omar handed me a travel mug of coffee when I got to the kitchen. He had the small television on low.

"We'd better get going if I'm to get you to the office by seven. They're saying traffic into the city is already stacking up."

Fudge's sneezing announced his presence in the kitchen. *"That ogre smells as bad as your employer. But I am going with. I may be able to discern something human noses cannot."*

Once in the car, I rolled my window all the way down and Fudge stuck his head out just like a dog. I privately laughed at the sight.

Traffic was indeed bad. It took nearly twice the time to get to the office than it normally would. But just a couple of minutes after seven, we pulled up to the burned-out husk of the building. Cassandra and Tommy were waiting on their front porch next door.

I hugged my best friend, who was nearly in tears. "The fire marshal says it's almost a total loss. The only thing keeping it from being so is the structure is full brick, rather than just brick siding," she choked out.

"Do they know what caused it?" I asked.

"It's arson," Tommy answered. "It didn't take long for them to find the remains of a Molotov cocktail that had apparently been thrown through the side door. They'll be back today to investigate in daylight, but they think someone broke in and sprayed gasoline or some other accelerant because it shouldn't have spread that quickly."

"But why?" I mused. "Everyone seems to like the deli. I know Ev doesn't get along with some people, but I've never heard of anything that would cause someone to do something like this."

"Take a closer look at the brick between the two doors," Cassandra sniffed.

I walked back over, ducking under the police tape that cordoned off that part of the sidewalk. Smudged with soot but still quite visible, someone had spray-painted "WITCH" in bright yellow, then covered it with a red interdictory circle, the universal sign for "no."

Holy shit. What Perchaladon had been talking about just came home to roost. My heart started pounding as I stared at it. I felt an arm go around my shoulders.

"You, me, or both?" Cassandra asked. "And why us? You'd think the pub would be more of a target. Cork isn't exactly your run-of-the-mill human."

"For all I know, he might be next," I said. "This is what the elf had been trying to tell me. People are getting bolder in their dislike of the paranormal community.

"What are you going to do?"

"Rebuild and reopen. I won't give in to bullies," she said with a grimace. "Arson is a mundane matter and I have faith they'll catch whoever it is. What are *you* going to do?"

"Set up shop in Ev's home office until you get rebuilt, then move back in. He won't give in any more than you will. But first, a shower, more coffee, a call to the insurance agent, then one to Gregory. Then…to Ev's, I guess."

The entire time we'd been talking, Fudge had been sniffing around the building, with an occasional sneeze.

*"It's difficult to tell on this public walkway, but there is relatively fresh were-something-rodent spoor,"* he told me.

"Do you know if any of your regulars are a were rodent of some kind?" I asked Cassandra.

She screwed up her face in concentration. "Not that I can think of. And since weres usually look sort of like whatever it is they turn into, I can't even think of someone who resembles a rodent. Why?"

"Because Fudge is smelling one."

She frowned. "That may change things. What in the hell have you — and by extension, me — gotten yourself into? I'll call the office downtown and let them know. They'll have to coordinate with the mundane authorities."

Just then, a couple of Cassandra's regulars came strolling down the walk, coming to a dead stop when they saw the building and police tape. They both ducked under the tape and rushed to give Cassandra a hug. She repeated her vow to rebuild and reopen.

They promised to keep an eye out and be the first returning customers when she did. That, at least, put a smile on her face.

I hugged her again and headed toward my apartment. I had a lot of stuff to do but a shower was the first thing on my agenda. Omar caught up with me.

"I will be your shadow until Gregory tells me otherwise," he said. "I don't like the look of this."

"Nor do I," I replied. "I'm going home to take a shower and change clothes. Will you give me a lift back to Ev's afterward?"

"Of course. I'll be outside when you're ready."

A shower and coffee did wonders to revive me. It was just after eight, so an appropriate time to call the insurance agent. He was flabbergasted when I told him of the spray paint. "You'd think people would leave those who bother no one alone. Apparently not. I'll get the paperwork started. I presume I should call your or Ev's cell phone if I need you?"

I cleared my throat. "Ev is out of cell phone range at the moment so I'll have to do."

"Gotcha. Talk with you soon." He hung up.

Then I called Gregory to fill him in. "Ev's home office is perfect," he said. "He never uses it. There's also a laptop already there so you won't be completely computer-less."

I snorted. "I'm using mine. The last time I looked at his, it had all sorts of porn on it. Not exactly what I or Sally want to see."

"Point. I presume Omar told you I want him shadowing you, right?"

"He did. And I appreciate it. I'm not certain of anything or anyone right now."

"Good. Omar has a key to both places, but you and Fudge stay at the cottage."

"Why? You only have one bedroom and will need it when you come home. Ev has four and only uses one."

"Because first of all, my cottage has food. Ev probably has something in the refrigerator but you won't be able to tell what it is due to the mold. Second, it has more protections on it than Ev's house or even your apartment building. Omar is big, strong, and scary, but he can't fend off a magical attack on you. Especially one from a distance. Until we know exactly what's happening *and* have Ev back to his old self, I want to ensure your safety. Get me?"

"Yes, sir," I answered but privately thought I'd rather stay in the big house and sleep in a real bed. We'd talk about that later.

"Good. I'll call you after the council meeting. If you need me before that, just call. I have excellent cellular service in this otherwise sylvan setting."

We hung up. I re-packed my overnight bag, put my laptop and charger into its travel bag, then asked Omar to come get Fudge's food. That I bought over the internet, but we could get litter and a spare box at a local store. As much time as Fudge spent at the cottage with me, it seemed reasonable to have one there, rather than ask Gregory to continually transport it for me.

As we headed down the road toward the freeway back to Ev's, my phone rang. It was Sally.

"The office burnt down!" she asked. "It's all over the news! Where are you and what are you doing?"

"I'm home. Cassandra called me last night and the elves very kindly lent me their cushy private jet, so I got in shortly before two. The place is almost a total loss but she's rebuilding. We're setting up shop at Ev's until that happens."

"Okay. How's Ev? What do I need to do?"

I filled her in on the happenings the day before, then told her to pick up a laptop, printer, cat box and litter, and to meet me at Ev's as soon as she could. "On my way," she said, and hung up.

# CHAPTER EIGHTEEN

Thanks to going against rush hour traffic, we arrived at Ev's in record time. Omar let me into Ev's house, then tried to scoop up Fudge, who had trotted at my heels. "Come on, little kitty. I'll let you into the cottage."

That earned Omar a hiss. *"Little kitty? Please. And I do not wish to be any closer to him than is necessary. I will stay with you for the time being."*

I chuckled. "Omar, he's taking offense to your 'little kitty.' His name is Fudge. And he prefers to stay with me for the moment."

"Okay. I just thought he'd like to be near his food and stuff. I'll put everything in the cottage and come back."

Omar closed the door behind me and I wrinkled my nose. The entire house smelled faintly of ogre. That would have to change. I called Sally back.

"Hey, you're not done shopping yet, are you?"

"No. What else do you need?"

"Room freshener. Enough cans to do the whole house. Or at least the first floor. It's going to be too hot to open the windows."

"Ew. I hadn't thought of that. What do you think? Will six cans do it?"

I mentally calculated the space. "Should. At least until we can get a supply of candles."

"On it." She hung up.

First things first. I dumped my laptop bag in the office and headed toward the kitchen. I knew Ev had a Keurig so it was just a question of finding his stash of coffee for it. Surprisingly, it was logically located in the cupboard above the coffeemaker. While it was brewing, I put a bowl of water on the floor for Fudge.

Once I had caffeine, it was time to set up shop and figure out what all needed doing. I set his laptop aside and put mine in its place. Then had to go into the living room to scrounge up throw pillows so I could sit in his chair and still reach the desk. My feet dangled, so I sighed and sat cross-legged. I dug around in his desk and finally came up with a notepad on which to make a very long list. Item one: regular coffeepot and coffee. Item two: human-sized desk chair.

I logged into the company email and spent the next hour answering frantic queries from our guards and clients who'd heard of the fire, assuring them we were still in business and, although the location had temporarily changed, we would indeed be moving back to the same space. I expected my phone to start ringing with calls on the same subject shortly. Item three: second phone line in Ev's house to give my cell phone a rest.

Then I started the tedious chore of installing the software the company used onto my computer. Omar poked his head around the office door. "I'll be in the kitchen if you need me." Shortly, I heard that television go on and smelled more coffee brewing.

By the time I was down to item twelve on my list, the doorbell rang. Omar ran to answer it before I could even get out of the chair. Sally came in with a laptop box in her arms. "Where do you want me to set up? Oh. Hi, Fudge."

I had to think. "Kick Omar out of the kitchen and use the breakfast nook table until we can rearrange things here a bit. I think there's enough room in the basement for an office for both of us, but I'll need to get furniture and all that. Hey. You can do that while your computer is downloading and updating software. Go down and figure out how to arrange everything and get Omar to shift whatever furniture and other crap needs to be moved."

"Gotcha. It's early for me. Does he have a coffeepot?"

"A Keurig. We're using that until I can get a real one."

*"Please ask the nice lady to let me out. I will make my business quick."*

"Fudge needs to go out. Can you open the kitchen door for him?"

Sally smiled. "Of course. Come on Fudge. It's still cool enough I can leave the door open for a bit. While you're out, I'll spray the house. Hopefully, it'll have dissipated enough when you come back in, so your nose doesn't get clogged up."

*"She is thoughtful, this one. I will return shortly."*

Item thirteen: business checks, rush delivery.

By one o'clock, I had a list of things to do or get that was two pages long. Sally, Omar, Fudge, and I had eaten delivery pizza for lunch. (Gregory was right: I couldn't tell what was in Ev's refrigerator. Item forty-five: clean out the fridge.) I was going over my list, separating it out between me and Sally when my phone rang.

"I'm almost on my way home," Gregory said.

"Well?"

"I gave my testimony in front of twelve of the sternest looking elves I believe I've ever seen. The fact that a non-elf was there was upsetting to them, even with Nelion exercising his authority as head honcho in the United States. Three of them didn't even want to hear what I had to say.

"It was a fairly cut-and-dried case because everyone could see the spell around the bat, as well as my beacon spell, which bears my magical signature. They even called Howard to verify it. However, I had to leave the room after answering their questions and was taken immediately to the car to be transported to the Lake Charles airport. I have no idea what was said afterward. *And* I had to leave without Ev. They decided they're going to be caretakers and will let me know *if,* not *when* the spell wears off. Only then will I be able to get Ev back."

Gregory was *not* a happy camper. And I didn't blame him. I was more than a little pissed about their attitude toward Ev, too. But right now, sad to say, that was the least of my worries.

"On another note," he said, "how are things there? I presume you're at Ev's. I should be home in about four hours and will be at your disposal."

"I'm in Ev's office, fielding calls and emails about the fire, trying to remember everything that was in the office and what needs to be done. Sally and Omar are arranging an office for us in the basement. When they're done, we're knocking off for the day. Sally's been on the clock since nine and I need a nap something fierce!"

He chuckled. "Stretch out on my bed. I will wake you when dinner is ready."

I'd take a nap there, but I was going to piss him off at dinner when I told him I was staying in the big house. I wasn't quite as helpless as I'd been a little over a year ago, before my magic manifested. The doorbell rang, which was ominous because I hadn't yet ordered anything and Ev always had packages delivered to the office.

"Do *not* answer it. I will," Omar yelled at me from the basement stairs. I heard him thunder the rest of the way up the stairs, through the kitchen and into the living room.

"Yes?" I heard after he'd unlocked and opened the door.

"I have a delivery for a Miss Amy McCollum," a voice said.

"I'll take it," Omar answered.

"I'm sorry, but she needs to sign for it."

"Then you'll need to come back because she's not here right now."

The voice sounded exasperated. "But it's a rush delivery!"

"Sorry. You need her signature; she's not here to give it. It's either me or you wait."

"May I ask when she'll be back?"

Omar growled. "I'm not her secretary. I don't know. Come back tomorrow." The door slammed.

After a few moments, he came into the office. "You didn't order anything, did you?"

I shook my head. "Not yet. Did you get a glimpse of whatever it was?"

"Yeah. It was a box. UPS uniform but a regular sedan, not one of their delivery vehicles, was in the driveway with someone else driving. And the guy looked like a weasel. Skinny. Pointy face. Your kitty said he smelled a were-rodent at the office, right?"

My phone rang. Caller ID said it was Marge, one of my upstairs neighbors. I held up my hand in the universal "I have to take this" sign. "You had a visitor about an hour ago," she said when I answered.

"I did? Did you recognize them?"

"Nope. Guy dressed in a UPS uniform but there was no corresponding truck or van outside. After the fire last night, which we know was arson, we decided you should know. And also that you should stay away from the apartment for a while. We didn't like the way he looked."

"We" probably meant all five of my upstairs neighbors. They, unlike me, were all retired and like most retirees, kept an eye on the neighborhood through their windows, gossiping about everything and everyone over coffee. It was like having a building full of grandparents looking after you, which was nice – most of the time.

"I had already planned on staying at Ev's for a few days until I get everything set up. Fudge is with me, of course. Thanks for the info, though. Let me know if anything else unusual happens, will ya?"

"Will do, hon."

This was getting creepy. Maybe I'd stay in the cottage after all. "I need to call Ms. Fitzsimmons," I said after hitting the 'end' button.

"Who?"

"Head Witch in the Midwest. My boss, for lack of a better term. That was my upstairs neighbor. I think your delivery person tried my apartment first. I don't have a phone number for the security arm and Gregory's probably on a plane with his phone in airplane mode, so she's my best bet."

"Good idea. Here's the license plate number. It's Wisconsin, not Minnesota, by the way." He handed me a matchbook cover on which he'd scribbled an alpha-numeric number, turned and headed back down to the basement.

I called Ms. Fitzsimmons but got her voice mail. I had no choice but to leave a message, so I tried to make it as succinct as possible and remembered to include the license number Omar had gotten. I ended it with, "Please have someone call me with an update."

An hour later, I was yawning, despite repeated infusions of caffeine. Omar and Sally emerged from the basement, Sally still looking fresh as a daisy, Omar covered in dust and cobwebs.

"We cleared enough space for two desks and a couple of filing cabinets," Sally said. "The software has all been loaded on the laptop, but I haven't pulled the data down yet. I've got the furniture ordered – it'll be here Monday between nine and noon. What else can I do today?"

"Go home. You've been here long enough. I'm going to knock off in just a couple minutes myself and go get a nap. I'll finish configuring both computers over the weekend. Can you work all day Monday?"

She looked at the calendar app on her phone. "I can probably be here by about ten. I have a coffee meeting early."

"Good enough. Thanks for everything."

"No worries – it's my job, you know! See you Monday." She grabbed her purse from the chair where she'd thrown it and left.

"I need a shower," Omar said. "Ev's is a lot bigger than the one in the cottage. Stay here and don't answer the door. I'll be down in fifteen."

Almost exactly fifteen minutes later, he was back. He obviously had planned on staying away from home because he was in clean clothes. Or, he'd just raided Ev's closet. They were close to each other in size, although Omar was taller. On closer inspection, he'd been into Ev's closet. The pants were a little short.

I'd finished what I could get done without having to *think* too much. It was past nap o'clock. We shut all the lights off, and after Fudge and I walked out the back door, Omar set the alarm system.

"On second thought, hang on a minute," Omar disarmed the alarm and motioned us back into the house.

"What?" I asked.

"Gonna put a couple of lights on to make it look like someone's here. Maybe our weasel will try something." He flicked on the light to the breakfast nook then disappeared from the kitchen. I heard him tromp up then back down the stairs.

"Okay, we can go now." He motioned us back outside. Two minutes later, we were in the cottage.

"I didn't know where else to put it, so the kitty's litterbox is in the bathroom. I put his food and water in the kitchen. I hope that's okay."

"It's per-perfect, thank you," I said in the middle of another yawn. "I'm going to lay down for a while. It was a short night and stressful day. Gregory should be home in another hour or so."

"I know. I got a text from him. Sleep well. I'll keep an eye out."

I retreated to the bedroom, Fudge in my wake. We curled up together and just before I conked out, I heard, "*He is not the only one who will keep watch. Sleep, my human.*"

# CHAPTER NINETEEN

"Amy, wake up. Dinner's ready if you're hungry." Gregory's voice penetrated my sleep.

"Huh? Oh. Hi. What time is it?" I tried to pull myself awake.

"Six-thirty. If you're not hungry, I will put yours in the oven to keep it warm."

My stomach growled. "I think there's your answer. I'll be out in a minute."

I rubbed the sleep from my eyes and padded into the dining area. Two places were set with steaming food on the plates. "Where's Omar?" I asked.

"I sent him home for the night. I can handle anything he can and then some," Gregory said as he spread his napkin over his lap. "He filled me in on the fake UPS driver. Have you any idea why whoever this is might be targeting you?"

"No," I mumbled through a mouth of something tasty and beefy. Swallowing my food so I wouldn't talk with my mouth full, I added, "The only people I've pissed off lately that I know about are elves. Obrist because I wouldn't pay his stupid ransom, and Perchaladon because I wouldn't join whatever rebellion he's fomenting. But they're in custody all the way down in Louisiana."

"We know whatever it is goes beyond the elves. You did well to call Althea, by the way. I spoke with Ed while you were sleeping. The mundane police have an APB out for that car and they're looking to see if it shows up on the traffic cameras for the time they think the fire was started. I suspect it will. Ed's people are going through their 'known bad guys' file for a were weasel or rat."

We were about half way through our meal (made all the more delicious because I didn't have to cook it) when a loud beeping, similar to a smoke detector, came from the hallway.

"Smoke? Where?" I asked.

"No, that's my perimeter alert for Ev's house. Stay here." He ran out the door.

Not on your life. I ran after him.

As he was running, Gregory keyed something on his phone. The house floodlights came on and illuminated a figure crouched at the back door, fiddling with the alarm keypad.

"Stop right there!" Gregory shouted. The crouching figure stood, took one look at Gregory, then started running around to the front of the house. Gregory raised his hands, preparing to throw a spell. I did the same.

Two spells flew. The one with forest green sparkles opened up a large hole in the ground, into which our potential robber fell. The second, carmine sparkles, cast a net over him. The sparkles faded from my sight as we approached our now-immobilized perpetrator. He was lying face-down, attempting to spit dirt out of his mouth but with his arms at his sides, there wasn't much he could do about what covered the rest of his face.

"Oh, well done, Amy," Gregory patted me on the back. "Would you mind burying him a little? It'll hold him more securely while I get the dirt off his face to see who we have."

Gregory flipped the guy on his back and I moved enough dirt to plant him about a foot deep, covering everything but his face and torso. At the same time, loose dirt moved off his face as if a blow-dryer had been aimed at him.

"Definitely a were rodent of some kind," Gregory mused to himself as he hit a speed-dial number on his phone.

"It's Gregory," he said when whoever it was answered. "I have someone here I think is one of the fire perps or at least our mysterious UPS guy. You or the mundane cops?" A pause, then, "Of course. Ev's house, side yard. See you in about thirty."

Gregory took one peek around the corner of the house. "There's a strange car in the driveway but this one is apparently alone. That's good."

"Who are you?" I asked the partially-entombed were. All I got was a growl in reply.

"Wait for Ed and his people to arrive," Gregory admonished me. "Let's go finish dinner."

"Shouldn't we watch him?" I asked.

"No. You've got him well covered and that dirt is heavy. It's also wet from the sprinklers, which makes it even heavier. And undoubtedly more uncomfortable." He snickered. "It would take more than a half hour to extricate himself and even then, all he can do is wriggle like a worm. Besides, I'm still hungry."

So we left our man in the ground and went back to eating.

"*You did well,*" Fudge said. "*You thought quickly and utilized your magic as you have been taught.*"

"Thank you, oh wise familiar," I answered. I could at least speak with Fudge without worrying about a mouth full of food. "I didn't feel you. You didn't help?"

"*There was no need. I monitored but you were fine without me.*"

We'd just finished cleaning up when there was a knock at the door, the bolt turned on its own, and it opened without any invitation. Ed Bartz stuck his head in.

"We're taking him down to HQ now. Want to watch?"

"No. You will call with whatever you find out, anyway. Amy and I have had a rough couple of days and need our beauty sleep."

"Okey-dokey." Mr. Bartz was very relaxed. "We have him, so you can release your web. And we've covered over the hole, but you might want to encourage the grass a little."

Gregory's eyes went blank for a moment, then he made a slashing movement with his right hand. "Thanks. Web's gone. We will deal with the grass in the morning." Ed's head left the door opening and a moment later, the door closed.

"He has a key?" I asked.

"No, but the door is keyed to him, just in case something should happen to me. We go back a long way and given the scrapes we tend to get into, it makes sense for someone to be able to get in without a key. All he has to do is put his hand on the knob. The reverse is true at his apartment."

That made sense. I yawned again.

"We both need sleep," Gregory said. "I prescribe a full, uninterrupted ten hours for both of us. Go to bed. I'll see you in the morning."

"Where are you going to sleep? You don't fit on your couch!"

"I'm going to import the bed from one of Ev's guest bedrooms for the night. It'll fit just fine between the back of the couch and the dining room table. I'll give you the bathroom, first."

I was brushing my teeth when I heard a "thump." Not quite a perfect landing but then again, Gregory was probably just as tired as I was.

I awoke the next morning feeling like a new person. I woke my phone up and saw that I had had the prescribed ten hours. It felt wonderful. The smell of coffee wafted in and had me scrambling into some clothes.

"I know it's Saturday and supposedly lessons but I'm guessing you have work to do," Gregory said after I'd had a full cup and was on my way to the pot to refill it. I didn't even have to dodge the bed because it wasn't there.

"Yes. I need to finish configuring the computers, download all the data, and figure out what's lost forever and what can be recreated."

"Omar will be here in about an hour. Then you can go over to the house to do whatever needs doing. I have permission to go into the ruins of the building to see if anything can be salvaged. I suspect Cassandra and Tommy will be doing the same thing. I also want to go down to headquarters and have a chat with Ed. Order lunch in. I should be back about three."

"Now that we've caught weasel-man or whatever he is, can I go home?"

"Not yet. We know your weasel-man had at least one accomplice and probably more. Until they've drawn the net closed and figure out where you fit into their plans, I'd prefer you stay here."

I sighed. It was nice having someone cook for me, but I missed my apartment. And the solitude that came with it.

*"What am I? Chopped liver? That is a phrase I do not understand. Chopped liver is very tasty yet this implies something less than delectable. Speaking of chopped liver…"*

"It means… Oh, never mind. I meant no people. I'm used to it being just the two of us. And I suppose I have to go shopping for you?"

*"You have been instructed to stay here so I will have to wait. But yes, when you are able…"*

Spoiled cat.

Omar arrived within the hour, we headed over to the big house, and Gregory left for the office. I put both laptops on the desk and started the process of restoring data backups. While they were working, I cleaned out Ev's refrigerator for him. When I'd finished, Omar took the trash bag out, holding it at arms' length. You *know* it's stinky when an ogre can't handle it!

Grub Hub delivered sandwiches for lunch and as I was finishing up the computers, Gregory returned.

"Thank goodness you bought fireproof filing cabinets," he told me. "They had fallen into the basement but with only a few dents, are still intact. I'll rent a truck on Monday and bring them here. I have the safe in the back of the Hummer."

I heaved a huge sigh of relief. All our original contracts were in those cabinets, and checks were in the safe. I crossed one thing off my to-do list.

"How are Cassandra and Tommy?" I asked.

"A lot of their kitchen equipment survived, as did all the wrought iron furnishings. There's a lot of cleanup to be done, naturally, but she thinks she only lost about fifty percent. That's not including food, paperwork, et cetera."

"And the building itself?"

"The shell is still there, although all the brickwork is covered in soot. It's a question of rebuilding the interior. My best guess is, depending on the contractor she hires, about three months."

Another sigh of relief escaped me. I knew she had business interruption insurance in addition to property insurance but nonetheless, it wasn't quite as bad as it had originally looked.

"Did you see Mr. Bartz?" I continued my interrogation.

"I did. The man we caught last night is indeed a were-weasel. His name is David Sainsbury, and he's part of a pack out of Chippewa Falls, Wisconsin. The license plate number on the car he used yesterday matches one on security cameras outside Cork's Pub, so he's probably one of our arsonists. He's been turned over to the mundane authorities."

"But why?"

"Ed's trying to get those answers now. Mr. Sainsbury wasn't talking so Ed has arranged to meet his pack leader in Eau Claire to see what, if anything, he knows. Remember, we're dealing with a conspiracy of some sort, so this isn't an isolated incident, directed solely at you, or Cassandra for that matter. If there are no answers forthcoming there, the next step is the Were Council."

If they were as frightening as the Witches' Council, I wouldn't want to be brought before them, were I the were-weasels.

Then again, I think I was a fairly sensible person. These people didn't seem to be.

"Any news about what the elves are doing? Is Ev still okay?" I was full of questions.

"Nelion has contacted Althea. They believe they're getting to the bottom of things but will need a few more days. Specifically, they want to hear what Ev has to say when he turns back into himself. Because ogres have no ruling council, there's really no one to force the elves to give him up.

"On the other hand, they have the ability to confine the bat to a particular area. That leash Alberon mentioned on Thursday. We can't do that, or at least I don't know how, so it probably is best he stay with them. The bat can do what bats do, while still having an eye kept on him."

Poor Ev. I hope he didn't remember a lot of what happened. Ev didn't like bugs (at all) and that's what bats generally eat. Not to mention five hundred pounds of ogre crammed into about an ounce of bat. He's used to being the biggest thing around and now could be easily squished by someone as small as me.

Gregory and I spent the rest of the day in his garden, taking out all the weeds that had popped up in his nearly week-long absence. After the sun was low in the sky, we hand-watered everything.

"Why not use sprinklers?" I asked.

"Because this ensures that each plant gets the amount of water *it* needs, rather than a generic amount that a sprinkler system would provide. The fruiting plants, like tomatoes, need more than the herbs. Make sense?"

"I guess so."

We spent the evening playing Chinese checkers, and a bed from the big house plopped, more gently this time, into the living room when it was bedtime.

# CHAPTER TWENTY

Gregory's cell phone rang in the middle of breakfast the next morning. His eyebrows raised when he looked at the caller ID.

"Good morning, Nelion," he answered.

I about spit out my coffee. I hadn't expected to hear anything from the elves for about a week – at least that's how long they implied the spell would last on Ev.

Gregory listened for a moment, then said, "Of course. I can be there later today."

Then, "Thank you. I will let you know my arrival time."

I stared at him as he finished his conversation. "What?"

"That was actually Alberon using Nelion's phone. He believes he has figured out how to remove the spell from Ev without killing him. Because my beacon spell is pretty much woven into Ev's DNA due to the way the transmogrification spell works, he needs me to do something. Therefore, I have to go back to the enclave."

"You mean *we* have to go back to the enclave."

"Why? There is nothing you can do. Stay here and I will, hopefully, bring Ev home with me."

I shook my head. "Nope. I'm coming with. I don't know why but I have to be there when Ev comes back to himself."

"*If you are going, then I am going, too.*"

"Fudge says he's coming with, too."

Gregory sighed. "But it may be a few days before we return. What about recreating the office?"

"Sally can do that. She just has to be able to get into the house."

"Very well. I know when you get something between your teeth, you won't let it go. Call Sally. I will call Omar about access to the house *and* getting the file cabinets, as well as making our travel arrangements."

He looked over at my cat, who was curled in the corner of the sofa. "Fudge, I'm afraid you will have to travel with us. I have no idea where we will be."

"Something I've been meaning to ask. Can't you just get him like you do his litterbox and stuff?" I was confused.

Gregory put on his lesson face. "Inanimate objects can be pushed or pulled through the ether. Familiars, who can traverse the ether on their own, can only be pushed *to* it. I don't know the whys and wherefores, but I cannot *feel* him on the other side, as I do with his litterbox. Therefore, I can't *get* him, as it were."

*"It is a failsafe device to prevent other magical beings from stealing us from our witch or wizard."*

I looked over at him. "That's happened?"

*"No, but it has been attempted. In the long ago past. It did not go well for the would-be thief. I will travel in that box with holes, but I expect a reward for doing so. Chopped liver still sounds delicious."*

Gregory and I made our respective calls. I also ran a load of laundry since I hadn't planned on being gone from home more than a couple of days. By noon, we were packed and ready to go, Fudge reluctantly curled up in the carrier.

At four o'clock on the dot, our plane landed at the airport in Lake Charles. The same guard was waiting for us at the terminal. "The car is this way," he greeted us.

As soon as we were out on the freeway, blindfolds were once again handed over the driver's shoulder. Fudge snickered as I put the small one over his head.

*"Elves think they are so smart, but they are no match for a familiar."*

I didn't bother repeating that. Almost an hour later (it seemed like twice that when you're left with only your own thoughts), we were driving over a gravel road, which meant we were near our destination. Finally, the car came to a halt and we were told we could remove our blindfolds.

I stepped out of the car into a fairy tale. Huge trees, hundreds of feet tall and thirty or more feet in diameter, surrounded us. Craning my neck, I could see swing bridges between branches, leading to what could only be described as elaborate tree houses, some two or three stories high, nestled in among the branches. On the ground, other structures were cradled between protruding roots, built to appear as part of the tree.

Nelion, Alberon, and a female elf emerged from one of the ground buildings. "Welcome," Nelion said. "I trust your journey was uneventful?"

"Yes, it was, thank you," Gregory replied in a somewhat solemn tone.

"Miss McCollum, we welcome you as well. Your familiar, too," he said to me, then looked down at Fudge. "I trust you will abide by our conventions while in our enclave."

Fudge just looked at him. *"Please tell him I will do nothing to upset their balance. In those exact words."*

Bewildered, I repeated what Fudge had said. Nelion nodded and motioned for us to follow.

"What was that about?" I asked my cat.

*"It has to do with our…disagreement. If Waldo deems it appropriate, I will share the story with you at some point. In essence, it means I will not interfere with their magic."*

Huh. "You can do that?"

"I'm looking forward to hearing that story. This is a side of you, and your compatriots, I didn't know existed."

We entered the structure Nelion and his people had come out of. It was much larger than it appeared from the outside and was set up like a conference room. All the furnishings were carved from wood, the table still in the irregular shape of a tree. The backs of the chairs were bas-reliefs of trees, plants, and woodland animals. The chair cushions appeared to be hand-embroidered in the same motif. It was gorgeous.

"Refreshments are on their way. Please, take a seat," Nelion said.

Alberon cleared his throat once we'd all sat. "I will address the reason for your presence, Mr. Tremaine. I believe I have found a way to bring your employer back to himself without waiting for the spell to wear off.

"It involves an arcane method for extracting the failsafe before unwinding the spell. However, your beacon spell, as you call it, interferes with what I need to do. I need you to temporarily remove it. It can be replaced immediately upon his restoration."

One of the guards I'd seen trailing after Nelion entered the room with a silver tray laden with a couple of carafes, cups, and a bowl of fruit. After placing it in the middle of the table, he retreated only as far as the wall next to the door.

"Coffee, Miss McCollum?" The female elf reached for the carafe and one of the cups.

"Yes, thank you," I replied, wondering who she was.

Once everyone had a cup of coffee or tea, Gregory answered Alberon. "I didn't look closely at the bat when I had him. Is the tattoo still completely intact?"

Alberon nodded. "Yes. It's there in its entirety, just sized for a bat rather than an ogre. We looked at it through a magnifying glass to be sure."

"Then I can do it. I was concerned because I didn't spell *Ev,* I spelled the ink in his tattoo. That's what I have to remove the spell from."

Curiosity got the better of me. "You know, I never saw his tattoo. Thank goodness. What is it?"

Alberon snickered, the first evidence of a sense of humor I'd seen from him. "A heart with the initials E and A within."

My jaw dropped. His own initials inside a heart? I looked at Gregory, my mouth still wide enough to collect flies.

He shrugged. "I told him he had to get a tattoo. He didn't like anything the artist had in his book, so chose that. You can't fault the man for loving himself."

Well, no, but…

"Ahem," Alberon said, a smile still trying to move a few muscles around his mouth. "Back to the matter at hand. I need a waning moon and tonight is the third night after it was full. It will work. I suggest we break until moonrise. Nolari will escort you to a place where you may rest."

I gulped down the rest of my coffee and stood with the rest of them. "This way, please." The female elf motioned us out the door.

We followed her around the curve of trees surrounding the clearing and to a similar door in another ground-floor building set among tree roots. I privately wondered where all the other elves were because I saw no one about.

"These are our guest quarters," she said. "Mr. Tremaine, I know you have been here before, so nothing should come as a surprise. We would be pleased to have you join us for dinner. Our guard will come to escort you."

We stepped inside and once again, it was larger than it looked from the outside. Similar to a hotel room, it had a bed, a sofa, and a small table with chairs. Like the conference room, the furnishings appeared to be handmade – and exquisitely so. Light came through a small window in the outside wall, as well as wall sconces and several hurricane lamps. Our bags were on the floor next to the sofa. The door clicked behind us.

"Don't bother trying to open it," Gregory said. "It's locked. Presumably so we don't go snooping around.

"The 'no surprise' part is the bath. The toilet doesn't flush because it's a composting toilet. If you need to shower, pull the chain once to start the water flow and pull it again to stop it. The temperature is preset but it's comfortable."

Fudge padded around the room, into and out of the bathroom, continually sniffing. *"The wizard is the only non-elf to be here in a long time. The only other spoor is full elf."*

"And this surprises you why?" I asked. "They obviously don't allow outsiders in very often."

To Gregory I said aloud, "Who is that lady? She acts like royalty or something."

He smiled. "In a way, she is. She is Nelion's spouse and also a member of the council. From what I can gather, they share the responsibility for running this enclave. Perhaps a little more on her side since he also has to deal with the rest of the country. But she is not as aloof as some of the others you will see."

*"I can use the human toilet if you leave the cover up and they have put down a bowl of water, but I could use some food. There is no tuna in the bowl next to it."*

Oh. I'd forgotten. "Gregory, can you get Fudge's food, please? Cat food doesn't seem to be on their menu."

"Of course. My apologies for the delay, Sir Fudge."

I grimaced. "Please. Don't encourage him."

The container of cat food materialized on the floor next to our bags. I dutifully filled the extra bowl, lifted the toilet lid, then plopped onto the sofa. Gregory had already stretched out on the bed, cell phone in hand.

"I would love to learn more about this place. There's no electric lighting, no electrical sockets, yet some have mobile phones. Those have to be charged. And there's a full signal, too."

I looked at mine. "If we're here more than a few hours, we'll have to find out how to charge our phones. I'm down to seventy percent battery and amusing myself with it while we wait will drain it even further."

"We will find out at dinner." He turned back to whatever he was doing. I pulled up my Mahjong app and started playing. Fudge finished his nosh and curled up next to me.

Countless games later, there was a quick rap on the door, then it opened. The now-familiar guard stuck his head in and said, "Dinner will be in about ten minutes. I have been asked to escort you."

"My cat?" I asked.

The guard sighed, looked at Fudge, then said, "He is invited, as well."

We followed the guard out, back around the circle of trees, and around the base of one of the largest ones. There, the bottom hidden from the clearing, was a staircase that wound around the tree, and up into the branches. It appeared to be partially carved into the tree and partially attached to it by some invisible means. This, too, was exquisitely carved and painted with vines and leaves, made to look as if the tree had somehow formed the staircase on its own.

We followed the guard up, and up, and up. The men were simply walking. Fudge and I, with our shorter legs, were climbing. I was nearly breathless by the time we reached a landing high up in the tree's branches.

To our right was an open door. This led into a large house, once again seeming to be a part of the tree, yet not. The main trunk of the tree rose through the center of the house, and I could see hallways leading out and away from it to various rooms.

"Welcome to our home," Nolari greeted us in the entranceway. "The dining room is this way." She led us around the tree trunk, down a hallway, and into what, in any human house, would be a banquet room. The table could easily seat twenty, but elaborate settings for six were at the closest end. Something niggled at my brain. It took me a moment, but I realized it was set for a formal dinner, exactly as the etiquette books taught.

"Please, take a seat. Nelion and the others will be here momentarily. Would you care for a glass of wine?"

Although I had always assumed one should never take food or gifts from elves (perhaps from my reading of fairy tales as a youngster), Gregory thanked her and took a glass. Mentally shrugging my shoulders, I did the same.

My first sip turned into a second, then a third. Like everything else I'd experienced while in the enclave, it was *good*. A pinot noir, if my tastebuds didn't deceive me. Nelion, Alberon, and another woman entered the room and were handed a glass of the same wine by Nolari.

"Thank you for joining us," Nelion said. "Alberon you already know. May I introduce Laendra, his spouse?"

I fought the urge to hold out my hand. Gregory and I both inclined our heads. I think I was getting the hang of elven social graces.

"Greetings," she intoned but the expression on her face indicated she wasn't really pleased to meet us at all. She was older, almost as white-haired as Alberon, but not a single wrinkle creased her face.

"Laendra is as talented as Alberon," Nelion continued. "We are fortunate to have *two* such mages in our enclave."

The older woman said something in what I presumed was Elvish. "Human English, if you please," Nelion said. "We should not exclude our guests from conversation."

*"She wanted to know why they had to dine with humans."*

She was probably one of the ones Gregory said didn't want to hear what he had to say at the hearing. "Probably why she said it in their language instead of English, huh?"

Just at that moment, Leandra spied Fudge. "A *familiar*? What are you playing at, Nelion?"

Nelion frowned. "The cat and Miss McCollum are as one. They are *guests* and will be treated as such."

Fudge narrowed his eyes. "*I do not like you either, lady. But we are stuck with each other for the time being.*"

"Hey. She didn't hear that, did she? Chill pill. You don't have to curl up in her lap. Just sit near me and stay calm." That was all I needed – my familiar picking a fight with an elf on their ground.

"*I will not 'pick a fight' as you say. And no, she cannot hear me unless I allow her to. But if she should start something, I will finish it.*"

"She *won't* start anything. Nelion won't allow it. Whatever animosity is between you and elves is in a time out, okay?"

I had tried to keep a bland expression on my face while conversing with Fudge but apparently had failed.

"Is anything wrong?" Nelion asked me.

"No, everything's fine." I said as we all sat at the table, Laendra ensuring she was on the other side from me. Fudge curled at my feet, still huffing a little.

To my surprise, Nolari and the ever-present guard brought in trays of food. Apparently, they didn't have servants. One tray was piled high with fruit, another with what appeared to be sautéed vegetables. Yet another had a large bowl of mixed white and wild rice.

"*There is no meat.*"

"They know you are here and know cats are carnivorous. They'll bring you something, I'm sure."

The trays and bowl were passed around and everyone helped themselves. It was like an old-fashioned family-style dinner.

Nolari gasped. "My apologies. I forgot one plate in the kitchen. I will return." She stood and hurried out the door. A moment later, she returned with a small silver dish. Heaped on it was what appeared to be flaked white fish. She put it on the floor next to my chair.

"We very rarely eat flesh. This is fish from the stream that borders the enclave. I hope it is satisfactory," she said to Fudge.

It must have been because he dug in immediately. *"Please thank her."*

I relayed his thanks and the humanoids went back to eating. When we were finished, Nolari and the guard cleared the table, then returned with two carafes and a plate of small cakes.

"Nelion, I have a question," Gregory said after coffee, tea, and cakes had been served. "The enclave obviously does not have electricity but some of you, including yourself, have mobile telephones. How do you keep them charged?"

"My abject apologies," Nelion said. "I'd forgotten humans were so dependent on them.

"Yes, the enclave is far from the modern world. However, as you have noticed, we have been forced to adopt some modern-day conveniences not only to conduct our business, but also to blend in when out in the wider world. Therefore, just outside the enclave proper we have a… farm, I believe is the term, with electricity, motor vehicles, and the like.

"If you will allow Arl to take your phones, he will have them charged. They should be returned to you before the moon reaches its zenith."

The same guard came to stand by our chairs with his hand out. I had a name for him now! I wasn't thrilled about giving someone else my phone but since I had nowhere to plug in the charger, I had no choice. Gregory and I both powered them down.

"How do you maintain such a strong signal?" Gregory asked as we both handed our phones over. "I would think your magic would disrupt it."

"On a normal basis, it would and did. However, one of our younger women who has studied human science has modified the signal coming from the tower at the farm so it can pass through many magical fields. Unfortunately, that modification does not work for telephones outside the enclave. Once outside our influence, the signal goes dead for about a mile until you can pick up the next nearest tower. She tried explaining it to me, but it has to do with human science, which I do not understand. Suffice to say, I am glad it does as it allows me to more easily communicate with the humans who run our outside businesses."

As soon as Arl exited the room, Alberon began talking.

"Tonight will be difficult," he began. "It is a spell that hasn't been worked in about a thousand of your years. It will also involve the blending of two types of magic, human and elf, which, to my knowledge, has never been done. Mr. Tremaine, I appreciate your willingness to assist us."

Gregory nodded. "It is my employer – and my friend – we are trying to retrieve. Of course I am willing."

"Then, shall we repair to the healers?"

"Healers?" I asked.

"They have been taking care of the bat. Our healers combine the skills of human physicians and veterinarians. They know better than any other what a bat needs."

I shrugged my shoulders. Whatever.

Instead of tripping back down the stairs, we exited the house and from the landing, took one of those swinging bridges to a landing in the neighboring tree. While I'm sure it was safe, I was extremely uncomfortable walking across it and vowed to never repeat the experience if I could help it. Thankfully, there was no wind to speak of, but it wasn't called a swinging bridge for nothing!

Once we got to the happily-solid landing, we took another set of stairs down one flight, and entered a room that looked very much like an infirmary, with beds and cages, small and large, lining the walls. It was open to the elements and I wondered what happened when it rained. Without a roof, it seemed to me anyone in that room would get soaked. Unlike a human infirmary, there was no medicinal smell.

"Evalon, we are here," Nelion called.

A man who could be Perchaladon's twin emerged from another room. "I am at your service," he said with a slight incline of his head.

"We will need a small table," Alberon told him.

"Everything has been prepared. Please, follow me." Evalon turned and went back the way he'd come in. We duly followed him into a room almost as large as the first, with a table similar to a vet's examination table in the center. In the middle of the table lay a small brown bat. It appeared to be asleep.

"I will leave you now. Please call if I can be of further assistance." Evalon left. The six of us crowded around the table and observed the bat.

Alberon looked up through the branches. I looked up as well, couldn't see anything but tree, but he said, "It is time."

# CHAPTER TWENTY-ONE

The bat stirred as we all stared down at it. Alberon put his hands gently on its back and rubbed, similar to the way you'd rub a crying baby's back to calm it. But the movements weren't random. They were counterclockwise, then clockwise, all in a set pattern.

"Mr. Tremaine, when I say 'now,' please remove your spell," he quietly said, continuing his caressing motion. "Now."

Gregory moved his left hand to the bat's shoulder and made a pulling motion with his fingers. I saw carmine red energy flow up to his fingers and there was no longer a tingle of magic.

Alberon ceased his stroking and with a furrow in his brow, started to trace something, as if following a maze with his finger. All of a sudden, there was a loud rustling noise, a squeak, a squawk, and a hiss. All except for Alberon looked around.

"What was that?" he asked. "I cannot stop to look."

On the floor behind me, Fudge had a hawk pinned, his claws partially extended into its back. *This one is an elf. What shall I do with it?*

"A red-tailed hawk," Nelion said. "An elf. Who transforms to such a bird?"

Alberon continued his tracing and without breaking his pattern replied, "Rimadur."

"One of our rebellious younglings," Nelion said for our benefit.

"Fudge wants to know what he should do with the bird," I interjected.

"Rimadur," Nelion addressed the bird, "this cat will hold you until Alberon has completed his work. Should you struggle, he has my permission to do whatever is necessary to continue his hold on you, up to and including death. Therefore, I suggest you remain as still as possible because I am certain control of his natural instincts is most difficult.

"Familiar, my thanks. I understand this is challenging for you but Alberon will take charge as soon as he is able."

Fudge audibly growled. *This is not easy. Tell the mage to make it quick.*

Alberon finally stopped following a maze and lifted his finger into the air. A chill permeated the room. He moved his hand as if his finger was a whip and there was concussive 'boom' with an attendant wind, blowing everyone's hair back. The bat shuddered a little but remained quiescent.

"The failsafe is destroyed," he said with an air of relief. "I can now remove the transmogrification spell. I suggest we all move back a step or two because not only will an ogre take up much more space, but he will probably be angry as well. Laendra, please prepare yourself to isolate him."

We all stepped back, Gregory and I to either side of Fudge and his prisoner. Alberon once again placed his hand on the bat's back but this time, pulled it up almost immediately. In the blink of an eye, there was a naked ogre sprawled face-down across the table, butt high in the air. Eau de ogre washed over us. I quickly averted my eyes. I *so* did not need to see that!

"Sloppy," Alberon said. "Clothing should have transformed along with the body. Allow me."

"What. The. Fuck." Ev choked out every word, as if his vocal cords weren't used to working. Which they weren't.

I raised my eyes. Ev had on a white bathrobe with the Omni Hotel logo embroidered on the chest. Phew!

Ev stood, holding onto the edge of the table for support. He cleared his throat, then roared, "Would someone explain what the hell has happened to me?"

Gregory stepped forward. "Ev, it's a long story. You have questions; we have questions. Please, calm yourself and let's sit down to talk."

"I will not calm myself! I have been flying around eating *bugs*! And enjoying it!" He looked around and started flailing his arms. "Elves! I might have known. They're sneaky bastards!" Ev's face darkened from puce to a deep purple.

Gregory and I both cringed. Gregory went to restrain Ev but ran into an invisible barrier. Leandra smirked. "He is contained within a three-foot circle. He cannot harm us."

"Mr. Angelich," Nelion began in a calm voice. "What has happened to you is not sanctioned. Please allow us to explain, then perhaps you can help us by answering some questions."

"Ev, please," Gregory admonished.

"*I am about to have a feast of bird,*" Fudge whined.

"Alberon, can you take the bird from Fudge now? He's about to lose control," I said.

"My apologies. Of course." Alberon bent down and put his hands around the bird, pinning the wings, careful to avoid Fudge's claws. When he was certain Alberon had a good hold, Fudge sprang off the bird's back and ran out of the room. Sounds of hacking came from down the hall. Alberon also left, taking the bird with him.

Gregory put his hands up in a calming gesture. "Ev, if you will please get yourself together, we can sit and have a civilized conversation. Yes, I know you are upset. We all are. But yelling will get you no explanation and I know you'd like one."

"I will never get a direct answer from these bastards," Ev roared.

"In that, at least this time, you are incorrect," Nelion said, still calmly. "Believe it or not, we are as distressed at your treatment as your friends are. If we can sit and have a quiet discussion, I will answer your questions to the best of my ability."

"And who the hell are you?" Ev's face had lightened somewhat but not completely.

Gregory sighed. "Ev, this is Nelion, the Head Elf in the United States and the father of Perchaladon, whom you have already met."

It was my turn. "Ev, get a grip. These people helped us find you *and* they're the ones who removed the spell. Not Gregory, not me. A little gratitude wouldn't go amiss."

He turned to me. "You're here, too? Who's minding the shop?"

"First, it's the weekend so the shop isn't open. Second, Sally has everything covered and knows to call me if there's something urgent." Now was not the time to tell him about the fire.

Nelion was anxious to move things along. "Please, Mr. Angelich. Let us move to a more comfortable area, sit, and have a reasonable conversation. I wager you are hungry because your stomach has now expanded to its normal size. We have food ready for you."

Ev visibly calmed even further. "Now that you mention it, yes, I am hungry. Let's go, then." He started walking toward the door and stopped abruptly after one step. "Hey! What the hell?"

Leandra smirked again. "If you promise no harm to us, I will release your cage," she told him.

Ev glared at her. "I make no such promises for the long term. But in the short term, I won't pound any of you to dust."

"That will be sufficient," Nelion told him. To Leandra, "Release him."

She huffed. "Very well," looked hard at Ev for a moment, then flounced out of the room.

Nelion apologized to us. "It's not you. She does not like anyone who is non-elf. Were she younger, I am afraid she would join our younglings in their rebellion.

"Now, please follow me. We have a more comfortable place than this in the room below."

We joined him in the infirmary, where Fudge jumped into my arms. "Are you okay now?" I asked.

*"I am still somewhat shaken but will recover. I am unaccustomed to exerting that much control over this body's instincts. Will there be more fish?"*

I chuckled. If he was asking about food, he was fine. But he stayed in my arms out the door, down the flight of stairs to the ground, and around the clearing to the conference room we'd originally met in.

Somehow, during the intervening hours, an ogre-sized chair had replaced one of the normal-sized ones at the head of the table. In front of it sat a platter with a roasted chicken accompanied by the same sautéed vegetables we'd had at our dinner. An ogre-sized mug held something frothy. Four other chairs faced glasses full of the same frothy something.

Nelion gestured. "Please, sit. Mr. Angelich, while you eat, I will tell you what I know. Then, if you don't mind, I have questions."

Ev nodded, sat, and started tearing into the chicken with his hands. I desperately wanted to apologize for his eating habits but didn't want to antagonize Ev any further. Instead, I took a sip from the glass in front of me. It was beer, but unlike any I'd ever tasted. It didn't have the bite of hops but wasn't overly sweet, like mead. It wouldn't be something I'd drink on a regular basis, but it wasn't bad.

*"Food?"*

Oops. "Nelion, my apologies, but Fudge is hungry again. Is there any fish left?"

"I don't believe so, but I will ask. If not, we can get something suitable for him."

"Please don't go to any extra trouble," Gregory said. "We have his regular food with us. With your permission, I will retrieve it from our room."

Gregory didn't wait for a response but momentarily, Fudge's food and water dishes appeared on the floor next to the wall behind my chair.

"*It is not fish or tuna, but will suffice, I suppose.*" Fudge immediately started devouring his food, rivalling Ev for inhalation rate.

"At that rate, you'll whorf it back up immediately. Slow down," I told him. "I don't want to have to apologize to elves for cat vomit." Thankfully, he started to pace himself but in no time, the food dish was empty.

Without even batting an eyelash at Ev's table manners, Nelion started talking.

"I am not certain of the *whys* of what happened to you. But this I will say: There has been unrest in the younger generation of virtually all species, ourselves not excluded. Apart from full humans, paranormals seem to want to shake up the status quo. Although humans, who outnumber us all, for the most part accept non-humans, the younglings want what they are calling 'parity.' I am not certain I completely understand their grievances.

"My son and some of his friends are part of this… movement, I will term it. Elves have always glamoured themselves when out in the wider world. Mostly to protect our privacy but also to more easily interact with humans and other species without suspicion. Weres are feared, regardless of their species, due to the violent nature of the more predatory species, especially as portrayed in the human cinema.

"I am sure there are other issues of which I am not aware. However, the younglings with whom we have spoken no longer wish to glamour themselves when in public. They are determined to force the humans to accept us. This can lead to problems."

"I saw it first-hand," I interjected. "Perchaladon met me on the bike path at the lake. He was not glamoured and it caused all sorts of problems. Several accidents, actually, as people rubber-necked at him rather than watch where they were going. You must admit, you are definitely stare-worthy from a human perspective."

"*That* is one of the reasons for the glamour," Nelion continued. "We accept that humans find us attractive, excessively so. Many years ago, a woman of my generation walked the streets of New Orleans unglamoured – once. This was in the days before New Orleans was truly civilized. She was accosted by several men at once, found a need to protect herself, and damaged several of the men. She escaped with a deflection spell but there were ramifications when it was discovered one of the men was a wizard and they contacted my father with a grievance.

"To continue on in the present day. I believe there is an inter-species conspiracy to cause an uprising of some sort. Somehow, I believe, you got caught up in it."

Ev swallowed the last of his food (he'd eaten the entire chicken) and wiped his mouth with the sleeve of his robe. I cringed.

"I may have overheard something," he began. We all sat forward in our chairs.

"You know I was on the set of the movie, right? And that there was an elf or two hanging around?"

Gregory and I nodded. Nelion just steepled his fingers.

"Well, I was walking to the porta potty and almost bowled over two guys talking in whispers. One elf, one somebody else. I didn't exactly stop to listen because that would have been rude, but caught the words 'demonstration' and 'August first.'

"That night, after saying goodnight to my date, I decided to go over to Frenchman Street for a drink before heading back to the hotel. The same elf was in the bar, at a table with a couple of other guys. I nodded at him because I knew I'd seen him on set and went on to the bar. I had my drink, decided to go back to the hotel, and left. Those same three guys followed me out.

"The next thing I knew, I felt kinda like I'd been trapped in something. Hard to describe. Then there was a feeling like I wasn't alone in my skin. I was shoved into a cage of some sort. I tried yelling, but nothing came out."

He took a swig of his beer. "I discovered I really wasn't alone in my skin, and that I had no control over anything. There was another something thinking there, but it only thought with emotions. It was scared. I couldn't talk, couldn't walk, couldn't move my hands. Nothing. Some time later, the cage door opened and the body I couldn't control flew. Scared the crap out of me.

"All I could do was observe. We flew, we ate *bugs*, we slept, we shit. For how long?"

Gregory grimaced. "Two weeks, give or take a day."

"Two fucking weeks? I lost two weeks thanks to whatever happened?"

"An elf, by the name of Obrist, cast a transmogrification spell on you," Nelion almost whispered. "It is not exactly forbidden but is severely frowned upon to cast such a spell on another being without their permission. My assumption is that you overheard the end of a plot and to prevent you from telling anyone else, Obrist ensured you couldn't.

"Now that we have a date, all we need is details," he continued.

"And will this Obrist fellow pay for what he's done?" Ev was starting to get riled up again.

"He is already in custody and has confessed to transforming you – after Alberon identified him as the caster. The council will decide his fate, which will hopefully be unpleasant. I am working now to change our laws to expressly forbid such actions."

"They haven't *yet* come to a decision?" Gregory was getting mad, too.

"As you may have noticed, there are some on the council who care not what happens to other species. It continues to be an intense debate. *If* I can tie this incident to something larger, especially something that may involve violence, that may convince them."

"What about the office?" I asked. "Wouldn't that convince them?"

"What *about* the office?" Ev stared at me.

"Um. The building got fire-bombed on Thursday."

Ev started turning purple again. "*What*? When were you going to tell me this?"

Nelion cleared his throat. "If I recall what you said correctly, that was a member of the weres, not elves. Therefore, no, it will not convince the council."

"The office*?*" Ev wouldn't be put off.

Gregory put his hand on Ev's arm. "Ev, the structure is essentially still there. Amy and Sally have recovered the electronic files and Amy's foresight in purchasing fireproof filing cabinets saved most of the paper. The office has been moved to your house until Cassandra can fix up the building. There is nothing to worry about on that front. We are more concerned with wider matters at the moment."

Gregory turned toward Nelion. "Ed Bartz, Head of Midwest Security, is investigating the fire. Because we had one of the weres in custody, he believes he can tie everything together. Hopefully, he can make a case that will hold up with your council."

"My stuff! All my stuff!" Ev wailed. Gregory made shushing noises; Nelion just looked at him out of the side of his eye.

"I would be most pleased to have an, as I believe is said, airtight case. I am certain Althea and Howard will keep me up to date," Nelion said.

"Now, I believe it is time to rest. Your friends, Mr. Angelich, have had a very long day, and I believe you will be better for a night's rest. We have put a bed appropriately sized for an ogre in the guest room next to the one Mr. Tremaine and Miss McCollum are occupying. I am afraid, however, that you will find the shower cramped as we did not have enough notice to enlarge it."

Nelion stood and we followed suit. "Allow me to wish you a pleasant night. I will see you in the morning before you depart."

Arl stood at the conference room door and ushered us out, Fudge surprisingly quiet at my feet. Ev shuffled along in the rear, bemoaning the loss of his memorabilia, his pictures, and stuff in general. At the adjacent doors, Gregory told me to go on in, he'd be there in a moment, then followed Ev into the other room.

A few moments later, there was a knock at the door. Surprised that Gregory would be knocking, I opened it. Arl handed me two cell phones and quietly wished me good night.

The elves apparently still assumed that Gregory and I were a couple because there was only one bed. I liked the guy, but I was *not* sharing a bed with him. Their sofa had the same issue as Gregory's – it was too short for a man to sleep on. Nor did it pull out to a sleeper. So I stripped the top sheet off the bed, grabbed one of the pillows, and made up a bed on the sofa. I took off my jeans and bra but left the t-shirt on, crawled between the layers of folded sheet, powered up my phone, and checked email while waiting for Gregory. Thankfully, nothing serious had arisen. I sent a quick text to Sally, letting her know we had Ev back as his smelly-ogre self and if we didn't return the next day, I'd call her.

It took about twenty minutes for Gregory to return. I cocked an eyebrow. "Well?"

He looked at my makeshift bed, shrugged his shoulders, and sat on the regular bed. "He is, naturally, still upset. It will take a while for him to come to terms with two tragic events in such a short period of time.

"I also had to replace the beacon spell. Getting into the tattoo without affecting the rest of him was a little more difficult than spelling the bottle of ink the tattoo artist used. Strangely, Ev didn't argue at all, especially when I told him that was how you identified him in your true dream.

"What took the longest is I had to get him some clothes. That robe will be gone with the sunrise and he had to have something to replace it. He couldn't decide what sort of image he wanted to project to the elves in the morning so vacillated between casual and business. I finally convinced him that since *we* were casual, he ought to be, too. Then it came down to which shirt he wanted. The man is an ogre, for goodness' sake. In this case, clothing does *not* make the man. I swear!"

"Before we go to sleep," I started in. "I need a question answered."

"Yes?"

"I can see your energy when you perform a spell, although it usually fades from my sight quickly. I usually feel a tingle when there's some sort of magic around. Fudge tells me elves *are* natural energy, yet I can neither feel them, nor generally see any of their spells. You tell me you can see at least the glamours. Why?"

"I can see everything they do, including a faint magical aura around them, even in their true forms. It has to do with age. Although you have come into your powers and can now use them fairly effectively, your subconscious brain hasn't quite adjusted to it. What the elves are and do is considerably more subtle than what we are and do. You can see and feel the, for lack of a better word, blatant magic. When your brain grows into your magic, you will be able to see and sense *them*, too."

*"Gregory is correct. I have observed human children learning to walk. First they crawl, then they toddle, then they walk, sometimes falling, then they can walk without falling. It is the same with magic. You are to the toddling stage in magic. Does that make sense?"*

I sighed. "But it would be so much easier to know who's what, and who's doing what, you know?"

*"That is what you have me for. I will always tell you."*

"It will come with time. Go to sleep. I will wake you at sunrise because the elves will be here shortly thereafter." Gregory powered up his phone and looked at it. I laid my head on the pillow, Fudge crawling behind me to make his usual nest in my hair. I slept.

# CHAPTER TWENTY-TWO

"Amy, it's time to wake up," Gregory's voice penetrated my dreams. I blearily opened my eyes to find Fudge staring into my face, a paw raised as if to take a swipe at my nose.

"I'm awake. I think," I mumbled.

*"Good. The wizard has been calling you for five minutes. I was about to take drastic measures."*

"Sunrise is in about five minutes. I suspect we'll be called shortly thereafter. I suggest you make your morning ablutions quick."

I sat up, dislodging Fudge from his perch on my chest. Untangling myself from the sheet, I realized I was just in a t-shirt and my underwear. "Look out the window or something," I implored.

Gregory duly turned his back while I grabbed my overnight bag and took the whole thing into the bathroom with me. Five minutes be damned. I needed a shower. As advertised, pulling the chain let out a stream of water that was only tepid. Not my favorite temperature but it would have to do. I hurriedly washed everything, including my hair, dressed, pulled the wet hair into a ponytail and exited the bathroom.

"I am informed that breakfast will be in the conference room we were in yesterday," Gregory told me, then started chuckling. When I asked him what was so funny, he told me that Arl had been reluctant to wake Ev, fearing some sort of retribution from the ogre, so had asked Gregory to do so. Gregory was amused that a supposed guard didn't even want to knock on a door.

"Come on. We don't want to keep the elves waiting."

Gregory opened the door, nodded at Arl, knocked on Ev's door, then went in. Arl, Fudge, and I waited outside. And waited. I heard voices coming from Ev's room and it sounded like an argument. Finally, Gregory and Ev came out, neither looking happy. When I looked at Gregory, he shook his head and mouthed, "Later."

Breakfast was just the three of us and of the continental sort, with coffee, juice, fresh fruit, and mouth-watering fresh-baked bread with marmalade. Ev grumbled about not getting bacon and eggs.

"They are feeding us, so be grateful," Gregory admonished. Ev continued to grumble while demolishing an entire loaf of bread.

We were finished eating, drinking more coffee from the magically-refilling carafe when Nelion entered.

"Good morning. I trust you slept well?" he asked.

"We did, thank you," Gregory replied. "May I ask what the plans are for today?"

"Althea has already called with news and has suggested a meeting at her office. I know you are anxious to get home so unless you have other plans, we will take our jet back to Minneapolis. You should be receiving a text or call from Howard shortly, requesting your presence at the meeting. It seems your Mr. Bartz has some ideas."

"*Waldo has communicated with me,*" Fudge told me. "*Our presence is requested as well.*"

Gregory nodded at Nelion. "Of course. And thank you for the offer of a ride. It will be much quicker than a commercial flight."

"Excellent. The plane will be ready to leave in about thirty minutes. Arl will help you collect your things then convey you to the airstrip. I will meet you there."

As soon as Nelion had left, I let Gregory know about Waldo's communication with Fudge.

"It seems we are all in the middle of another train wreck," he said. "Ev, I will drop you at the house on our way downtown."

"No way. After being turned into a bat, I want to know what's happening. I'm going with you."

Gregory looked at his phone. "It's only shortly before eight. Too early to call people but we can send texts now, before we're airborne. I'll text Omar. Amy, please text Sally. Have them meet at the house at, say, ten, and Omar can let her in. As well, he can keep an eye on things until this mess is solved, one way or another."

So, I sent a text to Sally, asking her to get to the house by ten so Omar could let her in and telling her we'd be airborne shortly, arriving in Minneapolis before noon but we had a meeting downtown immediately thereafter. Also to remind her that furniture was getting delivered that morning and the telephone people were supposed to be out to install a second line in the afternoon. I'd try to call her once we were in the car.

"Hey," Ev said as we trotted behind Arl back to the rooms. "What happened to my phone?"

Gregory shrugged his shoulders. "No telling. I don't know if, on a normal basis, electronics transform along with the body, but given Alberon's reaction to you not having clothing, I'm guessing Obrist couldn't change your phone. Perhaps it's in the ether; perhaps it landed on Frenchman Street and someone picked it up."

"I know it hasn't been used because it doesn't appear on my locator application. We will have to get you another one. There is a phone store just off the interstate exit for home, so we will stop there."

Ev pouted. "But what am I supposed to do until then? I'm certain I have all sorts of missed calls, texts, emails, all that. Two weeks' worth. I need to catch up!"

"Ev, calm down," I told him. "I forwarded your cell phone to the office, and that's been forwarded to my phone. I've also been monitoring your email, answering where I could and telling everyone else you were out of touch and would get back to them as soon as you were able.

"Thankfully, there have been no real emergencies while you were…gone. Your female friends are a little miffed at you, though. They didn't like getting a reply from me. You'll have to deal with *that* on your own."

Ev sighed. "This is disastrous. Even when I get a new phone, it won't have all the missed calls and texts. And I'll have to re-enter all my contacts."

"No, you won't. I had your phone set to back up everything to the cloud. Your contacts will download during the process of setting up the new phone," Gregory told him. It was a good thing Ev had Gregory. He'd flounder his way through life, otherwise.

We grabbed our bags (Ev, of course, didn't have one) and walked over to the SUV that had driven into the clearing a moment before.

Gregory looked down at Fudge. "I know you don't want to fly and I doubt very much the elves want you on their plane. Ready for a boost?"

Fudge nodded at him. *"I will be with Waldo when you arrive at their office,"* I heard just before he dematerialized.

While being driven to the airstrip, I asked Arl about the lack of other elves around. It seemed to me there ought to be more people inhabiting what was, in theory, a city.

He chuckled. "The area you saw is just one part of our enclave – the part that belongs to the Head of the enclave. They live near what to you would be all the administrative offices for convenience.

"There are other such clearings in our forest, which include housing and workshops. Anyone who was not associated with what happened yesterday was told to stay out of that clearing, to avoid being seen by humans – or your familiar."

I guess that made sense. They still preferred their privacy.

The plane ride was quiet. Nelion was absorbed in something on his phone. Alberon looked like he was meditating. Gregory and I read books on our phones. Ev started snoring.

When we landed at Flying Cloud, a black SUV, identical to the ones in Louisiana, was waiting outside the terminal. "This is our ride," Nelion said. "We will meet you at Althea's office in one hour's time."

"Our car is in the car park," Gregory said. "Come on."

The Hummer had been sitting in the hot sun for almost a week and was stifling. Add to that Ev's aroma (which I really hadn't missed) and I had to have the window open, even with the air conditioning going full blast. Ev complained about the noise but I didn't say anything. My comfort, at this point, was more important.

We were on the outskirts of downtown when I hollered at Gregory over the sound of the wind. "Hey, aren't we supposed to be blindfolded or something? Last time, we weren't to know the location of the office."

"I have no instructions to that effect," he answered. "My guess is that they deem you, even Ev, trustworthy enough not to divulge the location."

Ev snorted. "As if I care. It's another damned office."

We drove into a parking garage, went down to the lowest level and parked. Gregory herded us to a different elevator than the bank used by the general public. A guard stood next to it. No uniform, no visible weapon, but he was a guard nonetheless. I could tell by his bearing.

"We have an appointment with Althea, Ed, and I think Howard is there, too," Gregory told him.

Eyeing Ev, the guard nodded. "You are expected." He hit a button on the remote in his hand, and a moment later, I could hear the elevator whooshing its way downward. When the doors slid open, there was no corresponding 'ding' as one usually hears.

There was only one button in the elevator, too. The doors slid closed. I remembered it being an express and was grateful because I'd only have to hold my breath against Ev's smell in that enclosed space for a few moments.

The door opened to a familiar sight – plush carpeting, wood paneling, and Ed Bartz, the Head of Security waiting for us. "I'm to take you directly to the conference room. You're the last to arrive," he said.

We trooped into the conference room where nearly a dozen people sat at the table. I recognized Ms. Fitzsimmons; her familiar, Waldo (currently in the form of a rottweiler); Mr. Sharretts; Nelion and Alberon; but none of the others. I nodded my head at a lady sitting on a chair in a corner. She was the Witches' Council secretary, one who could remember everything verbatim without taking notes.

Fudge came trotting over and jumped into my arms. *"I missed you. This is an important meeting. These are all very important people."*

As we sat, Althea cleared her throat. "Most of us know each other well, but there are faces unfamiliar to others. I would ask, therefore, that we go around the table and introduce ourselves for the benefit of all. I am Althea Fitzsimmons, Head of the Midwest Witches' Council. This is my familiar, Waldo, Head of the Familiars' Council. On speakerphone is Maximillian Finck, Head of the Midwest Vampire Council."

"Howard Sharretts, Head of the Midwest Wizards' Council."

"John Martin, Head of the Midwest Were Council."

"[unintelligible] but you may call me Penelope, representing the non-elf fae on this continent."

Gregory added "wizard" after his name, so I added "witch" after mine. Ev just said his name. His species was rather apparent.

When the circle was complete, Ms. Fitzsimmons asked Ed to give his report.

Ed stood. "Thanks to some quick work by Mr. Tremaine and Miss McCollum, we were able to get our hands on a were-weasel who, we have found, has been the instigator of several violent crimes here in the Twin Cities over the last several months, including the arson at Mr. Angelich's office. Which, Amy, was supposed to upset you enough to join their cause.

"It took a while, but we finally broke him. There is a small group of young paranormals who are trying to take an upper hand in the wider world. Despite overwhelming numbers to the contrary, we believe they want to cow the humans into submission, with the elves ruling, the vampires having unlimited snacking ability, and such.

"Naturally, as all here agree, that is an insurmountable task. But it won't be for lack of trying. There are activities planned all around the United States for Wednesday, and they aren't peaceful demonstrations. There are plots to take over local and state government houses and if they kill a few lawmakers in the process, they don't care.

"Thanks to all investigative arms working together, we have the names of more than three dozen perpetrators and they are being closely watched. While we would like to confine them, it is simply hearsay at the moment, so we have no grounds to do so.

"The reason for this meeting is to decide how to prevent these plots from coming to fruition, preferably without violence, and also to determine how to deal with the unrest going forward."

I listened to what he had to say, then wondered why Gregory and I were wanted at this meeting. We weren't on any council and really had no say-so in what they decided.

As if reading my mind, Ms. Fitzsimmons spoke to me. "Everyone at this table is at least a century or more older than you, Amy. As a young witch, your input would be most valuable."

"I'm happy to help wherever I can," I replied, still unsure of my role.

"Ahem," came from the speakerphone. "May I ask why the ogre has been included in this conversation? They, as far as I know, are no part of the conspiracy."

"I inserted myself into it," Ev replied. "I was turned into a *bat* because of this shit and I never want that to happen again. To me, or anyone else for that matter. I'll be happy to help break some heads."

I winced. Profanity and the offer of violence. Just what was needed. Not.

"What?" the voice on the speakerphone exclaimed. "Nelion, it must have been one of your people. No other magic can touch an ogre as far as I know."

Nelion sighed. "It was. Mr. Angelich apparently overheard something he should not have in regards to this matter. We have detained my son, three of his elven friends, and a werewolf. Although I suspect there are more involved, I am being thwarted somewhat by my own enclave council because some of them agree with what the younglings are thinking. They wish to return to the old days, as well."

"I suggest you explain to them they are in error," Mr. Martin said.

"I have tried. I am afraid it will take more than turning an ogre into a bat for them to come around to my way of thinking, no offense to you, Mr. Angelich."

"Do they condone violence as well?" Mr. Sharretts asked.

"No. But I believe violence would have to actually be done for them to believe there is an issue."

Gregory sat forward in his chair. "Is there a way to allow *one* of these incidents to happen in a controlled manner, simply to prove a point to the disbelievers, of which I am certain there are many among all species?"

Everyone turned their eyes to Ed. He mused a moment. "Perhaps. Just like humans, most paranormals do not lead, but only follow. *If* we could actually detain our known perpetrators, whom I believe are the main instigators, chances are the rest of it would fall apart. However, that would be up to the individual councils. Laws on such differ and security forces must follow those.

"Nelion, for whatever reason, your son and his friends seem to be mostly involved here in the Upper Midwest rather than New Orleans."

"New Orleans humans are accustomed to the out-of-the-ordinary. Perhaps that is why," Nelion said.

"Yes. Of course. Anyway, if they could be released and somehow found their way back up here to act out their part. I have a good working relationship with the human security team at our state capitol and I'm sure we could come to some arrangement."

He looked at me. "I believe you could be helpful in this regard."

"Me? What could I do?"

"Lure them back. You told me Perchaladon had approached you about the discontent. Tell him the fire changed your mind and you want to be part of whatever it is they're doing."

I cringed. "I'm not a very good liar. On the phone, sure, I can handle it. But in person? That's another matter altogether."

Waldo barked. Once. In my direction. His deep voice made everyone jump.

*"As long as I am with you, I can ensure you tell an untruth with a convincing facial expression."*

"You can what?"

*"By controlling your emotions, just as I am able when you cast a spell. It is your emotions that give you away. If you feel guilty about lying, which you usually do, that shows on your face. I suppress the guilt and you lie convincingly."*

"I suppose you are getting the same information from Fudge that I received so many years ago from Waldo," Ms. Fitzsimmons said to me. To the rest of the group, "For those unacquainted with familiars and their abilities, they can suppress our emotions for brief periods. It is useful when casting a delicate spell. The same skill can be used to ensure Miss McCollum's facial expressions do not give her away."

I made a face. "Well, okay. I suppose. I call Perchaladon and, in theory, join him. Then what?"

"We know the state capitol building is the target. What we do not know is the time or how many others may be involved, and what their species are. Time is short, and we *must* have that information in order to have enough personnel of the right species on site. So, see if you can ferret out his plans, then let me know. I can handle the rest."

"You are putting Amy in danger," Ev said. "I do not like that my assistant is being put in harm's way."

"She is more than capable of protecting herself now," Gregory answered. "In addition, I will be there with Ed's people."

"If she's going to be involved with a mob, I will be there as her bodyguard," Ev said emphatically. "Only elves can touch me with their magic, and that's if I don't get to them first. Any other species doesn't bother me."

He looked at me. "This Perchaladon fellow must understand I'd want to protect you and I'm the best man for the job."

"But how are we going to explain me being pissed at society in general but not at them for turning you into a bat? And how do they know you won't kill them on sight?"

"Hm. That is a problem. But I want to help!"

"You can help by going back to work and ensuring Amy's presence is not missed," Gregory told him. "In addition, there may be some stragglers who escape our net. It is known Amy is now working out of your house after the fire. Someone may come for her, or perhaps try to deliver a suspicious package, as they have already done. We need an ogre there as a deterrent and Omar has to leave the city tomorrow."

"Then it's settled," Ed said. "As soon as the elves are released, we will let you know so you can call Perchaladon and get the ball rolling. Gregory can guard you and let me know what you are doing."

That sounded like a dismissal and it was. Gregory touched my arm, indicating we were leaving. He did the same to Ev. There were noises along the lines of, 'It was nice to meet you,' and 'Thank you for your help' as we exited the room.

Once we were back in the car, I kept the window rolled up so I could hear, leaned over the front seat (right next to Ev, eeeww), and asked Gregory what else was happening in the conference room. Before answering, Gregory popped the sunroof and although I saw nothing, I felt the tingle of magic. He was doing his fan thing again. My nose – and I'm sure Fudge's – was grateful.

"They are undoubtedly working out how to detain the people on their list. Although witches and wizards pretty much follow human law, weres, vampires, and others do not. Just as Nelion told you, there are many in his enclave who see nothing wrong with turning Ev into a bat and are still debating releasing the four elves they've detained.

"Once that is settled, they need to coordinate with the human authorities around the country to ensure that if something does happen, everyone is prepared. And Ed will have his own work cut out for him, ensuring the planned demonstration or whatever it is goes off the way *he* wants it."

It sounded like a lot of work in a short period of time. I did not envy security their task. On the other hand, I was going to be very busy myself. I had to get Ev back into the swing of things, in addition to infiltrating a mob. Was it Friday yet?

# CHAPTER TWENTY-THREE

After a stop at the cell phone store, we were back at Ev's house. It was controlled chaos. Omar was directing the furniture delivery guys, who were grumbling about having to haul large pieces of furniture down a flight of stairs. Sally was trying to get the telephone man to put the second line where *she* wanted it, rather than where he wanted to put it, and at the same time telling Omar just *where* in the basement each piece of furniture needed to go.

"Oh, thank goodness you're here," she said to Ev. "Mario's been trying to reach you for two hours. He's left five messages. Something about his charge going off the deep end."

"My phone's still not set up," Ev grumbled. "And I wouldn't be able to hear anyway, with all this ruckus going on."

I snickered. He wasn't thinking. As usual. "Go up to your bedroom and use the extension there."

"No," he told me emphatically. "The home phone number will show up on his caller ID. I don't want any of them having that."

I sighed. "Fine. Take my cell phone, then. As much as I dislike it, they all have that number in addition to yours. I'll set your phone up and we can switch when I'm done. But call him. Mario doesn't get twitterpated easily."

Ev took the phone I proffered and headed up the stairs. "How can I help you?" I asked Sally.

"I'm good," she said. "You should be able to work in the breakfast nook until I get the office downstairs finished." She eyed the next piece of furniture coming in the door. "That's the last one. I should have everything set up in an hour or so."

I grabbed my laptop off Ev's desk and headed toward the kitchen. First things first. A pot of coffee was in order. My stomach also reminded me it was lunch time.

"I've ordered sandwiches for lunch," Gregory's voice spoke over the rumble. "Give me Ev's phone. I'll set it up while you get started on your Monday."

As soon as the coffee was done, we both sat at the breakfast table and worked on our electronics. The weekend had been fairly quiet as far as work went, so I was able to make quick work of the email part of my morning. *This* Monday I got to forward a bunch of them to Ev for his answer. What a relief!

Omar brought a huge box into the kitchen. "Lunch is served!" he bellowed. That brought Ev into the kitchen, as well as Sally. Two ogres in a relatively small space. I opened the door and windows, bugs be damned. I wanted to taste my food.

"What was Mario's problem?" I asked in between bites.

"Enh. Nothing I couldn't handle," was all he said. "Is my phone ready?"

"It is." Gregory handed it to him. "Everything that was on it before is on it now. The only thing you're missing is new calls and texts in the last two weeks. But all your voice mail messages are there."

Ev sighed. "It will take forever to catch up." He handed my phone back to me.

Gregory's phone chimed as we were cleaning up from lunch. "Yes?" he said, then listened. "Of course. I'll tell her." He hit the 'end' button.

"That was Nelion. He received a call from Nolari. The council voted to release Perchaladon and his friends. Nelion is not happy but also says this what we wanted to happen, so… The only saving grace, he says, is that the elves were banished from the enclave for a period of a year. Not for turning you into a bat, Ev, but for getting caught by non-elves!

"Nelion suggests you call Perchaladon in about two hours, Amy. Nolari believes they are probably en route back up here. Unless they were able to get a charter flight out of Lake Charles, which is doubtful, they will be on a commercial flight and be in the air, so you can leave a message and sound appropriately angry."

I nodded. "I have to figure out what to say. 'You creep!' probably isn't it."

Gregory chuckled. "No, I wouldn't think so. *Not* if you want to worm your way into his affections."

"Yeah, I know."

"*They do not know* we *know their friends are the arsonists, not humans. Use that. Pretend you think it is humans perpetrating the crimes.*"

"I *know*," I told him. "But an actress I'm not."

"I need a few minutes of quiet to write myself a script of sorts," I told everyone. "And this house is not quiet. I'm going to the cottage for a bit, okay, Gregory?"

"Of course. It's unlocked. We will not disturb you unless it's an emergency."

I took my laptop and coffee to the cottage, Fudge trotting behind me. Once seated on Gregory's sofa, I opened a blank Word document and started to write. I'd done it before – ten times in novel format. I could write a short story.

"Perchaladon? Hi, it's Amy. We need to talk. Yes, I'm still pissed at Obrist, and by extension, you, for turning my boss into a bat and thereby making my life hell for a couple of weeks. But you probably don't know that our office was firebombed last Thursday, and whoever it was spray-painted 'no witch' on the outside wall.

"I don't know if it was directed at Cassandra, or me, or both. But neither of us have done anything to deserve something that drastic. You remember telling me you wanted to shake up the humans? Well, after last Thursday, I'm interested in doing so. Please call me as soon as you can."

I sat back and re-read my work. *"That may pique his interest,"* Fudge said. *"But you will need to ensure you* sound *angry. How will you address the fact of his freedom?"*

I'd forgotten about that part. Ah, I had it. Nelion had called Gregory, who'd told Ev, who'd yelled about it loud enough for me to hear. I could use that in conversation. In the meantime, I added, "I don't know if you'll get this but…" in the opening.

Satisfied with my opening salvo, I made my way back to the house and down to the basement. Sally and Omar were still tweaking the furniture arrangement. While the delivery guys were complaining about hauling it all, Omar simply picked up and moved each piece until it was situated to Sally's satisfaction.

"It's going to be cramped no matter what I do," she said. "And we'll be able to hear each other's phone conversations. But it's the best I can do under the circumstances."

"It's fine and we'll manage. Which is my desk?"

"That one there, over next to the filing cabinets. They were in your office to begin with so…"

This was my first trip to the basement since the fire and I looked around. All of Ev's junk was piled in one corner all the way to the ceiling. That had to be Omar's work – no one but an ogre could have lifted all that quite so high. Sally had been busy cleaning. Nothing was dusty and the carpeting had obviously been vacuumed, yet dents from boxes and furniture were still visible.

Our desks were only about three feet apart, with extension cords running between them to power everything. As a klutz, I'd have to watch my step to ensure I didn't trip on them. The desks and chairs were clones of what we'd originally had, brand new cordless phones sat on the desk, and there were four boxes from the office supply store on the floor, waiting to be unpacked.

The phone rang and, just like normal, Sally answered it, "Angelich Security. How may I help you? One moment, please." Looking at the cordless phone in her hand, she punched another button. "Ev, John's on the phone for you. It's line two on these phones."

"I'm impressed," I told her. "Three days and we're pretty much back up and running."

"Thanks to paying premium prices for what's effectively next-day service, it wasn't hard," she grinned. "The only problem is the coffeepot. I can't get the pot under the spigot in the bathroom to fill it."

"Again, we'll deal. Gregory thought it would take Cassandra about three months to get everything rebuilt. Knowing her, it'll take even less than that. Then, we get to do the move all over again."

I looked at my phone. "Time to make my call. I have to go upstairs for a stronger signal, so I'll be right back."

I made my call, and thankfully yes, got Perchaladon's voice mail. I think I sounded convincing, if I do say so myself. I just channeled my anger at the whole situation into it.

Once back downstairs, Sally and I tried to settle back into a work routine. A few times I heard Ev stamp on the floor right above my head and wondered what had him mad – this time. But I still had my work to do: re-downloading bills from the internet, calling people as I thought about it to temporarily change the mailing address, and things like that.

By four o'clock, I was missing my afternoon nap. I had a routine of getting into the office early and leaving early, thereby having time to catch a few winks before I changed gears in the evening. My after-nap activity used to be writing my romance novels but recently, had been studying. However, everything was back at my apartment, which I dearly missed.

"Take a break," Sally said when she caught me yawning. "If your text message was any indication, you've been up since dawn. It's past your normal quitting time anyways."

I nodded. "Gregory woke me just before dawn, actually. I wonder if I can go home."

"Not yet," Gregory said as he made his way down the stairs. "Not until I'm satisfied you're completely out of danger. Has Perchaladon returned your call?"

"Dunno. Signal crapped out down here. Sally, thanks for everything. I'll see you tomorrow *afternoon*. Don't come in until your normal time. You've worked hard these last few days."

"Needed doing and you've been busier than a bee. But okay, I'll see you tomorrow."

Gregory accompanied me back upstairs. As I got to the top of the stairs, I got a strong enough signal that my phone pinged to let me know I had a voice mail. From Perchaladon. I silently showed Gregory the phone.

"Let's go to the cottage. I'll pour you a glass of wine and you can return it there. I want to hear at least your side of the conversation."

"No wine. I'll fall asleep on him. I may even without it."

"Coffee, then. Come on."

We made our way back to the cottage and while we were walking, I hit the voice mail button, putting it on speakerphone so Gregory could hear. "Amy, what a pleasant surprise," Perchaladon began. "I am actually in Minneapolis at this moment. Do please return my call as soon as you can."

I waited while Gregory made a pot of his heavenly brew. I took a swig from my cup, heaved a huge sigh and said, "Here we go" while hitting the 'return call' button.

"Amy, I am so pleased to hear from you, especially your message," Perchaladon said upon answering. "I am sorry for your troubles, though. These humans really do have to be taught a lesson."

"How do you plan on doing so?" I asked.

"We can start this evening. We can go to a human nightclub with some of my friends."

I shook my head. That wasn't what I had in mind. "My apologies, but I am simply too tired to go out clubbing tonight. As you might imagine, recreating the office quickly so we can get back to business is a lot of work."

"Ah, yes. I had forgotten that would be one of your responsibilities. Hm…" I could hear the wheels turning. Was I trustworthy?

"If you are serious about paying back humans for their treatment of paranormals, there might be something else."

That was more like it. "I'm listening."

"Those friends I mentioned? They are planning a demonstration at the state capitol. Virtually every paranormal species will be there. There is a meeting tonight to go over the final details, make signs, things like that. Would you like to attend?"

I made a thumbs-up gesture at Gregory. Fudge nudged my arm, nearly making me drop the phone. "I'm not very artistic but yes, I'd like to help. Would you mind if my familiar accompanied me? I'm still sort of shaken up after Thursday and he helps to calm me."

That wasn't a lie. Sort of. I think most people who lived with cats found them a calming influence.

Perchaladon sighed. "A lot of paranormals who can read auras, especially elves, don't like familiars. Can you not be away from him for a few hours?"

"Not right now, no. I don't like crowds so that would be an added stress. If he can't come with, I'm afraid I'll have to bow out of tonight."

Gregory frowned. I shook my head at him. I was certain I had Perchaladon right where I wanted him.

"If you must, then all right. But please put him in a carrier. It will help keep the animosity in check. Shall I pick you up at your apartment at seven-thirty?"

"Until everything is settled, I'm staying at Ev's," I told him. "For a few more days. I'll have to work longer hours and not adding a commute will help a lot."

"Of course. And where is that?"

He was as good at lying on the phone as I was. I *knew* he had Ev's address stored away somewhere thanks to his friends, but I gave it to him anyways.

"I am farther away from there than your office. I will see you at seven forty-five." He rang off.

I sighed. "He's picking me up at seven forty-five for some sort of a planning meeting."

"That's perfect!" Gregory exclaimed. "Do you have clothing that will support wearing a brooch?"

When the answer was, "Yes", Gregory called Mr. Bartz. "Ed, we're a go. Need a mundane spy brooch by seven-thirty. The usual delivery method will work."

# CHAPTER TWENTY-FOUR

Two hours later, after a quick nap and dinner, there was a clatter on the kitchen table and a lovely enameled silver brooch appeared. It looked almost antique, in the shape of a daisy, with a piece of citrine as the flower's center.

Gregory picked up the pin. "The citrine conceals a camera. We usually just charm something to record but with elves around, we don't want to chance them picking up on anything magical. If you can, ensure you face each person in the room so it gets a full-face shot. Don't forget to keep your phone on so I can track you by GPS. I will be nearby."

"A question," I said, my voice shaking a little with nerves. "Magic always screws with electronics. With elves around, won't this pin short out or something?"

While pinning it to the lapel of a blazer I'd had him get out of my closet, he answered, "Except for the lens, everything else is shielded by rubber, which is concealed by the metal. I don't know if it's been tested with elves, but I do know it works when being worn by a witch casting a spell. Hopefully, it will continue to do so. It's the only way I know."

"Okay. Let's get this show on the road." The three of us trooped back to Ev's house. Once there, Fudge reluctantly entered the carrier I'd left by the door. Gregory patted my back and told me he'd be around. Ev came into the living room as I sat fidgeting on the couch, waiting for the doorbell to ring. (What? I'm old-fashioned enough that a man can come to the door for me. I refuse to answer to a car horn.)

"Are you sure about this, Amy?" Ev asked, watching me squirm as he considerately sat in a chair across the room. "They can find some other way, you know."

I shook my head. "Time's too short. And I've already committed to doing it. Gregory said he'd be tracking me and I have Fudge to help. We'll be okay."

Precisely at seven forty-five, the doorbell rang. Ev motioned me to stay seated as he answered the door.

"Good evening, Evander," Perchaladon's rich voice reached me. "Amy should be waiting for me."

"She is," my boss answered. "You have to know I'm not happy about this. You'd better bring her back in one piece or there will be hell to pay."

I had a flashback of being back in high school and my dad giving my date rules for the evening. I stood, grabbed Fudge's carrier, and pushed my way past Ev.

"Let's go," I told Perchaladon. The same driver stood with the passenger door open, and as I approached, he moved to take Fudge's carrier from me. "Thanks, but I've got it," I told him as I crawled inside and put the carrier between my feet. Perchaladon slid in beside me.

"You are nervous," he said as the limo pulled out of Ev's driveway.

"I've never done any protesting before. And I'll be around strangers. Yes, of course, I'm a little nervous." That was the absolute truth.

"Not to worry. My friends are all good people. You'll be comfortable in no time."

*Yeah, right*, I thought. "Good people" who apparently didn't mind a little violence. I concentrated on my breathing to calm my heart rate. In moments, I felt Fudge at the back of my mind, pushing out calming waves of his own.

*"You will be fine. I am here."*

We both subsided into our own thoughts and the rest of the ride was quiet. Almost an hour later, we were in Dinkytown, an area near the University of Minnesota. It is a neighborhood with roots going back more than a century and has a history of being the site of student protests and other activism. A fitting spot, then. The driver pulled up behind another limo in front of a house that looked like it could use a facelift – or at least a good scraping and a new coat of paint. The limos looked out of place among the older compact cars on the street and in the driveway. Bicycles were locked to a stand on the front porch.

"Ready for your first protest meeting?" Perchaladon asked.

I took a deep breath and nodded, grabbed Fudge's carrier, and followed him to the front door. Surprisingly, he didn't ring a doorbell or knock, just walked in as if he lived there. He turned to the right, into what was probably the original parlor, but now, cleared of furniture with mis-matched chairs forming a circle, was obviously a meeting room. Most of the chairs already had butts in them and those butts were attached to very young-looking people. College-aged, I'd say, although in the paranormal community, looks could be deceiving. I saw four elves in their unglamoured state, at least six were-somethings, and some more human-looking people who I assumed were either glamoured elves, or witches and wizards. Conversations halted and they all stared at me.

"Greetings, everyone. This is my friend Amy, who wants to join us."

There were murmurs of "welcome" but some grumbling filtered its way through.

"Why does she bring a familiar among us?" one of the female elves asked. All the elves and a couple of the more human-looking people nodded in agreement.

I felt Fudge tamp down my emotions so rather than reply with a smart remark that might turn people against me, I simply said, "He is an emotional support animal." Fudge snickered in my mind.

Some of the humans nodded in understanding. Some of the not-humans grimaced.

"Please, everyone. Amy needs her cat. Now, we have business to attend to," Perchaladon said with an authoritative voice as he sat in one of the empty chairs, then motioned for me to sit next to him. "I see we are missing a few. Shall we begin or wait?"

"Wait a few more minutes. Richard texted to say he and his roommates are caught in construction traffic on 94," said one of the weres, who looked like he'd change into a cat of some sort. At least, he had the look of a lion to him, with a wild mane of black hair.

Conversations slowly started back up, but I knew I was the topic of a few, given the glances and glares directed at me. "Pay no attention," Perchaladon said quietly. "Once they get to know you, they will welcome you with open arms."

*"Based on what I am sensing, I sincerely doubt his statement. Be prepared. Notice all the natural substances around you: skin, the wood floor, cotton shirts, which I believe you call T-shirts. The rug smells like a combination of synthetic and wool. You can use the wool in it."*

I sat quietly and followed Fudge's instructions, noting who was wearing cotton. Then, although I hoped everything would go smoothly, prepared myself for what I would do if things got out of hand.

A few moments later, four men tromped through the door. "Sorry we're late," one of them said. These, too, had looks of a were about them: a canine, another feline, and a couple rodent-somethings.

Perchaladon cleared his throat loudly. "Would someone call Mason and put him on speakerphone?"

One of the (probable) wizards grabbed his phone out of his pocket, hit an apparent speed-dial number, another button, then put his phone on the floor in the center of the room.

"We're here, Perchaladon. Why could you not have had this meeting in another two hours?" a deep voice asked. Obviously, a vampire who was waiting for dark.

"Because some people have jobs to go to tomorrow and we need some shuteye before then," the same wizard answered.

Perchaladon cleared his throat again. "This was the best time for the majority, Mason. Now, we have things to discuss. Warren, what have you discovered about security?"

One of the werewolf-looking men spoke. "As with most government offices, there are six armed guards at the main entrance, with three metal detectors. The guards do not change from day to day during the week, at least, not most of them. I presume if someone's sick, they have a replacement ready. Once past the main entrance, there are six more patrolling the rotunda, also armed. The metal detectors are no problem because we don't need metal. We…" [He gestured to the two men to either side of him] "…can take out the ones in the rotunda if you all can handle the ones at the doors."

I nudged Perchaladon. "What does he mean, 'take out'? I thought this was a protest?" I whispered.

"It is. But in order to get into the chambers en masse, we need to eliminate the guards," he whispered back.

This was *so* not good! While I could feel Fudge tamping down on my emotions, I couldn't let the threat of violence pass without saying *something*. I stood, moved to the center of the circle, and turned, looking at each individual as I did.

"What are you hoping to accomplish? Violence will only make humans dislike you more, not less! Have you tried working *within* the system to change it?"

There were growls, both figurative and literal, coming from nearly everyone. "Miss. Amy. We have waited centuries for humans to *like* us, as you say. We're not looking for them to *like* us. It's time the humans went back to being subjected to *our* will, not the other way around," one of the were-somethings said.

"The only way to accomplish that," the vampire on the phone added, "is to take control of governments. Start local and work our way up."

I'd gotten what I came for: pictures of everyone in the room, except for the vampire on the phone. It was time to end my participation in something so foolish.

"My apologies. I thought this was a *protest*, not a revolution. While I agree with you in principle, violence is not my way of doing things. Have no worries, I won't talk to anyone. But I'm out of here."

I turned to walk out the door, grabbing Fudge's carrier on my way, and suddenly was unable to take another step.

"I'm sorry, Amy, but I cannot allow you to leave now that you've seen everyone here," Perchaladon quietly apologized. "You will be taken to my condominium until we've completed our task."

Fudge burst through the door on his carrier, the impact knocking me off balance. With my legs frozen, though, I was unable to fall. Thankfully. As I watched, he arched his back, fluffed his fur more than I'd ever seen, and turned a complete circle while baring his teeth and hissing. I felt the spell on my legs break.

*"Run! I have told Waldo what has happened, and he will get word to Gregory. I will keep them away from you until the wizard has come."*

"No way, José. We're in this together."

He might be able to interrupt elven magic but wasn't immune to other magic or mauling by weres. I turned to see weres shifting, witches and wizards raising their hands to cast a spell, and elves looking frustrated. Thanks to Fudge's heads-up, it only took a thought to bind fur to wood floor, and the wool in the rug to cotton clothing. Weres belly-flopped onto the floor in mid-change. Magical folks lowered their hands as they tried to disengage themselves from the rug that had slapped them in the face.

The front door burst open and Gregory came pounding into the room. He stopped to survey the scene and started chuckling. "I guess I didn't have to be in quite so much of a hurry. I thought you were in trouble, Amy."

"I almost was. Fudge saved the day. But I do need to leave. I don't want to be involved with these people and their hare-brained schemes. Let's go."

I left the cat carrier where I'd dropped it and backed out of the room. Fudge backed right along with me, hackles still raised. Gregory preceded us out of the room and opened the front door.

*"I can only disrupt their magic while they are within my sight. We will need to run."*

Once out the door, we ran for the Hummer, which Gregory had pulled onto the front lawn all the way to the porch stairs. The engine was still running. As soon as Fudge had hopped in, Gregory put it into reverse and hit the gas. Elves crowded their way out the door onto the porch, the magical folks right behind them, sans rug and pieces of their clothing. Fudge stood on my lap, paws on the dash, and the elves once again looked frustrated as their powers were taken away.

Once in the street, Fudge ran to the back window so he could still keep the elves in sight. As Gregory sped away, I felt the car lurch as spells hit it.

"Bumps in the road," Gregory said. "Those youngsters aren't strong enough to penetrate the protective spells on this baby."

Once we'd turned a couple of corners and were well on our way out of Dinkytown, Fudge came back up front, curled up in my lap, and promptly started snoring. I'm sure he expended a lot of energy doing what he did and I didn't begrudge him a nap, although I wished I could join him.

"Ed has asked me to take you directly to HQ. Are you okay with that?"

"Sure. Better there than home or Ev's. They know those places."

So, squinting against the setting sun, Gregory drove us toward downtown. I leaned back in my seat, exhausted.

"That was some quick thinking, Amy," Gregory said. "I'm proud of you."

"Thanks, I guess, but Fudge was the one who told me what to look for. I hope I got what you needed because I never want to do that again. People like that scare me."

"I hope you never have to do it again, too. Without Fudge, we both would have been in a world of hurt. At least for several sunrises."

Less than a half hour later, we were once again in the conference room at Magical HQ (as I'd come to think of it), surrounded by the high muckety-mucks of the paranormal world. Fudge had woken briefly when I cradled him in my arms to carry him but had gone back to snoring. Mr. Bartz had taken the brooch off me the moment we got off the elevator and disappeared down a corridor.

"I'm sure you're hungry after so much stress," Ms. Fitzsimmons said to me, "but I'd like to postpone your meal long enough to learn what you heard and saw."

I related the conversations at the house, describing the wizard who'd called the vampires in the hopes they could trace his phone or something. I also apologized to Nelion when I told them it appeared his son was the ringleader. He seemed to take it in stride.

Once I'd said my piece, I was dismissed from their discussions and escorted to the same hotel-looking room I'd occupied about a year earlier after Ev and I had been released from our kidnapping. I laid Fudge on one of the bed pillows; he still didn't wake. As before, I spoke an order of a cheeseburger, fries, and soda for me, and tuna for Fudge at the phone, never even picking up the handset. Ten minutes later, a serving tray shimmered into existence on the table with a plate of mouth-watering food on it, as well as bowls for Fudge.

Just as I was about to chomp down on the burger, there was a knock at the door. Answering it, I saw Gregory standing there with a plate of food in his hand. His appeared to be hummus and pita chips. He, apparently, wasn't as hungry as I.

"Hope you don't mind. I thought we could eat together, and I'd tell you what I know of what's happening."

He didn't even have to ask. *Of course*, I wanted to know what was going on! I ushered him into the room and we both sat at the table.

In between bites, he relayed that Fudge and I would be staying at HQ until at least the next night, possibly for a couple of days, until whatever it was had happened, and the perpetrators were caught. Mr. Bartz had printed out the photos taken by my lapel pin and they were in the process of identifying everyone. At least one of the weres (another rodent, fittingly, a weasel) was already on their radar for other crimes.

"My understanding is that all the planned *revolutions…*" [He used air quotes around the word.] "…in other cities had nearly fallen apart by the time the authorities had rounded up everyone. The one in the Twin Cities seems to be the largest and most well-organized. That's not surprising, given our large paranormal population.

"I believe your actions may change, delay, or precipitate their plans. We won't know for certain until they can get mobile phones tapped. Thankfully, my association with paranormal law enforcement is unknown to that generation so perhaps not too large a monkey wrench has been thrown into the works."

"I hope they stop it," I said. "As I told them, I sort of understand where they're coming from. Oh, not the whole world-domination thing, which is stupid, but the lack of acceptance by humans. But violence is *not* the answer. Never has been, never will be."

Gregory nodded. "I'm headed home. Ev will *not* be happy that you will be here tomorrow but there's no help for it. Can I get you anything from home before I leave?"

I *still* didn't want that man rummaging around in my underwear drawer. But I needed clean clothes. "I didn't have a whole lot at your place and have worn most of it. Let me call Cassandra and ask her to pack a bag for me. Can you pick it up from her house tomorrow morning?"

"Of course. Get some sleep. You've had a rough few days and as you're completely safe here, you should be able to sleep as soundly as Fudge appears to be."

*"I am not sleeping that soundly. I heard every word he said and as soon as I feel like moving, will eat the delicious tuna I can smell."*

I relayed what Fudge had said. Gregory chuckled, and with a 'sleep well' closed the door behind himself.

I called Cassandra, who didn't seem surprised that I'd been sequestered again. "You do seem to get yourself into situations that require it," she laughed. "Of course I'll get some clothes for you. I'll go over now and have it ready whenever he gets here in the morning. Sleep tight and don't let the bedbugs bite!"

After ringing off, I once again stripped off my jeans and bra, and clad only in a T-shirt, crawled between the sheets. Thankful that Magical HQ had cable television, I tuned into the west coast baseball game, lay my head on the pillow next to Fudge and drifted off.

# CHAPTER TWENTY-FIVE

It seemed I'd barely closed my eyes when my alarm went off. It was just beginning to get light, which was my normal wake-up time, established long ago thanks to Fudge shredding my drapes. I debated going back to sleep since I apparently wasn't going to work, but habit took over. The magical phone delivered a large pot of coffee, which I slurped while checking social media and email from my phone.

Around six-thirty, there was a knock at the door. Hoping it was Gregory with a bag of clothes and toiletries from Cassandra, I pulled on my pants to answer it.

"Good morning," Mr. Bartz said. "I hope you slept well?"

When I nodded, he continued. "I know being stuck here is extremely inconvenient, especially given the turmoil Mr. Angelich's business is probably in after last week's events. Therefore, we have determined to protect Mr. Angelich's house so you can go to work. If that's acceptable, of course."

Was it?! It seemed strange, but I was actually excited to be able to go to work. "That would be marvelous!" I replied. "But I'm waiting for Gregory to bring me some clean clothes and toiletries."

"I spoke with him moments ago. He is on his way and should be here within a half hour or so, depending on traffic. He'll take you back with him."

I heaved a huge sigh of relief. I could pretend normalcy for a few hours. "Great. And thanks."

Mr. Bartz turned back down the hallway as I closed my door.

*"Nothing about your life is what you would consider normal,"* Fudge twined around my legs. *"And working in the ogre's house is definitely not so. But we will make the best of it."*

I refilled my coffee cup. "So, now that I've seen you in action, care to explain what you did last night?"

A sigh escaped him. *"I suppose I must. A moment while I communicate with Waldo."* He closed his eyes and opened them a moment later.

*"As long as it goes no further than you and Gregory, I have permission to share.*

*"We have already discussed how the elves* are *the magic you perceive around you, yes? Familiars are that same magic, but older. It is how we are able to traverse the ether without getting lost, move from host body to host body, and keep that body healthy until it is no longer needed. The oldest among us, myself and Waldo included, are strong enough in our magic to speak to our witch or wizard in their mind. It is that same strength that allows us to interrupt any magic the elves project outside themselves. Waldo and a few others can even disrupt elven magic to the extent that an elf will dissipate."*

"You mean kill them?" I was flabbergasted.

*"Yes. It is why elves fear us. I do not know how much they know of us, but they* do *know we can destroy them. Hence the necessity of my promise at the enclave."*

Wow. Not that I didn't already think it, especially after the previous night, but my cat was a bad-ass. Since Fudge knew basically everything I was thinking, he preened.

Another knock at the door, and Gregory was standing there with an overnight case in his hand. "I'd have sent it along earlier, but nothing can transport into this building," he told me as he handed it to me. "I have to speak with Ed so that should give you enough time to shower and change. I'll be back here in a half hour."

Cassandra had packed everything I'd need and then some. Of course, she didn't know I was going to be allowed to leave my prison – at least for the day. So I showered and got ready for work.

On the ride out to Ev's, I filled Gregory in on what Fudge had told me, with the admonishment that it was for his ears only.

After I'd related Fudge's revelation, Gregory whistled, then said, "Fudge, may I say, that is an extraordinary ability. Amy, and by extension, I and her other friends, are quite lucky to have you around."

My cat just preened a little more. Not that he needed any encouragement to have a big ego. I said as much.

Gregory chuckled. "I understand most familiars have no humility. The fact that Fudge is a cat just augments it."

Fudge snorted. *"I am what I am. I know my own abilities. Why should I be bashful about it?"*

I gave him a scritch behind the ears. "I know. But I still love you."

We pulled into Ev's driveway, Gregory maneuvering the Hummer between two police cars, both marked.

Gregory explained their presence. "Although the cars say 'Edina Police,' they are actually paranormal cops. While we hope the presence of the police will deter anyone, the four cops are trained to deal with anything except elves. Fudge, that's where you come in. I'd like you to patrol, if you would."

*"That will be unnecessary,"* Fudge said as Waldo emerged from the back of the house.

"My apologies," Gregory coughed. "I did not realize the extent of Althea's involvement."

*"It is not Althea's idea. It is mine,"* a voice boomed in our heads. *"As a Rottweiler, I am frightening to most species and as a large one, am*

*capable of taking down even a bear or wolf. And* I *have capabilities the youngling does not.*"

It seemed odd to have my couple-thousand-year-old familiar referred to as a "youngling." And it was disconcerting to have another voice in my head. I'd learned a few months ago that Waldo had the ability to speak to anyone's mind if he chose to do so. But to have the oldest familiar in the world taking an interest in my well-being was enough to make me blush.

"*It is not just your well-being,*" the voice boomed again. "*It is the principle of a paranormal attacking another paranormal which sets my teeth on edge. I will prevent that from happening.*"

Oops. He could read minds, too.

Fudge's familiar voice answered, "*He cannot. I relayed your thoughts.*"

"And you did that why?"

"*It seemed the right thing to do.*"

Familiars. There was no figuring them out. But at least I only had one of them digging around in my brain.

So, confident I was fully protected, I made my way down to Ev's basement, Fudge at my heels. First things first: I had to go upstairs to get water to make coffee, then start the pot to perking. Fudge curled up under my desk as I fired up my laptop and started my day.

Despite the different surroundings, it felt great to have a normal workday. Sally had done a marvelous job of setting things up and I quickly got back into the swing of things: checking emails and voice mail messages, and making a list of things to talk to Ev about when he finally announced he was ready to work.

About an hour later, I heard him bellow from the top of the stairs, "Amy? You down there?"

I hollered that I was and I'd be up to his office in a moment. I refilled my coffee, grabbed my notes and made my way upstairs.

"Who're all these people and why are there cop cars in my driveway? The neighbors probably think I've done something bad," he asked as I pulled a chair up to the front of his desk and sat.

"They're paranormal cops. Making sure the creeps I met last night don't come here and try something. And in case you're wondering, the Rottweiler is a familiar who's stronger than Fudge."

"So what happened last night? Gregory was close-mouthed about it, just telling me you were okay. And that I couldn't go clubbing last night because of whatever the hell it is that's going on. It was a boring night."

To Ev, staying home at night was tantamount to imprisonment. For some reason, I didn't feel bad. Instead, I gave him an overview of the previous evening, the fact that I couldn't sleep in my own bed as he had been able to do, and that, hopefully, it would all be over in twenty-four hours or so. Then, to business.

We got everything sorted between us and just before I left to go back to my desk, I reminded him to either use his cell phone or the office line we'd had installed.

"Shit. Thanks. But what do we do if someone calls while I'm on the phone? We don't have a second line anymore."

I sighed. He could be such a putz at times. "Voice mail will pick up if the line is busy. Just like it did when both lines were in use in the old office. You're going to have to make adjustments for the next few months. Use your cell phone if you're so worried about it."

Sally arrived shortly after lunch (I missed Cassandra bringing mine to me and foresaw GrubHub getting a lot of business) and we continued as best we could.

Somewhere mid-afternoon, as I was beginning to yawn and contemplating my usual nap, a roar penetrated all the way to the basement. Fudge bounded up the stairs more quickly than Sally or I could. The front door was thrown open and Ev stood on the step. We could see his agitation even with his back to us. My cat was nowhere in evidence.

I shouldered Ev aside so Sally and I could see what had him so tense. On the front lawn, a large Rottweiler and a much smaller dark brown cat had a bear pinned down, the dog sitting on the bear's chest and my cat on his face. The bear was bleeding from multiple wounds, but still managed to bellow out his anger, or frustration, or whatever.

"*Desist or I will destroy you!*" Waldo's voice reverberated in my head. Sally's eyes widened.

"What the hell was that?" she asked.

"You heard that? And you're fully human? It's the Rottweiler," I replied. "That's Waldo, the head honcho of all familiars. I guess he's not bothering to concentrate his voice."

The bear continued to struggle and roar. In the blink of an eye, it shimmered and vanished from beneath Waldo and Fudge, who casually stepped down as if coming off a platform. They both started grooming the blood off their claws and fur.

The four cops, who had been standing at the four corners of the front yard with their hands raised, lowered them simultaneously, as Gregory came running around from the back.

"What the hell happened?" he yelled.

"An elf just tried to do *something*, probably bad, to the occupants of this house. He unveiled in the middle of the yard and transformed into a bear. Waldo had us mask the yard from sight and sound while he took care of the intruder," one of the cops said.

Gregory turned to Waldo. "Well?"

Waldo didn't stop licking at the blood spots. "*I do not know who this was except that it was a fairly young elf. Anyone who feels the need to veil and subsequently shift is a menace. He did not stop his advance with warning and continued to struggle to free himself even after he had been stopped from entering the house. Althea and the others have been notified. You may continue what you were doing. I will stay.*"

"Show's over, Ev." Gregory motioned him back into the house. Ev kept staring at Waldo.

"Who is that dog and what did he just do?"

I sighed while shoving Ev in the direction of the door. "I told you. He's a familiar who's stronger than Fudge. He just proved it by killing the elf. And you met him last year, anyways."

Ev looked down at me. "He killed it? As in, didn't send it anywhere but it's dead?"

I continued shoving, this time into his office. "Yes. Dead. Better that than you having a brown bear rampaging through your house and/or attacking any of us, isn't it?"

Ev dropped into his chair, running his hands through his hair. "What the hell is happening around here? First, my office gets burned to the ground, and now an elf, bear, whatever, tries to attack me. What's going on, Amy?"

I grabbed a Coke from the small fridge in his office and handed it to him. (Ev disdained plain water.) "Drink. And calm down. Somehow, we got on the radar of a group of radicals. Even though we really have nothing to do with them, and nothing to threaten them with, I guess they figure eliminating *anyone* on the periphery of what they're doing is better than not. They're obviously a violent bunch, which is why we have magical protection. For which I'm grateful. You okay now? Can I go back to work?"

Ev wordlessly nodded so I turned to go back to the basement, and ran smack into Sally, who had been standing behind me. She looked a little pale. I grabbed her arm and propelled her toward the stairs.

"Do I need to get something to calm you down, too?" I asked her.

"Um. No. I think I'm good. But what the hell?"

"You heard what I told Ev?" She nodded. "Then there's your explanation. I'm sorry you're caught up in it and I'd understand if you want out. All this truly weird crap wasn't in your job description."

"I think I can handle it. I'm just a little overwhelmed. Stuff like this doesn't generally happen to someone like me, y'know? I've never had another voice in my head, and never seen a bear in person, much less one that disappeared into thin air."

I could empathize. The first time Fudge spoke in my head was more than a little disconcerting. My heart rate was up, too, because of the elf/bear. Bears belonged either in the zoo or in the wild, according to this city girl. But I was learning to deal with weird shit, which this whole week-plus definitely qualified as.

"Take the rest of the afternoon off, go home, and pour yourself a glass or two of wine. It's only a…" I looked at the clock on my computer "…little over an hour, anyways."

She nodded and, reaching under her desk, grabbed her purse. "Thanks. I think that's a good idea. I'll see you tomorrow."

I sighed as she headed up the stairs. Good help was hard to find and if these creeps cost me an assistant, *I'd* be the one doing some ass-whooping. Just then, the phone rang, reminding me I still had a job to do.

An hour later, Gregory hollered from the top of the stairs. "Time to go, Amy!"

"Back to my prison?" I asked as I shut everything down for the night.

"Unfortunately, for at least one more night, yes. Today's events just highlighted the need for your security," he replied as I trudged up the stairs, Fudge trailing behind me.

"Someone keeping an eye on Ev?"

"We think *you're* the target because of last night. But the police will stay until it's all over to ensure his safety. He is not pleased because he can't go out again tonight, even though I've explained the dangers."

That sounded like my boss. As an ogre, regular magic bounced off him and he usually partied at paranormal clubs, where the bouncers could handle anything he couldn't as far as a physical attack went. He should remember that elven magic *didn't* bounce off him, though.

"Poor guy," I murmured. "Not being able to go partying but still able to sleep in his own bed surrounded by his own stuff. I don't feel sorry for him in the least."

"Nor do I. But I feel sorry for me when he finally *can* go back out. It will be some long nights, to be sure, because he will feel he has a couple of weeks to make up for."

The ride downtown was quiet. Fudge stood in my lap with his paws on the dash, watching traffic. Gregory sighed several times as traffic thickened but said nothing until we pulled into the parking garage and up to the solo elevator.

"I'll let you off here," he told me. "Ed has shanghaied me for tonight, so I have to go to work. I'll come by your room later if there's any news."

Ms. Fitzsimmons and Waldo met us at the elevator. "My apologies for keeping you from your home once again," she said. "But we feel it's necessary for your safety."

I only nodded and turned down the hall to where I knew a room awaited me. They followed, Fudge falling back and trotting alongside Waldo.

As we reached my room, Ms. Fitzsimmons put her hand on my arm. "I know this has been a difficult few weeks for you. I just wanted to tell you that we are proud of the way you have comported yourself, even put yourself in danger for the greater good."

"I guess it comes with the territory, huh?" I replied. "I have an ogre for a boss, who seems to get himself into pickles all the time and drags me with him. I'm just looking forward to being able to sleep in my own bed for more than one or two nights at a time and getting my routine back. Until the next time he does something stupid."

She chuckled. "I know several ogres. None of them are quite as, shall we say, accident-prone? as your employer. My hopes are the same as yours because I, too, value my routine."

Waldo nudged her hand with his head. "We must go. There are things to attend to. Please, make yourself as comfortable as possible and don't hesitate to ask for anything that will help that."

Fudge and I went into our room. A second suitcase sat on the bed with a note in Gregory's handwriting: "Cassandra wasn't certain how long you'd need to be gone or what you'd want. She packed more for both you and Fudge and asked me to bring it to you."

In the bag was more clothing and Fudge's favorite toys. He snatched one filled with valerian root out of my hand and started chewing on it while I put the rest of the toys on the floor and the bag in the closet. I kicked off my shoes and lay down on the bed, determined to get a short nap in since there wasn't much else to do. Fudge hopped on the bed next to me, the somewhat worse-for-wear toy in his mouth. We curled up together.

# CHAPTER TWENTY-SIX

It was dark when I opened my eyes, which meant my nap was longer than a "quick" one. The clock on my phone told me it was nearly ten o'clock. My stomach told me it was well past dinner time. I asked the magical phone for a garden salad, ranch dressing, and a small piece of salmon that I shared with Fudge.

*"You are the best human ever. You give me more treats than any other witch I've had."*

"If by 'best human' you mean the one who spoils you the most then yes, I guess I am. But you've worked hard the last couple of weeks and deserve a little pampering."

We'd just finished eating, the plates disappearing when I told the phone we were through, and there was a knock on the door. I opened it to find Gregory and Mr. Bartz, both with grins on their faces.

"Would you care to sleep in your own bed tonight?" Gregory asked.

"Would I? You bet. But how? What?"

"May we come in and tell you what happened over the last three hours?" Mr. Bartz asked.

"Of course." I opened the door wider. Both men came in. Mr. Bartz went to the phone and ordered three bottles of beer while Gregory sat in one of the chairs and splayed his legs.

When the beer had arrived and the first sips were duly taken, Mr. Bartz started his narrative.

"Thanks to you, we were able to identify all the parties in the room last night, as well as the vampire on the phone. Working with the mundane police, thirty-two members of this little clique have been rounded up and charged with making terroristic threats. Some were even stupid enough to boast of what they were doing on social media."

"I don't understand. I mean, I understand making a threat is illegal, but…"

"One of the witches you saw last night was a timid little thing, going along with her boyfriend to make him happy, although she didn't agree with the violence. She noticed her tail (who has since been reassigned) and confronted her. She's the one who spilled the beans.

"The Minnesota Senate was in a night session tonight, supposedly for some important vote. It turns out the Majority Leader is a were-coyote and is sympathetic to their 'cause.' He's the one who engineered this evening meeting.

"The idea was to storm the capitol building, use magic to subdue as many senators as possible, and turn them either into weres or vampires. The theory being if they were paranormal beings, and making up a majority, they'd, oh, I don't know, start making laws to subjugate humans. Or something. What they didn't think completely through is the Senate usually meets during the day. Vampires wouldn't be able to be politicians among humans!"

Gregory snorted. "I'm not certain politicians *are* human, but be that as it may, the plan was set for nine tonight. We were able to set up a trap, utilizing police from every major species but most especially, the elves. When they entered the capitol, there were no human guards at the door but all elves. Were species and magical people were the guards in both the rotunda and chambers. It was a simple matter to subdue them even before they got to the Senate chamber and haul them out. The senators didn't know what was happening until the Majority Leader was arrested."

"So that's the end of it?" I asked.

"Pretty much," Mr. Bartz said. "You are already under the aegis of the Vampire Council, so none of them will bother you without severe repercussions, which they already know because of your prior run-in with one. There may be a stray elf, were, or wizard, but between your familiar and Gregory, you will be guarded for the next couple of weeks until we're certain there are no more stragglers. But I honestly think we got them all in one fell swoop."

I was relieved beyond belief. A small smile crossed my face as I looked at Gregory. "It's early. Are you taking Ev out?"

"Are you kidding? I need some sleep, too. I will tell him tomorrow. Now, pack your things and I will take you home."

I almost cried as we pulled up to my apartment building. I'd only been gone four days, but it seemed like a lifetime.

"I will pick you up at seven-thirty in the morning, okay?" Gregory asked as he helped me haul the two bags filled with clothes, toiletries, and Fudge's toys down the stairs and into my apartment.

"Okay. But does Fudge have to stay awake all night? That's tough for him."

"*I can do it if need be, but it is not necessary. There are added protection spells on the building. They feel like elven magic.*"

I looked down at my cat, then glared at Gregory. "Wait. Elven protection spells? So they know where I live, too?"

"Nelion thought it prudent. He said he purposely made them to degrade in about a week, which should be plenty of time. If not, he will return and refresh them. I agreed with him, as did James." James was the owner of my apartment building, and a wizard to boot. "James' wards won't keep an elf out. These will."

I mentally shrugged my shoulders. Nothing I could do about it now. I said as much and bid him good night. I closed the door behind him, then plopped my butt down on *my* sofa, Fudge hopping up and curling next to me.

*"It is good to be home. You need to order more of those smelly candles if I am to accompany you to work each day. They stink but are better than the ogre."*

I gave him a long, massaging back scratch. "You know we're still figuring out what we need to replace. I'll add them to Sally's shopping list."

He nuzzled me, then moved to the other end of the sofa for bath time. I padded into the kitchen, put my morning coffee together, set the timer, and headed for bed. It *was* good to be home!

# EPILOGUE

**Three months later.**

We were celebrating. Thanks to Cassandra's mother's connections, the building had been completely reconstructed in record time. Ev had allowed Sally and me to decorate the office, so it looked less like a man cave and more like a business establishment. I was looking forward to returning the rental car and resuming my walk to work in the early mornings, getting a latte from Cassandra to drink while my coffeepot perked, and having her deliver my lunch. I had missed those five or ten minutes of "girl time" each day.

The revolution-that-never-took-place didn't make the papers. The big news was the arrest of the Senate Majority Leader, but that had nothing to do with the "revolution" and everything to do with the fact that he'd been caught in a compromising position with a girl the same age as his teenage daughter. I suspect the powers-that-be in the paranormal community engineered the scene as an explanation for his arrest, rather than allowing his were status and his involvement with insurgents to be made public. Like most news stories nowadays, there was about three days of outrage on social media, then the story faded away. No one questioned the lack of a trial in human court.

I was never told what happened to the creeps I'd confronted and their friends, but Nelion was apparently comfortable enough to allow the extra wards on my apartment building to vanish without refreshing them. Fudge was wary for the next week or so after that, but even he finally calmed down and resumed being less of a familiar and more of a cat. I was finally allowed to drive myself to and from work at Ev's house and get back to my normal life.

The deli's grand re-opening was a resounding success. The weather was typical for October – somewhat cool with a light rain – so everyone squeezed into the store. Cassandra probably made more that day than she did in a regular week, which said something about how popular her place was and how much it had been missed.

Ev, Gregory, Sally, and I were squeezed into a corner, out of the traffic, and enjoying watching Cassandra and Tommy get hugs from all the regulars.

Gregory touched my arm. "I have some news for you."

"Yeah? What?"

"After discussion with Althea, we have decided to graduate you from witch school. Between how you acted during the latest crisis with Ev and how you've progressed in your lessons since then, we don't see a need for me to teach you any longer."

I was almost at a loss for words. I was free on Saturdays? "Uh. Thanks," I said. Then realized more was required. "I really appreciate all your efforts, Gregory. I hope I can live up to your expectations."

He chuckled. "I never had any doubt. And although I would admonish you to stay out of trouble, it seems to follow our employer and we get caught up in it. So, I will not say that. But know if you ever have questions, I am here." He squeezed my arm.

*"The wizard need not worry because you have me."* My cat may have been physically three blocks away, but he was never out of my brain.

"And I'll always be grateful for you, you spoiled little thing."

Ev cleared his throat. "This is nice and all, but we have work to do. Amy, I'd like to talk to you – I'm thinking about buying another security firm whose owner wants to retire and there are some logistics to go over. So, come on everyone. Back upstairs."

I glanced sideways at Gregory and mouthed, "Uh-oh."

He smiled, shrugged his shoulders, and opened the door for us. As I passed him, he quietly said, "Never a dull moment."

## About the Author

A semi-retired accountant, Master Herbalist, author, and witch, Deborah J. "DJ" Martin is the author of non-fiction books about herbs as well as this fiction series.

She abandoned frozen Minnesota many moons ago and now lives in the woods of the southern Appalachian Mountains with her husband, four cats, and numerous woodland creatures. If you can't find DJ in the garden or visiting her grandchildren, check Facebook http://www.facebook.com/authordjmartin, Twitter @authordjmartin or her website http://www.authordjmartin.com.